WHATEVER YOU NEED

S. JONES

Editing:
Marla Selkow Esposito

Proofreading:
Virginia Tesi Carey

Formatting:
Leanne Clugston at Irish Ink

ONE

AMELIA

"THIS CAN'T BE HAPPENING," I HISSED, SLAMMING MY HEAD down on the pillow. I squeezed my eyes shut and tried to pretend that this was nothing more than a bad dream. But when my eyelids opened, the burn from the metal digging into my wrists was a sharp reminder of my stupidity.

I was normally a very level-headed person, so how the hell did I think having a one-night stand with a stranger that I met at happy hour would be a good idea? Oh, I knew why, because I followed my best friend's advice. Something I would never do again. When I accepted her dare to be spontaneous for "just one night" this was not what I had in mind.

Ava knew I didn't have an impulsive bone in my body. My need for calm and predictability was established when I showed up at the bus stop in third grade with my twenty-five-pack of pencils already sharpened. Now here I was handcuffed to a bedpost because I felt like I had something to prove. Not only would I be looking to replace my childhood friend, but I was also never drinking vodka again. I was sticking to wine from here on out.

"I'm so sorry," my date Parker repeated for the tenth time,

while pacing a path along the brown carpet. "The key must have fallen out of my pocket on the way back from the bar."

"Right." I sat up and looked across the room, not acknowledging his apology. "Do you have a paperclip or a bobby pin handy?"

"Er..." He walked over and inspected my wrists again, looking as if the lock would just magically pop open on its own. "I can't say that I have either of those."

"Well, have you looked around? I'm sure there must be something you can use."

"Right." He jumped up and scurried around the apartment. Doors flew open, and drawers were rummaged through in haste as he searched for something that would free me from his fuckup.

Jesus, this was a shitshow.

He pushed his sandy-blond hair out of his eyes, looking defeated. "Do you want me to call the cops or something?"

"What?" I shrieked. "No, I want you to find the fucking key and unlock me."

This seemed like a good idea a few hours ago. I had just downed my second shot and ordered my third drink. Parker came over and introduced himself as a rescue pilot for the Coast Guard. He seemed fun when I was filled up on vodka. Now, it was clear that he couldn't even rescue a poodle stranded in an above ground pool, let alone a human being.

Rescue pilot my ass.

They say you can't judge a book by its cover, but I highly suggest reading a few chapters first before buying a copy.

"If I could help you, I would, but I can't." He pinched the skin between his brows. "I think our best option would be to call the police."

I exhaled slowly, trying to calm myself down. It was so stupid of me to put myself in this position. "Fine, but can you at least cover me up before they get here?"

This was going to be mortifying, but at least I still had my bra and underwear covering up the important parts. Thank God, we didn't go all the way. Hell, Parker barely made it off second base, thanks to his ex-girlfriend unexpectedly showing up. He chased her down the hall and tried to explain that it wasn't what it looked like, even though it was exactly what it looked like. After listening to the two of them scream and yell at each other for over an hour, I was grateful that she stopped things from going any further.

Parker ran his hands through his hair, looking every bit as embarrassed as I felt. "Sure. Let me find something."

He moved to the dresser and then the closet, frantically searching for a solution to my problem. "The bed sheet on the floor will work," I suggested, pointing to the crumpled mess at the bottom of the bed.

It was as if a light bulb went off in his head. "Yeah, right. Good idea," he said, following my line of sight. "Would you like a glass of water or something?"

I licked my dry, chapped lips. "Yeah, that would be great. Thanks."

He immediately returned with a tall glass of water and set it on the nightstand beside me. "Uh, I am going to need a little help with that. I can't use my hands, remember?"

"Shit, I'm sorry, I forgot." He quickly picked up the glass and brought it to my lips.

Once I was finished, he pulled out his phone and dialed 911. I leaned back and closed my eyes and listened to Parker explain to the dispatcher what had to be one of the dumbest calls this person would get on their shift tonight.

"Uh, hello. I'm not sure if this is an emergency or not, but I have a woman handcuffed to my bed." His eyes widened. "Yes, she's all right. No, she's not here against her will." I tried not to cringe at his overpitched voice. "Yes, I'm sure. I somehow lost the key. Yes, she's conscious and awake. You want to speak to her. Okay, I'll put the phone on speaker."

Every muscle in my body tensed as I assured the

dispatcher that I was fine and we only needed someone to remove the handcuffs. I prayed that the recording of this call would never see the light of day.

With nothing left to do but lay there and wait for help to arrive, I gave Parker's room a quick scan. He had a pile of accounting journals and spreadsheets neatly piled on his nightstand and the dresser in the corner with a flat-screen TV mounted over the top. The small closet door hung open, revealing a handful of color-coordinated suits and dress shirts neatly hanging in a row. There were two dress shoes and a polish kit laying on the floor underneath.

He didn't have a lot, but his room was organized and clean. The only other thing I knew about him was that he was an accountant who worked too much. I gained that little piece of information from his ex as they tried to hash things out in the other room earlier. That's when I learned that Parker lied to me about being a rescue pilot for the Coast Guard. Instead, he was nothing more than a boring little bean counter.

"So, how long were you and the ex together for?" I asked, figuring I might as well make small talk while we waited for help to arrive.

He brought his palm up to the back of his neck. "Sarah and I dated for seven years."

I blinked, feeling my mouth hang open in surprise. "That's an awfully long time."

"She wanted marriage and kids, but I'm still building my career. We're both at different points in our lives."

"So, you're a workaholic?"

"I wouldn't say that. I would describe myself as ambitious. I believe that there's nothing wrong with wanting to succeed in life."

No, there wasn't. It seemed Parker and I had more in common than I realized. The life I presently lived on autopilot wasn't very fulfilling, but it was all I had and ever known. I was a no-nonsense, go-getter who worked hard in an industry filled with power hungry men. My career was something I could control and dictate. It didn't allow me time for relationships. I had tried a few times over the years, but I could never find the right balance between the two, so I gave up and fell in love with my career instead.

Parker sat on the edge of the bed, scrolling through his phone when a knock sounded at the door. He pushed himself off the mattress and went to answer it. It was difficult to hear their voices from the other room, so I stretched my head forward in time to watch two officers walk into the bedroom.

One was wearing a traditional blue patrol uniform and the other was dressed in all black. Black pants and black polo shirt with a black bomber jacket. The sight of him had my heart beating faster in my chest. There wasn't a doubt in my mind that if I had seen him before tonight, I would have noticed him.

His dark hair was swept in a tight wave along the top, falling down onto his forehead. I couldn't tell if he was Mexican or Italian, but whatever nationality he was, it worked for him, and he looked like the type that knew that too.

His eyes did a quick scan of the room as if he were looking for any sign of trouble. My gaze caught on the top button of his shirt. It was open enough to reveal a sliver of tan skin and draw attention to the gold rope chain dangling from his neck.

They both assessed me, and it took every ounce of self-control I had not to fidget under their scrutiny. I swallowed, feeling my muscles go tense. The one in uniform with a mustache reminding me of a younger Tom Selleck spoke first. "Good evening, ma'am. I'm Officer Peterson." His eyes did a sweep across my body as if he were making sure I was okay. "If you just give me one second, I'll get you out of these things."

He was polite and professional, and I was grateful for his calm demeanor. While I appreciated his attempt to put me at ease, I was still praying that the ground would open up and swallow me whole. This had to be the most embarrassing thing to ever happen to me.

Once Officer Peterson unhooked the handcuffs, I brought my wrists to my lap and started rubbing small circles along the red marks bruising my skin. Despite my fingers feeling slightly numb, it felt good to use my hands again.

I sneaked a peek at the hot cop. He stood tall, his jaw was clenched tight and his eyes were aimed straight at me. His stare was intense, and I was suddenly very aware of how hard my heart was pumping in my chest.

He pulled his gaze away from mine and narrowed it on Parker. "Are you going to help her?"

"Uh…" Parker glanced down at me. "Yeah, of course."

It took all my effort not to roll my eyes at his flimsy attempts to help me. I blamed it on his tall, lanky body. Where Parker's build resembled a swimmer's frame, the hot cop was filled out in all the right places. They were like night and day in every way possible, right down to caramel-colored skin versus ivory white. One was blond and boring and the other dark and dangerous. Now, if I had to guess who the rescue pilot was, it sure as hell wasn't "cuff boy."

I snagged my clothes from the end of the bed and practically ran into the en suite bathroom to change. I yanked on my jeans and sweater and shoved my feet into my high-heeled boots. If I thought I could quickly slide past the three men in the room and avoid eye contact, I couldn't have been more wrong.

All three heads snapped up at the sound of the door creaking open. Well, shit!

For some reason, there was only one set of eyes that I was focused on. The hot cop made me uneasy, an effect he probably had on most women. There was a good amount of confidence oozing off him without coming across as arrogant. But I really didn't like the way he studied me. His expression held too much sympathy and concern. As if I needed another reason to rethink my actions tonight. I could only imagine how bad this looked.

I straightened my shoulders and went directly to the chair to gather my things. I didn't know what my problem was, but I knew that I didn't want to stick around and find out.

I drew my scarf tight around my neck, trying to cover up as much exposed skin as possible. "Thank you," I said to Officer Peterson.

He gave me a kind smile. "Of course, before you leave, ma'am, I have to ask you a few standard questions. Let's start with your name." He reached inside his pocket to pull out a notepad and pen.

I forced a smile and pretended to be on board with answering these questions. I tried not to get too worked up thinking about this police report ending up in the wrong hands. Everything I've worked for over the past eight years would be gone in the blink of an eye. That was a risk I couldn't take.

Thankfully, the questions were pretty basic: name, age, address, birthdate.

I spoke slowly and carefully and did my best to not show how nervous I was. When the questions ended, I breathed out a sigh of relief.

Hot cop observed me from across the room. He barely said two words since he got here and I was questioning why he was even here to begin with. He stood a couple feet away, letting Officer Peterson do all the talking.

He looked like he was trying to figure me out, no doubt assuming the worst of me. He probably thought I was some kind of floozy who has casual sex with strangers all the time. Nothing could be further from the truth.

He turned his attention to Parker. "Next time you might want to be more careful." His voice was stern and sharp as he spoke.

His eyes shifted to mine and they softened. "Is there anything else we can help you with?"

I shook my head. "No, but thank you."

There really wasn't much more for me to do other than gather my things and get the hell out of there. The hot cop quickly moved to the side as I walked into the living room. A whiff of his cologne caught up with me as I passed by. It took every ounce of self-restraint to keep my feet moving in the opposite direction. I wasn't a stranger to Armani cologne, but for some reason it smelled better on him than anyone else. I wanted to go to the nearest store and buy a bottle to take home with me.

Parker was in the other room exchanging information with Officer Peterson, while the man who had me flustered followed closely behind me. I grabbed my black pea coat off the couch and nervously smoothed down the scarf once it was buttoned. I felt his presence at my back while I studied the floor for a long awkward moment. Hoping the uncomfortable silence would pass, I squared my shoulders and spun around to face him.

"Thank you both for coming to my rescue so quickly. I'm sure you have much more important things to do," I said, hoping he picked up on the sincerity in my voice. I was embarrassed beyond belief. There were probably people out there who really needed their help, but they had to take this stupid call instead.

"No thanks needed. It's our job and we are happy to help." His eyes had a certain sparkle to them that I hadn't noticed in the other room. Now that he was standing in front of me, I could see his face more clearly. "Plus, it's a slow night, so you didn't take us away from anything important. Unless you consider choosing between the glazed and jelly doughnuts we were about to buy. I just happened to be with Peterson when the call came through."

I laughed, feeling the mood in the room shift. I wasn't sure if that was meant to be a cop joke or what, but it was enough to relax my shoulders. And apparently, feeling less tense sent words flying from my mouth before I had time to think them through. "Well, from what I can see, you can afford to indulge yourself every once in a while."

My eyes widened. Did I really just say that? I sounded like an idiot. I was making a complete fool of myself.

He shoved his hand in his pocket and stared down at his dress shoes. He seemed so calm and collected while I wished I could forget this night ever happened.

I took an uncomfortable step back, thinking that a little distance would help me regain my bearings. "I'm sorry. I didn't mean it like that." My entire face burned with embarrassment. "I just meant that you appear to be in great shape, but I'm sure a doughnut of two won't change anything."

Jesus, take the wheel! This was the worst first impression ever.

His lip twitched and I couldn't help but stare at it. "Thanks. Keeping in shape comes with my job description. I don't really have much of a choice."

I nodded and did my best to keep myself from saying anything foolish. I'd already humiliated myself enough tonight. "That's as good a reason as any."

I slid my fingers inside my skin-tight leather gloves, hoping he didn't notice how much they were shaking. The weight of his stare made me nervous. I could see where he would be very good at his job.

Raindrops started to streak against the windows, while a burst of thunder sounded from the sky. Great, could this night get any worse? I glanced at the time on my iPhone and checked my Uber app. It said the driver Jorge was two minutes away.

"Well, I should probably get going." I held up my phone. "I appreciate all the help tonight."

"Wait," he called out as I reached the door. "Are you sure you have a safe ride home?"

He moved closer to me without even realizing it. Maybe it was just my imagination, but he seemed just as affected as I was. His close proximity was making it hard to ignore those butterflies that kicked around in my stomach.

I jumped when my phone dinged with a notification.

"That's my ride, and yes, it's safe." I held up my phone, letting him know that my driver was outside waiting for me.

"Okay." I watched the thick cords of his neck move as he swallowed. For some reason, I was noticing every little detail about him. "Because I don't mind giving you a ride home."

It seemed like he didn't want me to leave. Could he feel the chemistry between us too?

You're just imagining it, Amelia. He's just doing his job.

"I'm fine, but thank you for the offer. Have a good night, Officer."

Regret hit me the second I stepped outside. I've never been this affected by a man before and this felt like a missed opportunity on my part. I was torn between wanting him to drive me home and grateful that I turned him down. Temptation and distractions were something I didn't have time for.

A part of me wished that we had met under normal circumstances. One where I could give him my number and maybe go on a date. But it was pointless to even fantasize about things like that.

Sheets of rain coated the street as I carefully navigated through the muddy puddles so my feet wouldn't get soaked. It was just my luck that my Uber was parked three doors down on the opposite side of the street. Once I reached the waiting car, I slid inside and convinced myself that refusing his offer was for the best.

TWO

MARCO

The abandoned warehouse reeked of mold and dead fish. The sight and smell of decaying bodies caused me to slowly approach the scene. As the medical examiner stood over the dead bodies taking detailed notes, my thoughts were distracted by the repeated camera flashes recording the details of the gruesome scene.

"This is Jonnie Romas," Kevin Spencer, our crime scene specialist said, pointing to the first body. "He had a rap sheet that pretty much went all the way back to grade school. He started boosting stuff out of the local bodegas for fun and worked his way up the crime ladder from there. He's been in and out of the system since he was twelve. Six months ago, he was being looked at for the rape of a sixteen-year-old girl, but the witness refused to cooperate, and the charges were dropped."

"This guy over here." He walked toward the second body and reviewed his note pad. "Joey Ortiz. Age twenty-nine, just got out of Attica, released early for good behavior. He didn't make a lot of friends during the three years in the clink, but got really close to a guy named Benny Castro." I raised my eyebrows at that name.

Two years ago, I was the one who took down Benny for murder and extortion. He was a pain in my ass and we almost had the case tossed out by a dirty judge. The guy had greased a lot of palms at City Hall and paid a ton of cash to a scumbag lawyer that was just as dirty as Benny himself.

"This young guy here," he said, stepping over the yellow crime scene tape. "Is Alonzo Diaz. Age eighteen, been in and out of foster care his whole life. Not much of a record on him, but we did learn his sister, Juanita, was one of Benny's girls. She's been missing for over a month now." He drew his pencil around in the air, as if he were connecting all the dots. Clearly, there was a link between these three victims and Benny Castro.

"Our last friend over here is the most interesting of the bunch." He made a dramatic stop and looked down. "Perhaps you've heard of him? They call him the 'babysitter.'"

"Fuckin-A." I ran my hand along the back of my neck. The babysitter's real name was Cruz Carillo and he was a known human trafficker. This whole shitty mess was all connected to Benny somehow. I knew it in my gut. Like many powerful and well-connected criminals, it was likely Benny Castro was controlling things from the inside. And if that were the case, we were screwed.

I looked at the blood splattered across the concrete floor and examined all points of entry into the abandoned warehouse.

"I'm going to do a second walk through and see if the CSI unit collected anymore physical evidence." I patted him on the back and took another look around, searching for shell casings, footprints, anything important that may have been missed.

I was looking through my notes when I heard footsteps approach from behind me.

"Smells like our friends have been here for a while now,"

my partner, Logan Blake, said as I reflexively pulled up my foot to avoid stepping on a dead rat on the floor. Logan and I had been working together since we met at the academy. We bonded over the fact that we were one of the few that didn't have a military background. Which meant we had to do extra sprints and pushups to keep up. We became fast friends and hung out as much as possible outside of work.

"I think that's an accurate assumption, Detective." I turned and mentally noted the graffiti on the cinderblock wall and the mold along the ceiling. This place was a shithole and worked perfectly as an out-of-the-way torture chamber.

We had four dead bodies total. Each one shot execution style with a single bullet to their head. All at point-blank range and all somehow connected to Benny Castro.

I looked back to the four men, each with their hands zip-tied behind their backs and their arms and legs bound to a metal folding chair by silver duct tape. This had his name written all over it, but given the fact that he was still locked up at SCI Chester, he obviously didn't do the wet work himself. I wish I could say that this call was as much fun as the one I was on earlier this evening, but this was a long way from a barroom hookup gone bad. After closer inspection of their hammer smashed fingers, along with the foul smell, I'd guess this little party ended a couple days ago. Good thing it was winter and not summer or we would have needed gas masks to work the scene.

I rubbed the heels of my palms over my eyes, feeling a headache coming on. It was a little after one a.m., and also my third night in a row of overtime. I barely had time to eat, shower, and sleep before I was back at it again. Given the number of victims involved, this case was going to take up a good chunk of my time. I was the lead homicide investigator here, which meant that I would spend the next week chasing dead-end leads and interviewing uncooperative witnesses.

No one was interested in ratting out a guy as dangerous as Benny Castro.

Logan shook his head. "I say we got enough to start with. Let's get out of here."

"Lead the way." I held my hand out, pointing to the exit. I couldn't get out of that warehouse fast enough. As soon as we hit the sidewalk, a blast of cold air hit my face and I inhaled deeply for the first time since arriving on the scene. The ground was wet and muddy, but thankfully the rain had stopped. The flashing red lights from the cop cars lit up the dark street, reflecting off the windows of the surrounding building. There were bystanders and reporters gathered around the perimeter, whispering and watching for whatever would happen next. People loved gossip and a quadruple homicide would give the crowd a lot to chew on. Which was ironic because some of these spectators were no saints themselves and probably knew more about what went on in there than we did.

Logan handed me a bottle of hand sanitizer and we both scrubbed our hands raw. This place was disgusting. There was nothing nice about Nicetown. No matter how bad the city of Philadelphia tried to clean up the northern neighborhood, it would never be safe. Not with the drug dealers and gang bangers running the streets.

I walked over to my cruiser and started the engine to let my car warm up. I wanted to go home and take a hot shower to rid the rotten smell of death off my body.

Logan glanced at me, looking just as tired as I felt. "You wanna go grab a beer? We have about an hour before the bars close down."

"Nah, I'm going to circle the block a few times and make sure I didn't miss anything." I was hungry for answers and I wasn't going to sleep until I exhausted every lead.

"Okay. Suit yourself."

We shook hands and I said goodbye to the cops that were

camped outside. I slid into my unmarked car and drove through the streets looking for anything unusual. Working in homicide kept me on my toes. Even though the work could get dangerous at times, I couldn't imagine doing anything else.

I pulled into a gas station and scrubbed my hands down my face. A group of young kids, sitting on the half wall between Dazed Donuts and the local Wawa store, caught my attention. These "kids" were too young to be hanging out at this hour, but old enough to know what was going on in the neighborhood. My eyes scanned the area, taking in my surroundings. The streets were less crowded this time of night, but they weren't empty of the local gangs and homeless people scattered around. I got out of my car and headed in their direction. They sat up straight, their legs planted wide as they stared me down. They already had me pegged as a cop by my unmarked cruiser, and they weren't the slightest bit intimated or afraid of my presence. They sat there with their arms crossed over their chest, like they were waiting for me to give them shit.

I put my hand in my pocket and casually walked up to them along the littered sidewalk. "How you guys doing tonight?"

They sat perfectly still. Not one fidgeted, but I could still tell who the leader was and who the weak one was. The weak link avoided eye contact while the leader leveled his icy gaze on mine.

"Mind if I ask you guys a couple questions?"

The leader rolled a toothpick around his lips. "You can ask, man, but that don't mean we have to answer."

"I'm investigating a homicide at the warehouse on Nineteenth Street. You know the big gray building where they used to make wooden furniture. Just making sure you boys didn't see anything." The building was in their direct view and this was their nightly hangout. There was zero chance that they didn't know anything.

"Nope," the leader said, adjusting the Eagles ball cap that was turned sideways on his head.

"You a 76ers fan?" I asked the kid on the end who was wearing a Ben Simmons jersey.

"I live in south Philly, whaddya think?"

"I live in Philly too," I pointed out, "and I'm a Lakers Fan."

"You a LeBron fan too?" he asked, looking me over, not sure what to think.

"Nope." I shook my head. "I don't like bandwagon fans who jump from team to team just because they gain or lose a player. Plus, LeBron ain't got nothing on Kobe." He smirked, and I knew I had him at that moment.

Philadelphia fans hated LeBron James. With Kobe Bryant growing up right outside the city in lower Marian County, he had a giant local fan base. He was our hometown boy, and we mourned his loss hard when he died in that helicopter crash. True fans stayed loyal to the teams, no matter what. I wanted to present myself as someone who was loyal. Someone that they could trust.

One of the biggest hurdles cops faced today was convincing parts of society that they weren't the bad guys. Sure, we had our fair share, and the ones that did abuse their power deserved everything they got. Most of us just wanted to protect and serve.

The leader jumped off the wall, stood tall, and rose to his full height. He was probably an inch taller than me, but I still outweighed him by at least twenty pounds. "You guys keep asking questions about that warehouse. We don't know nothing about it because we didn't have shit to do with it."

I stepped closer, ignoring his attitude. I knew acting tough and staying quiet was the way they survived on the streets. It didn't make them bad kids; they were just defensive around cops. They assumed that we already thought they were guilty of something. It was ingrained in their heads since they were born, and thanks to a few shitty cops, I had to work harder to change their perception.

"I have no reason to believe that you had anything to do that. I was just wondering if you guys had seen anything."

"Yeah, well, we don't got no answers for you. And we sure as fuck don't want no trouble. So, whatever you're hoping to find, you ain't going to find it here."

"I believe you're telling the truth," I said, looking him straight in the eye and extending my business card. "But if something changes and any of you want to talk, here is my info."

It didn't surprise me that none of them accepted the card. "All right then." I smiled and slid the card back in my pocket. "You boys be safe."

I tucked my tail between my legs and walked back to my car. I wish I had more time to spend getting to know these kids so I could convince them to trust me. I wasn't one of the bad guys who would fuck them over. If someone helped me out, I had their back. I knew that they didn't choose this life and most just wanted to protect their family. I admired them for that, but I couldn't force them to talk to me.

On the way home, I took a last-minute detour. For some reason, I found myself driving by a brick brownstone in a much trendier neighborhood than Nicetown. Amelia West was the highlight of my fucked-up night. I couldn't even remember the last time I'd been on a call like that. It was times like tonight where I missed being on patrol. When I first started, I got a thrill from breaking up bar fights and handing out traffic violations. I was young and felt like king shit on Turd Island in my uniform. But as I matured, my taste for justice grew more intense and I needed more of a challenge. I loved being a detective, but going home to an empty house after a long grueling day was getting old fast.

I didn't know why I was searching for Amelia since she was long gone by now. Even though our interaction was brief, I couldn't stop thinking about her.

I've been attracted to women before, but never like this. Not even close. It was three hours and four dead bodies later and she was still in my head. How crazy was that? I needed to shut these thoughts down. The cost of her designer purse alone was enough of a reminder that she was way out of my league. Amelia West and I had nothing in common. So why the hell did my tired brain keep resisting the urge to look her up?

THREE

AMELIA

"So, tell me again how last night was my fault," Ava said as we sat, crammed in a small section of the cute little bistro we had chosen for our Saturday morning coffee date.

I set my latte down with a frown. "Because you are the one that suggested I take the pretty boy home for a no-strings hookup."

She laughed, drawing attention to our table. "Well, he was definitely pretty… But I never told you to let him shackle you to the bedpost. That, my friend, is all on you."

She had me there. What I did was stupid and reckless and so unlike me. For one night, I just wanted a little distraction, something to take my mind off of things. Instead of forgetting my problems, I ended up adding another one to my list.

"If last night's 'handcuffing' wasn't a sign from God that I was forever unlucky in the man department, I don't know what is."

Ava gave me a scolding look. "I think that's being a little dramatic, don't you think."

"Actually, no, I don't think so. This has been the curse that has been my love life for as long as I can remember. I've come to the conclusion that not all of us can have the perfect love story like yours."

Ava's life resembled a Hallmark movie. She met her husband Drew at a coffee shop on campus. He was a hotshot baseball player and strolled in with his teammates while she was studying for her calculus exam. He was the guy who could virtually have any girl he wanted on campus. However, the second he laid eyes on my best friend, it was love at first sight. She brushed off his advances and made him work for every date they went on. He loved the challenge and she loved the tease. Now, almost a decade later, she still keeps him on his toes and he still worships the ground she walks on.

"I think you're overreacting a bit."

"I completely disagree." I sat back and folded my arms in annoyance. "Remember Calvin James?"

"Oh, Calvin." She snorted and looked around to make sure no one was listening. "The chemistry major who didn't know how to use his little penis."

"Stop." I laughed, although that was an accurate description, so it really wasn't all that funny. "He was a sweet guy, but clearly he wasn't for me."

Calvin was cute and charming, but the longing was lacking during our six months together. We had zero chemistry in bed and lacked the intimacy I craved. Although I enjoyed our emotional connection, I wasn't looking for a close friend. So, I ended things and broke his heart.

I'll never forget when he stopped by my dorm to pick up his things. Right before he turned to walk out the door, he placed a set of 9-volt batteries on my lap and said, "Just in case you still don't think we have a spark."

I shook my head at the memory. "That breakup was the most awkward experience of my life."

"Oh my God, I forgot about that." She paused and her lips

turned into a grin. "How long did he stand outside the door and wait for you to run after him?"

I sighed. "He was like a guard at Buckingham Palace. I don't think he moved a muscle for two hours." I felt bad for the poor guy. It was after that experience that I decided to focus on my grades and enjoy my last two years of college. Sure, I dated a couple guys briefly after that, but no one worth mentioning. Once I graduated, I threw myself into the family business. It wasn't until I went on a blind date set up by a mutual friend that I met my next boyfriend. "And let's not forget Chad."

Ava made a sour face. Chad was the complete opposite of Calvin. He was a men's fitness model who drew me in with his beautiful stupid smile. He never met a mirror he didn't like. If he wasn't traveling to some exotic location for a photo shoot, he was at the tanning salon or having his teeth whitened at the dentist. I was infatuated with his looks and impressed with his bedroom skills. But then again, so was he. Looking back, I was definitely more in lust with him than in love.

"Ahh… Good old Chad. The idiot that spent more money on his clothes than you did. That cheating Fabio look-alike bastard."

"Stop." I laughed. "He did not look like Fabio. That's gross." I shivered. "I would also like to point out that you didn't always hate him."

"Just because I appreciated his ass in a pair of fitted jeans, doesn't make up for the fact that the guy was an asshole whose looks overcompensated for his lack of brain cells."

"True," I acknowledged while sipping my coffee. Speaking of fine ass, a smile touched my lips just thinking about the hot cop from last night. No matter how much I wanted to pretend that I wasn't attracted to him, the butterflies in my stomach just wouldn't quit.

Ava's big brown eyes flickered across my face. "Why do you have that look?"

A blush crept up along my cheeks and I tried to hide it by acting dumb. "What look?"

God. Having a childhood friend sometimes wasn't always fun. Ava knew my every facial expression, and sometimes it felt as though she knew my every thought. There wasn't anything I could get past her.

She gave me a knowing grin and propped her elbow on the table, cradling her chin on the tops of her hands. "Tell me about the hot cop who came to your rescue."

I shifted uncomfortably in my chair. "Do we really have to talk about this?"

"Yes, my life is insanely boring, I need to live vicariously through you."

If only that were true. "Your life is far from boring, Ava. Between the moms at Madison's school and the old ladies at the salon, you get your hands on more gossip than TMZ."

Not only did Ava have a family life that would make any woman jealous, she was also a successful business owner. Her upscale salon was situated right next to Tiffany & Co. She had an impressive clientele that paid big bucks that helped support her jewelry obsession.

She rolled her eyes. "I can tell you're deflecting, so give me some juice."

I looked down at my coffee and tried to keep my voice even. "There isn't much to tell, and he wasn't the one who rescued me, it was the other cop."

She coughed out a laugh and shook her head. "Only you that would happen to."

"Even if I did find him attractive, so what? It's not like I'll ever see him again." I looked down, not wanting to acknowledge how much that thought disappointed me.

She arched an eyebrow. "That's too bad because your eyes light up when you think about him."

I needed to shut this conversation down. If she sensed how hard I was crushing on the poor guy, she would never shut up about it. "My eyes do not light up."

She sat up and practically bounced in her seat. "I bet you went home and fantasized about him last night too, didn't you?"

"You're ridiculous." I scoffed, not bothering to even deny it. She was right. I went home and tossed and turned all night. No matter how exhausted I felt or how comfortable my mattress was, I could not get to sleep. My mind kept conjuring up images of him and those handcuffs. And there wasn't a chance in hell that I would ever admit any of that to her.

"Oh, this is awesome." She clapped and squealed like a young child who was just told she's going to Disney World. She reached into her purse to pull out her phone charger. "There has to be a way to find out his name," she said while plugging the charging unit into the wall.

If my head wasn't already pounding so badly, I would have banged it on the table.

"Ava." I put my hand out and told her with the same level of patience that she used with her five-year-old daughter. "Enough already! Okay."

She pulled her phone close to her face so she could see the screen better. "What was the other officer's name?" She all but ignored my request and I wanted to roll my eyes for the tenth time today.

"I don't remember." And that was the truth. Even if I did, there was no way I would contribute to her little Nancy Drew fantasy.

She set her phone down and sighed. "Well, there goes that idea."

My cell vibrated on the table, Owen's name flashed across the screen. I hit decline and put my ringer on silent.

Ava stared at me for a long moment while sipping her coffee.

"Just say it," I said, feeling my good mood evaporate. The sadness in her eyes got me every time. This topic made me uncomfortable, but there was no avoiding it with her. She hated this for me.

She flattened her lips and tilted her head to the side. "I hate the thought of you being miserable for the rest of your life."

I shrugged, trying to ignore the sting from her words. Although the thought of being stuck with Owen was pretty depressing. "Ava, this is what I want. My job makes me happy."

"Okay, so I guess we are going there. Have you and Owen made a decision yet?"

Owen and I had a long and complicated history. Even though we haven't been a couple (I use that term loosely) since we were in high school, it was always expected that the two of us would marry. It didn't matter that I didn't love him or that we could barely stand each other. My fate would be sealed the day I decided to step into my grandfather's role.

My fingers folded around the cup, thinking about the meeting that I was headed to after I was done with my coffee. "No. We haven't. Maybe this is the closest I'll ever get to a real relationship. Owen and I are both on the same page about what this is. We aren't in love, and I don't think we ever will be. Going through with this would be the smartest choice and the best option for me career-wise."

I hated admitting that out loud, but considering our families' close ties, this entire arrangement made sense. Owen needed to clean up his playboy reputation, and I had to follow through with my obligation to my family.

I glanced at the time and quickly gathered my things. "Shit. I gotta go. I'm going to be late." I stood up to throw away my tray and pulled her into a hug. "Try not to worry too much, okay?" I pulled back and held her at arm's length. "And next time you want to have a girls' night out, we are skipping the bar and going to the spa instead."

She laughed as I looped my arm in hers and strolled out of the cafe.

———

I slipped inside the conference room without a minute to spare. Thankfully, I had everything I needed in my messenger bag and was able to avoid a trip up to my office. I quickly grabbed a bottle of water, pulled my tablet out, and silenced my cell phone.

"I appreciate you allowing my private equity firm to perform the due diligence on the Autograph Hotels," said Michael Slate, from Black Heart Capital Management. He sat at the end of the conference room table, flipping through the pages of a thick, spiral bound business proposal.

"Mr. West, Mr. Eastan," he addressed my grandfather and his business partner, while Owen and I sat off to the side taking notes. "The two of you have built a very profitable business. My financial team did a thorough examination of your books, and we think your company would be a tremendous addition to our Titan brand of hotels. As you know, Titan enjoys an incredible reputation in the luxury hotel demographic, and we think their addition to the portfolio would drive our growth strategy and complement the tremendous brand your family has built over the last forty years."

Owen and I shared a glance. This meeting was bullshit. Our grandfathers scheduled this meeting to prove they meant business. Either we agreed to their terms and married or they would sell the company.

"Thank you for the compliment, Mr. Slade," interjected Owen's grandfather, Edward. "But I believe you came here to tell us how much Black Heart would be willing to pay for the properties." He sounded slightly impatient as he looked at his watch.

"Yes, of course." He cleared his throat and adjusted his glasses. "I know how personal this business is to you both. When we went through the survey reports, it showed that your guest and loyalty scores are off the charts. Your employees raved about how much they enjoy working for your company. Many of the comments stated that they felt like they were treated like part of the family, with the highest of praises extended to Amelia West."

My grandfather beamed at me with pride. "She's a major part of our success." He winked while Owen stewed in his seat next to me.

"Yes," Mr. Slade extended me a warm smile, "it's fair to say that she's a huge asset."

"Let's get back to the dollar figure shall we," Edward interjected.

"Of, course." He shuffled through a pile of papers. "It's quite difficult to give you an exact dollar figure. Based on the reports, however, we were able to estimate an all cash-offer of one point three billion if you were to sell to Black Heart."

A collective silence fell over the room; my grandfather and Edward stared at each other. It took me a minute to let the magnitude of that dollar figure sink in.

My grandfather stood from the table. "Mr. Slade, we appreciate your time, and Black Heart's generous offer. Clearly, we have no intention of making a decision today. However, I believe I speak for my partner and myself when I say that you've given us something to think about."

"Fair enough," Mr. Slade said. "I expected as much. The offer is valid for the next forty-five days. I know this is a lot to take in, but I look forward to speaking with you both in a week to see where your thoughts are on our offer."

Edward opened the door, allowing his assistant to escort Mr. Slade to the elevator bank outside the suite.

Owen shot out of his chair the second the elevator doors closed. "Damn it, old man. What the fuck are you playing at?"

Edward quickly pulled the door shut to the conference room and stalked over to his grandson. "Calm down, boy. You and your childish behavior have forced my hand in this situation. I told you that when this company was started that Jeffery and I both agreed that the firstborn son would take the reins and secure our family legacy. With Amelia's father no longer alive and your mother being nothing more than a socialite who is incapable of running a business, this is the plan." I wanted to cut in and tell him that Owen wasn't much better than his mother would be, but I stayed out of it. Everyone at this table knew that Owen unchecked would run this place into the ground if he were the only one in charge. He was better at spending money than making it.

Edward leaned forward and flattened his hands along the table. His stance was intimidating. "It is up to the two of you to lead this company into the next generation."

"You mean if I agree to an arranged marriage like the kingdoms were transferred in the medieval ages, for fuck's sake! It's like some crazy episode of *Game of Thrones*."

"Amelia is a beautiful and talented woman," he shot back and I wanted to sink into my chair. "You'll be lucky to have her as a wife."

"Okay." I stood up and put my hand out. This was embarrassing and a huge setback to the Me Too movement currently going on in our country. I didn't need them talking as if I wasn't here in the room. "I'm right here, everybody. I can speak for myself."

"Amelia, sweetheart," my grandfather said in a soothing tone. "You cared for Owen years ago. Maybe that fondness that you once shared could be rekindled. You know how much it would mean to me to be able to keep this business a family affair, but I want this to be your choice."

"Exactly," Edward added. "In order for this to happen, Owen will have to demonstrate a little bit more maturity than he does today." He turned to his grandson. "He will also need to give up his playboy ways and learn to keep his dick in his pants. The last thing this company needs is grainy photos showing up of you and one of your boat bunnies getting it on."

Owen cursed under his breath. His knuckles were white as he clenched his hands along the armrest of his chair. "Anything else?" He met his grandfather's cold eyes. It was safe to say that they didn't have the same kind of relationship that my grandfather and I had.

"Yes." My grandfather straightened his tie and turned his attention to Owen. "If you want to be a part of this business and enjoy the lifestyle that it affords, you will be loyal to my granddaughter and you will treat her with respect. That is non-negotiable."

Owen and I had our work cut out for us, that was for sure. I questioned if I could actually go through with this. Yet, I reminded myself that my grandfather needed me. He stepped up to the plate when my dad died. He's the only father figure I've ever known. I owe him everything. Now, with my grandmother in her final stages of Alzheimer's, he needed to focus on her. This business was his baby. I couldn't allow him to sell it.

I couldn't imagine what Eastan and West would look like if it were gobbled up by Titan Properties. This company was built from the ground up by these two men. There really was no other option.

"Don't worry, Grandfather. We will find a way to make it work."

After all, what did I have to lose?

FOUR

MARCO

I leaned forward, setting my elbows on the bar. "Did Mom put you up to this?"

My brother, Matteo, sat on the stool next to me. I left my mother's house with my brother hot on my heels. I just wanted to get shit-faced and not have to explain myself to anybody. Just me and my thoughts and no one to judge me or ask questions that I didn't want to answer.

"Mom didn't have to put me up to it, Marco. I figured you could use the advice of your wiser older brother right now. You know she would never choose her sister over you, but the grudge you're still carrying around is killing her."

My cousin and his family were going to be in town for the holidays, and my aunt wanted the entire family to get together. The problem was, my cousin's wife was my ex-girlfriend.

I sat up on my leather stool and glared at him. "So, now I'm an asshole because I don't want to sit across the dinner table from my ex-girlfriend who cheated on me, or the cousin who stabbed me in the back?"

Sienna and I were high school sweethearts. We fell in love during the time of puberty, braces, and spin the bottle. We were each other's first. First kiss, first time, first heartbreak. When she cheated on me with my cousin, it divided our close-knit family right down the middle. Everyone was forced to pick a side; you were either Team Marco or Team Antonio. Of course, my mother chose me and Aunt Connie chose her son.

He rolled his eyes while I tried to stay calm. "It's been over a decade. I get that you may never be able to fully forgive, and you're entitled to feel the way you do. But, dude, Mom lost her husband and is alone, she denied herself a relationship with her sister because of her loyalty to you. Don't you think she's suffered enough? Try to put your own personal feelings aside and do what's best for her."

His words gave me pause. I wasn't a selfish prick who didn't give a shit about his mother's feelings. The last thing I would ever do is bring her any more pain. Despite what I knew in my heart to be true, I hated the thought of her being sad. It wasn't my fault she chose not to talk to her sister.

"I'm not the bad guy here."

"No, you're not." He blew a breath out in frustration. "So, don't be the guy that keeps his mother from her family. Aunt Connie and Antonio want to make amends, it's time to put this foolishness behind us. Mom isn't getting any younger, and please don't take this the wrong way, but it's time for you to stop thinking about someone other than yourself."

"What the fuck." I pinned him with a deadpanned glare. This lecture was the reason why I wanted to be left alone. My brother, no matter how much I loved him, just couldn't help himself. He was only two years older than me, but always felt the need to keep me in line as if he were in charge of me.

He held his hands up in surrender. "What they did was wrong on so many levels, but it was ten years ago, hermano. Let it go. I'm not saying that you guys need to be best buddies like Matt Damon and Ben Affleck, but you can co-exist for a few hours in Mom's living room. They live on the other side of the country, so it's not like you'll see them very often anyway."

I have a lot of regrets over the years, but cutting my cousin out of my life wasn't one of them. He didn't just make a mistake; he crossed a line that he can never come back from. Even when my father died, he never tried to reach out to me once. If he was ever going to try to mend our relationship, that would have been the right time. If my aunt was still hurting, then my piece of shit cousin had no one to blame but himself. But my mom was a different story. I'm sure that if I took the time to look deep enough inside my fucked-up head, I would acknowledge that he had a point. Still, I was too headstrong to admit it.

"I'll think about it."

"Don't think Marco, do." He played with his watch on his wrist. "Maybe a few days to cool down and think things through will do you some good."

"Maybe," I grumbled and downed the rest of my drink.

Matteo patted my shoulder. "You need a ride?"

"Nah, I'm going to stay awhile. Go home to your family."

My brother was a good man, and I was a spitting image of him. We had the same dark hair, with the slight wave on top, identical brown eyes, broad shoulders, and the same height. But that's where the similarities ended. Matteo was a family man who dressed in suits every day to go to his big paying marketing job here in the city. He was the one who got good grades in school, married the girl who he met in tenth grade, and followed every rule to a T. No matter how hard I tried, I could never be half the man my brother was.

His strong arms came around my shoulder. "The roads are getting slick. You might want to head out soon."

"Thanks, Dad."

He chuckled and slipped his coat on. "I'll catch you later, bro."

I glanced around the bar; the place was empty. It shouldn't

have surprised me considering we were about to get hit with a big nor'easter tonight. I turned around in my stool and looked out the window. The snow was coming down hard. They were calling for two feet by morning, and by the looks of it, the weather was getting worse by the minute. The large flat-screen TVs mounted along the wall had journalists in their parkas reporting on how this was going to be the storm of the century. I sipped my whiskey and decided to book a room here at the hotel using my phone. I was already on my third drink and it wasn't like I had anyone home waiting for me.

Once I completed my reservation, I picked up the menu and figured I'd might as well order something to eat. As soon as I finished my order, I wrapped my hands around the crystal tumbler and scanned the lounge. My drink almost slipped from my hands when I saw the familiar blonde step into the restaurant.

Her long hair bounced along her shoulders in loose waves. She was wearing a sexy little black dress with matching high-heeled boots that carried her effortlessly across the room. Even in the dim lighting, there was still something about her that stood out. I couldn't look away even if I wanted to.

Her steps faltered when she noticed me, and her face colored in surprise. My shitty night just got a whole lot better. There was no way she could act like she didn't recognize me.

"Hello." I tried to suppress my grin as she stepped closer. My greedy eyes drank up every inch of her. I wanted to commit every one of her physical features to memory, and not just because it was an occupational hazard. It was for purely selfish reasons. I ran my hand along my jaw, trying to get myself to relax. "It looks like we meet again."

She set her purse down on the bar and gave me a suspicious once-over. "Hello, Officer." She flashed me a nervous smile and flicked her gaze across the room.

"It's Detective," I corrected her over the rim of my glass. "How are you, Ms. West?"

"I'm fine. Thank you." She dragged the stool out next to mine and took a seat. "I'm surprised you recognized me with clothes on."

A laugh slipped out of me, and I tapped my index finger to my temple. "I never forget a pretty face."

Shit! Was I flirting? The last time I saw her, I had to be a professional. Now, I was off the clock so all bets were off.

"This is crazy." She crossed and uncrossed her legs and attempted to pull down the hem of her dress. Interesting I thought. Most women would be pushing it up to get my attention. "I just realized that I never got your name the other night."

I grinned at her. "That's because you never asked me last time we met."

Her red painted nails fiddled with the paper cocktail napkin resting on the wood countertop. "It was a little awkward, don't you think?"

"Probably a bit more for you than me." I extended my hand. "Why don't we fix that and start again. I'm Marco."

"Amelia." She shook my hand. The warmth that spread through my chest from a simple touch caught me off guard.

"Nice to meet you, Amelia. Can I buy you a drink?"

Smooth, Marco. Real smooth.

"I'm not sure." Her lips twisted. "The last time I drank, it didn't end well."

"I don't think one drink will hurt," I said, trying to put her at ease. But then I just couldn't help myself, so I added, "Besides, I'm off duty tonight and I don't have my handcuffs with me. I'm pretty sure you're safe for now." I winked.

I could see the battle in her head forming over wanting to share a drink with me and wondering if she shouldn't. She had no reason to be nervous around me, but I was surprised at how much I liked that she was.

The bartender came over and leaned his arms along the bar. "Hello, Ms. West. What can I get you?"

I raised my eyebrow and looked between the two. "Hi, Charles, I'll have a dirty martini with extra olives, please."

"You can put that drink on my tab," I interjected, wondering how the hell she was on a first name basis with a fifty-something-year-old bartender with a British accent.

Charles and Amelia stared at each other. Something oddly familiar passing between them. "Thank you, but you don't have to do that."

"I insist." I reached for my drink while the bartender went off to prepare hers. Once he was finished, he placed the glass in front of her and walked to another customer. "You must come here often. Either that or Charles is a friend of yours."

"Actually, both." She leaned forward, and I noticed the black silk fabric of her dress tighten around her breasts. I forced my eyes upward, not wanting to come across as a creeper. "I work here at the hotel."

She dropped her gaze to her drink. I suspected something was troubling her, and I wanted to know the source of it.

I took a sip of my whiskey. "What do you do here at the Autograph?" I asked, hoping we would settle into easy conversation. Normally, I didn't have to put an ounce of effort into impressing a woman, but I was anxious to keep things going long enough to see if she felt the same spark that I did.

Amelia played with the napkin underneath her glass. "A little bit of everything, I guess."

A shadow flickered across her eyes, but it disappeared as quickly as it came. There was something about the way she said the words that had the detective in me wanting to push and prod until she confessed whatever she was hiding. She seemed to have the weight of the world resting on her shoulders, and I had a sudden urge to take it all from her. Which was ridiculous because I barely knew her. She wasn't my problem to worry about and I was off the clock. I had enough trouble of my own to worry about.

"Where's the boyfriend tonight?" I asked, feeling nervous and uncertain about this whole exchange. I was normally confident, but Amelia caught my attention and I was feeling off my game.

"Pardon?"

"The guy you were with last time I saw you," I said, choosing my words carefully.

She laughed, and the sound drowned out the chatter around us. I could listen to her laugh all day long. "He's not my boyfriend."

"No?" I assumed as much, but having her confirm it sent a grin sliding across my face.

She chugged the rest of her drink back and signaled for another refill. "That was a disastrous almost one-night stand." She cringed. "I should be embarrassed. You didn't actually catch me at my best moment."

"Trust me, I've seen much worse."

"I'm sure." She averted her gaze away from mine. "It's just that I don't make a habit of doing foolish things like that."

She didn't owe me an explanation. But I believed what she said. She didn't strike me as the type to participate in activities like that. Not that there was anything wrong with experimenting or going home with a stranger, but Amelia put herself in danger. I didn't want to make things more awkward for her, but I felt the need to address that.

"I can tell you're not that kind of girl, but you really need to be more careful. There are a lot of crazy people out there."

She swallowed, and I immediately wondered if I should have kept my trap shut. She probably came here to unwind after a long day and here I was giving unsolicited advice. "I know. Trust me. I'm done."

My jaw clenched just thinking about her and that idiot.

She had no idea that when my eyes landed on her handcuffed to that bedpost, my first instinct was to rush over, set the bed on fire, and cover her up. Although not in that exact order. The thought of the two of them together bothered me a lot more than it should have.

She watched the waiter place my plate of nachos down in front of me. "So, Marco, what kind of police work do you do?"

"I'm a homicide detective."

She leaned back. "Wow. That must be a grueling job. I can't imagine all the emotions and danger involved. Doing that every day must be exhausting."

"It does take an emotional toll after a while, but I couldn't imagine doing anything else."

An unsolved murder was like an open wound to a family. If I could put the pieces together and start them on to the grieving process, then it was worth it. I took pride in what I did and earned a steady paycheck, but I sensed she was more of a white-collar man than blue.

Amelia seemed like a sweet, down-to-earth girl with a great sense of humor, but she was obviously on the wealthy end of the spectrum. I might not buy designer clothes for myself, but that didn't mean I didn't know how much they cost. Judging by the silver watch around her wrist with the Tiffany & Co. blue surrounded by a dozen or more diamonds, I would say she was rolling in the dough.

And here I thought I was king shit wearing the latest version of the Apple Watch. "You mentioned that you worked here but never said what you did."

She reached inside her purse and pulled out a business card. "Here you go."

I flipped the card, noticing her job title said that she was President of Marketing and Sales Operations.

"President, huh?" I teased. "That's quite an

accomplishment for such a young woman. You're obviously driven and passionate about what you do."

"Thank you. My grandfather is part owner of the corporation, so this hotel is very special to me."

I choked on a tortilla chip and patted my chest with my fist, waiting for the sucker to pass. Once my throat was clear, I took a sip of my water. "Your grandfather owns this hotel chain?" I asked because, What. The. Fuck. I was struggling with how I felt about that because this woman was completely out of my league.

She grabbed a loaded chip off my plate without asking and starting munching away. "He does," she said, reaching for another chip.

I expected her to elaborate further, but she didn't. I was left wondering why she seemed to shut down whenever the topic of her employment came up. Clearly, it was time to move the conversation forward. "Does your family live here in Philly?"

"Yes and no. My dad died when I was ten. My mom moved to Palm Beach after I graduated high school and I am an only child. My grandparents still live here, and I consider Philly my home. It's not a big family, but it's all I have."

I took a hefty sip of my drink and watched her polish off a good portion of my appetizer. Shit. I ran a hand through my hair. That sounded depressing. I came from a big Italian family, filled with more aunts, uncles, and cousins than I could count. I couldn't even pretend to know what that was like.

"Are you close with your family?" she asked, dabbing the corner of her mouth with a napkin.

I leaned back in my seat and thought about how to answer that. "Somewhat," I said, not wanting to get into my family drama. Thankfully, she left the topic alone.

For the next hour, we ordered a couple more appetizers and shared some fun and light conversation. I noticed that she was ignoring her drink and mostly sipping from the glass of Diet Coke she ordered. Amelia was petite, but let me tell you, she had an appetite and a love for food that would make any Italian woman proud. My mamma would love her.

"So, what led you to sitting in a bar in the middle of a snowstorm?" Amelia asked, while licking sauce off her thumb. It shouldn't have turned me on, but it did.

I had a serious fucking problem when it came to this woman.

I cleared my throat and tried to shake off these weird feelings. "I was hoping to catch a buddy of my mine who works nearby, but he had already left for the day. I knew this place was here and figured it would be a good place to unwind after a stressful week."

She dragged her nail along the rim of her glass. "I understand."

A heavy silence took over us. Something told me she understood all too well. Maybe we were both dealing with the same shit.

"Can I ask you something?"

"Of course."

"I'm curious. How the hell did you end up going home with that schmuck?"

She rolled her lips together. "I didn't realize he was a schmuck at the time." The sarcasm in her voice was thick. "He told me he was a rescue pilot."

I drew back, squinting my eyes at her. "You bought that line? He didn't even look like he could rescue a golden retriever."

She pointed her finger at me. "In my defense, I was filled up on vodka, so clearly my judgment was impaired."

I titled my head to her martini glass. "Should I be concerned? I'm a whisky drinker, but I'm pretty sure those dirty martinis are made with vodka."

She plucked a green olive out of the glass with a toothpick

and sucked it in her mouth. "I'm on a two-drink limit from here on out."

"Ahh… I guess that explains why you switched to the soda." I grinned, and she grinned right back. Something soft settled in my chest.

Her big blue eyes flickered back and forth between mine, then down to my lips where they lingered before moving back up again. I didn't want her to shy away from me like the night we met. This intense need to take her up to my room and claim every inch of her took me by surprise. Maybe because I was afraid that I'd never see her again. If this was my only opening, I was taking it.

I scooted my chair closer to hers and draped my arm along the back of her stool. She shivered slightly at the barest touch of my fingers. If I could get her on board with my plan, this would be a night that we both remembered. "It doesn't look like we're going anywhere tonight. I got a text from my buddy at the station. The roads are already slick and they're only going to get worse."

She looked over to the white snow as it fell against the windows. The streets were covered in white fluff, and the lobby was nearly empty except for the few people that were stranded here like us.

She darted her tongue out and swept it over her bottom lip. "It's a good thing I know the owner. Maybe I should see about getting a room for the night."

"Actually, I'm already checked in. I was about to go upstairs. I've got a nice warm room with a king-size bed. No need to waste your money when I have plenty of space for both of us."

The line was pretty cheesy, considering she practically owned the damn place, but it was the best I could come up with.

Her eyebrows rose. "Is that code for what I think it is?"

I pretended not to know what she was talking about. "What exactly do you think it means?"

She didn't even try to hide the smile that played on her lips. "I think you're hoping to get lucky."

She had no idea about the things I fantasized doing to her. The sexual tension between us was as clear as the crystal chandelier hanging from the ceiling. I wanted her, and I wasn't going to pretend that I didn't. The only thing I wondered was if she wanted the same thing. Playing games wasn't my style.

As much as I enjoyed our flirty banter, I needed to make my intentions known. "I like you, Amelia, and I'm sure it's obvious that I'm attracted to you. If you want to put an end to this conversation, we can part ways now. No hard feelings. But if I'm being honest, I'd really like to take you upstairs to my hotel room." I reached out and stroked her palm. "So, what do you say? Will you spend the night with me?"

The bartender tried to act like he wasn't paying attention as he wiped down the mahogany bar top. When I turned in my seat to get closer, our knees brushed up against each other. The hitch in her breath sent all my blood rushing down south.

I was strung so damn tight because it seemed to take her forever to answer me. I'd never been the type to get nervous around a woman. Normally, I was confident, but she seemed uncertain and I didn't understand what her hang-up was. There was no question on whether or not she was attracted to me. And that wasn't me being vain. Her eyes were very expressive, and she looked pretty fucking interested. So, I was at a loss on what to think, and it was my job to read people.

She adjusted herself on the stool and seemed to tangle with her words a little bit. "I wasn't lying earlier when I said I don't normally do this kind of thing." Her eyes assessed mine as I prepared for a rejection. But then a sheepish smile tugged at the corner of her lips, and I got the impression that she didn't give it away very often. "And even though you were just lecturing me earlier about the dangers of one-night stands, I'm afraid that if we do go our separate ways that I'll regret it later."

"Is that a yes?" I asked for clarification as I ran my hand through my hair. By the way my palms were sweating, I might as well have been a teenage boy asking his high school crush to the prom.

She finally cleared her throat and put me out of my misery. "Yes, I'll spend the night with you."

I pushed my weight off the stool and reached for her hand. She eyed it with caution, but thankfully linked her fingers with mine and followed me out of the lobby.

FIVE

AMELIA

Marco frantically dug his key card out of his pocket. Fumbling it between his fingers, he almost dropped it three different times before waving it in front of the sensor. He impatiently pushed the door open as soon as we got the green light.

He pulled me into the room by the waist and pressed my back against the door. Soft lips crashed onto mine before I could prepare for the impact. I could taste the whisky on his tongue, and feel the desperation in his hands as they sifted through my hair. The sexual tension in the elevator was nothing compared to the level it was at now. I knew that I should have been worried that someone from work might see me, but I was too lost in the moment to care.

My hands twisted in his shirt as he rolled his hips into mine. I matched his movements, as if this was a dance we've done a thousand times before. His grip on me tightened, sensing the urgency flowing through me. I couldn't remember the last time I had felt so alive.

"I feel your need, Amelia." A strangled sigh left my mouth as he continued. "So, you better make damn sure this is what you want." His lips traveled down the column of my neck.

"Because you are going to get every fucking thing I have to give. All you have to do is say the word."

"I want this," I whispered. My voice was thick with emotion. I so fucking wanted this.

"I'm going to touch every inch of you," he whispered, turning that spark I felt earlier into a wildfire. "And I need you to promise that you won't hold back." Brown eyes locked on mine and I knew in that moment that I would give him whatever he asked for. "Promise me."

"I promise."

He slammed his lips back down in a frenzy. This was the kind of kiss that made everything else fade away. For once, I wasn't thinking about my future. I wasn't thinking about my career. I wasn't thinking about anything else other what was happening right here in this room.

"You're spending the night with me tonight," he whispered, moving his lips over my exposed shoulder.

"Isn't that the whole point of being here?"

His large palm reached out and cupped my face, he brushed his thumb softly across my bottom lip. "I meant the whole night."

Chills raced up along my spine as I stared at him. I didn't want to turn those words into something they weren't, so he needed to be clear on what this was. "This is just a one-night stand, right?"

His eyes searched mine. "Isn't that what you wanted?"

I didn't want to acknowledge the disappointment that grew in my stomach at the thought. I liked him more than I should have, which was why I was debating if this was a good idea. Developing feelings and attachments wasn't an option. But I knew if I didn't spend the night, I would be left wondering what it would have been like. The sensible and right thing to do would have been to turn around and walk out that door. But if I was going to make a bad decision, I couldn't think of a better one.

"I'm not sure what I want anymore, but I know I want this with you," I told him, desperate for things to continue. I wanted him to understand that I was ready for this. Whatever this may be.

His hand stilled. "I like you, Amelia, but tonight is all I can give you. I don't want to lead you on, but I'm not looking for a relationship. I need to know that you're okay with that."

I didn't know what was wrong with me, but for some reason that statement touched a nerve. "So how does this work? Am I expected to be gone before the sun comes up? Do I leave you my number on the nightstand?" I swallowed, suddenly unsure about what the hell I was doing and wondered if I should pull back. "I'm not trying to be difficult here, but I've just never done this before and I want to know what the expectations are."

He frowned at me. "You're thinking way too much about this. Just relax."

He was right. I was, and I needed to snap out of it before I completely messed this up.

I let out a resigned sigh, hoping he couldn't sense my embarrassment. "I'm sorry. I guess I'm not very good at this."

"Just to clear things up, there are no expectations, I'm not going to make you any promises that I can't keep. Let's just focus on tonight."

I smiled up at him, relieved that he was ready to get us back to where we were a few minutes ago. "I'd like that."

"Me too, beautiful."

He captured his mouth with mine. Our tongues tangled together, adding just the right amount of pressure with each stroke. He kissed me like it was what he was born to do, as if this moment was destined to happen.

There was no doubt that Marco knew what he was doing, because clearly, the men that I've kissed before have been doing it all wrong.

My head hit the wall as his mouth trailed along my neck. I

sank my teeth into my bottom lip to keep the curses from flying out of my mouth. I couldn't believe I almost talked myself out of this.

He let go of my wrist and pulled my dress over my head with ease. Next, he made quick work with unzipping my boots and tossing them to the side. I was wound so tight that I had to close my eyes and hold my breath. I don't remember being so eager for anything in my life.

He slowly unhooked my bra and dragged the straps along my shoulders, letting it fall to the floor. Once my lace thong was at my feet, he grabbed my hips and slid his hands down to my ass and carried me over to the bed.

He laid me down gently on the mattress and sucked in a breath. "You're beautiful," he whispered before placing a tender kiss to the corner of my mouth. The scruff from his jaw was foreign yet welcoming. I wanted to savor the feel of it against my skin.

He pulled away to kick off his shoes and quickly undress. The only light in the room was from the small lamp on the bedside table. The second my greedy eyes took him in, I wished that the lighting was brighter. Everything I could ever fantasize about was standing right in front of me. I practically salivated at the mouth.

He was hard everywhere, and grinned when he caught me catching an eyeful. My body shuddered with excitement at what was about to happen.

He crawled on top of me like he couldn't wait another second. His lips crashed to mine with desire and anticipation. I dug my fingers into his scalp, urging him on. Soft lips nibbled on my skin as his hands began their journey. He seemed to be taking his time, worshiping every inch of me. His hand brushed along my opening before dipping his finger inside. There was no question that he was paying attention to my sounds and movements. I got the impression that he was trying to give me exactly what I needed.

His finger moved in slow circles. "You are so ready for me," he whispered, as he continued to search for my most sensitive spot. My core muscles clenched and I felt the blood rush to my ears. I wanted to remember everything about this night. His touch. His voice. The smell of his cologne. I wanted it all ingrained in my head. I never wanted to forget a single second.

Marco took his time, drawing pleasure from me in a way I'd never felt before. My breaths were heavy while I held on to his shoulders in a death grip. I came fast and quick, never experiencing anything so mind-blowing in my life.

He swallowed hard as his eyes stayed on mine. His gaze was unwavering and I was struggling with trying to make sense of what was happening. I couldn't help but wonder what he was thinking.

I brought my hand up to cup his face. I could sense some type of struggle in his eyes as he peered down at me.

He brushed a piece of hair off my shoulder and rested his forehead against mine. The touch was intimate and soft and it confused me. "You are so unexpected."

"Is that a good thing or a bad thing?"

"I haven't decided yet." His brought his mouth down to my nipple and swirled his tongue around the peak.

"I hope it's a good thing." I smiled, as his hands and mouth moved around my skin, heightening my arousal.

"I guess time will tell." He teased me before moving over to my other nipple. "I'm going to make this a night that you'll remember," he promised as he positioned himself between my legs. Even though he was technically a stranger, I'd never felt so connected to anyone in my life.

I closed my eyes as he slowly eased himself inside. He was gentle at first before he grinded himself in deeper. I slid my hands down his back and lifted my hips to meet his. He groaned, moving into me, his thrusts grew hard and fast. His rhythm was controlled and measured as he filled me in a way no man ever has. All my nerve endings stirred back to life. Even though he just brought me to the brink a few minutes ago, I was ready to beg him for another release.

"You feel incredible," he said on a ragged breath before lifting my leg up to get a better angle. I wrapped my arms around his neck and pulled him closer. Everything about this moment was intensified. Sex has never felt this satisfying. Never in my life have I experienced so much pleasure and I knew I never would again. I curled my fingers into his back, my nails leaving marks along their path. The intensity hit without warning, shattering me as another orgasm tore through me.

Marco pinched his eyes shut as he barreled into me, chasing his own release. I couldn't tear my gaze away from him as he thrust one last time.

His head fell against my neck, and I ran my hands through his sweaty hair. I stared up at the ceiling wishing that things were different and wondered what they would be like if they were.

"You are amazing." He lowered his mouth to mine and kissed me sweet and slow.

We both laid there, neither one of us in a hurry to move. My chest rose and fell and I never felt more content in my life.

"I just need to…" His body went still. He jerked his head up to mine. His eyes were wide with panic. "I didn't use anything. Fuck." He climbed off of me so fast I didn't even have time to blink.

"Marco." He wouldn't even meet my eyes. This was absolutely humiliating. "It's okay. I'm on the pill."

He looked down and studied me. "I don't know what came over me. I'm always careful. I never lose control like that."

I pulled the white sheet up over my naked chest. "I'd like to point out that I don't do stuff like this either. Believe it or not, I've only ever had three partners up until you. And they were all men who I was in a relationship with. I don't make a habit of sleeping around. So, unless you tell me I have a reason to be concerned, we're good."

His shoulders relaxed. "I have to get physicals all the time for work." He scratched the back of his head and looked away. "I just had one last week."

"Okay," I said, still unsure how I felt about his reaction. He didn't owe me anything but it still didn't make me feel all that great. Talk about a mood killer.

"I'm going to go clean up. Be right back." He seemed nervous and skeptical. Did he not believe me?

I threw my head back on the pillow. This was why I didn't do stuff like this.

A few minutes later, Marco came back to bed and crawled in next to me. I rolled over, giving him space.

He brushed his thumb back and forth along my shoulder. "I'm sorry I freaked out."

"It's okay," I said, even though my feelings still hurt from his comments.

"Talk to me, beautiful." His voice was soft and tender, and it wasn't helping my emotions, which were all over the place.

I leaned into his touch. "You're going to think I'm stupid."

He kissed my forehead. "Try me."

"Your reaction bothered me. It feels like you don't trust me and I know that's stupid because we barely know each other. I just felt uncomfortable, that's all. What's even crazier is that I can't blame you for being concerned, considering the circumstances around how we met in the first place. God, I'm going to shut up now."

He grinned at me. "You're cute."

I narrowed my eyes at him. "I just rambled like an idiot and you think that's cute?"

He crawled over the top of me. "Do you want the truth?"

I rolled my eyes. "No, I want you to lie to me."

A burst of laughter tumbled out of him. "I didn't realize you could be so entertaining."

"I only act like this when I'm nervous."

He gave me a lazy smile. "Don't be nervous."

I rolled my eyes. "That's easy for you to say, Mr. One-Night-Stand."

The playfulness left his eyes. "I freaked out, because you make me forget about all my rules."

"What rules, exactly?"

"That's exactly my point. Most women know beforehand what to expect."

"Marco, I know what this is. You made your point loud and clear."

He let out a heavy exhale. "It's not just that. I lost control with you and that never, ever happens. I have my rules to protect women from being misled or hurt. I'm never this careless and that's nothing against you, so please don't take it that way. I don't know what happened. The only thing I could think about was being inside you, and once I was, I forgot about everything else."

I smiled up at him. "Maybe we both should just quit talking."

He laughed. "Yeah, clearly, I suck at pillow talk."

I smiled, remembering how amazing he was just a few short minutes ago. "Well, I can tell you with one hundred percent certainty that you do not suck at everything. My last two orgasms are proof."

He snaked a hand around my waist and positioned himself on top of me. "Two is nowhere near enough. We only have one night and I intend to make it count. I'm going to make this so good for you, you'll never forget me."

My palms flattened against his cheek. "And what can I do to make you remember me?"

He tucked a piece of hair behind my ear, a slow, lazy smile stretched across his face. "Trust me when I tell you I won't be able to look at another woman with blond hair and blue eyes again and not think of you." The tips of his fingers trailed down to my jaw. "You're pretty unforgettable, Amelia."

How was I going to let this man go? I didn't know how I was going to feel when the sun came up and I had to go back to my reality. The only thing I did know was that this was a one-night stand, and I wasn't supposed to feel a damned thing emotionally. But I liked the idea of him remembering me. What I didn't like was the thought of never feeling like this again. I fell asleep in his arms wishing that our circumstances were different.

The following morning came way too quickly. I snuggled close to his warm body, taking advantage of every second I had left.

I pushed the comforter aside and was thankful that he didn't stir. My body ached everywhere, it was a reminder of everything we did last night.

The last thing I wanted to do was leave this room. I had to face the real world at some point, didn't I? The one that was literally waiting for me right outside that door.

I quickly got dressed and stared at him. How could I feel something so strong, so quickly? There wasn't much I wanted for myself, but I wanted him. Unfortunately, he wasn't mine to be had. We lived in different worlds, and any thoughts about a future were nothing more than a fantasy. And I learned a long time ago that happily ever after's don't exist.

At least not for me.

SIX

MARCO

I LOOKED OUTSIDE THE WINDOW AT THE WINTER WONDERLAND laid out below me. I woke up this morning feeling relaxed and well-rested until I reached across the bed and realized that Amelia was gone. Normally, I would have been excited about being spared the awkward "morning after" goodbye, but this time was different. I wasn't sure what I expected when I invited her up to my room last night, but judging by how disappointed I was with waking up alone, I'd say I got way more than I bargained for.

I took a sip of my coffee and noticed the snowplows had been out all night, trying to clear the main roads, but the side streets were still pretty slick. I knew things would be a mess at Mom's house, so I took a hot shower, got dressed, and headed over to her place.

It seemed like every idiot in Philadelphia who had never driven in the snow decided to hit the roads this morning. When I pulled up to her house, I could see the city plows had packed the end of her driveway with a hefty amount of snow to remove. I trudged a path to her garage and grabbed the same shovel I used when I was a kid and began to clear out her driveway and sidewalk.

By the time I finished, it was mid-afternoon. I fixed myself a bowl of freshly made Italian Wedding soup and parked my butt at the kitchen table.

I sipped on my Diet Coke and scrolled through my phone. I got an email notification from the hotel telling me that my room charge was credited back to my account. My lips tilted up in a smile. Maybe I should stop by the Autograph this week and thank Amelia in person for taking care of my bill.

"Hey, Marco. Did you hear what I said?"

My head whipped up to see my mom standing in front of me. I didn't even hear her walk back into the room. She was wearing her usual black shirt and black pants. It was the only color she wore these days. Hell, even her apron was black. It was such a contrast to the colorful blues, yellows, and reds she wore growing up. Everything about her was brighter back then, even her smile. My father's death had been difficult for all of us, but for my mamma, he was her entire world. I searched her face, noticing lines around her eyes that weren't there before. She looked tired, and suddenly my conversation with Matteo the night before was fresh on my mind.

"I'm sorry, Mamma, what was that?" I couldn't even pretend to know what she had asked me.

Her brow furrowed. "I asked if you'd drop off some soup to your grandmother today. The food at the senior home isn't good and she needs to eat something. You know how stubborn she can be."

My grandmother was straight off the boat and moved to America when she was ten. Her stubbornness and love for good food was genetic.

"Sure."

She ladled the soup in a plastic container and wrapped up some fresh Italian bread in tin foil. She placed everything in a reused Macy's bag and set it in front of me.

She looked down at me staring into my soup bowl. "Marco, what's wrong?"

I reached for her hand. "Mamma, please sit. I want to talk to you."

She untied her apron and pulled out the chair next to me. "Tell me, *figliuolo*, what's troubling you?"

"I'm sorry about the way I reacted yesterday. I stormed out of here like a child."

She patted my arm. I noticed the smooth skin on her hand had wrinkled with age. Where does the time go? I stroked my thumb over her knuckles, wishing I could rid myself of the guilt I felt.

"Don't ever apologize for how you feel," she said softly.

I brought her hand up to my lips and kissed the back. "If you want to see Aunt Connie and her family at Christmas, I will be okay."

"Marco, you don't have to…"

"Please, Mamma, I do." I squeezed my eyes shut and shook my head. "Do it. It's the right thing to do. I know it's complicated, and I know you're worried about me, but I'll be fine. Right now, I'm more concerned about you."

She was the strength of this family. The anchor that kept us grounded. I'd spent the last ten years wrapped up in my own feelings that I forgot how important Aunt Connie was to her. I was so caught up hating my cousin that I didn't see how much my mother was hurting.

Concern tightened around the corner of her eyes. "Marco…" she paused, unsure if she should continue. "Do you still love Sienna?"

In all the years that the rift has been going on in our family, she's never asked me that. I'm sure she's wondered why I never brought any girlfriends home to meet her. "I promise you I don't love her like that anymore." This is where it got tricky. "Antonio's betrayal is what hurt the most. I know God wants me to turn the cheek and forgive, but I guess I haven't been very good at that." I exhaled slowly. "I don't know how I will feel when I see them, but that's for me to worry about. You need your family."

She shook her head sternly; the concern in her voice was strong. "My darling boy, you don't understand, they hurt you and when you hurt, I hurt."

"I know that, Mamma, but I'm not hurting anymore."

She looked up at me with worried eyes. "If you're sure about this…"

"I'm a thousand percent sure."

"Okay, I'll tell Connie we can do Christmas together, but that doesn't mean that I won't be cursing Antonio and Sienna out in my head." A tiny smile crept across her lips. "You know, I always had my doubts about that girl and after everything she put you through…" her voice trailed off.

"None of that matters anymore," I told her gently. If I could take one more worry off her list, or distract her from her grief in any way, I would in a heartbeat. "Honestly, even if I could go back in time and do anything differently, I don't think I would. Sienna and I ended up exactly where we were meant to be."

"She never appreciated you for who you were. I never should have allowed you to date her. She always rubbed me the wrong way. She always seemed so fast and promiscuous. Now your cousin is the stupid one who gets to deal with her."

A laugh tumbled out of me. "I love you, Mamma." I pushed my soup bowl to the middle of the table, so I could grab her hand. "I'm worried about you. You look so tired."

She looked at the linoleum floor before looking back up at me. "The holidays are tough for me. I miss your papa."

"I know you do. That's why I think spending Christmas with your sister will help."

Her lips thinned. "Do you think you'll find love again?

You are so handsome and have so much love to give. You have such a big heart, Marco. You need to share it with somebody."

"I'm not sure about that. I know I'm not looking for anyone right now."

She looked disappointed. I didn't have the heart to tell her that I didn't want to put myself in a situation where I would develop feelings for someone. Physical feelings were all I was interested in. Relationships were complicated and most of them didn't last, so why even bother? Why risk going through all the bullshit and risk getting hurt again? Why hand my heart over to someone when it will only get broken in the end? Been there, done that.

Rising to my feet, I pulled her out of her chair. She opened her arms and I fell into them. Her eyes watered over. "Thank you for doing this, Marco. Thank you for being so selfless. Your papa would be so proud."

I wish more than anything I could bring my father back to her. Very few people have what my parents had. Their love for each other is a tough act to follow.

The moment was interrupted when the kitchen door slammed shut behind Matteo. He shook the cold from his shoulders and stomped the snow from his boots. "Sorry to barge in and break-up your little happy moment." He smiled, but it fell when he saw our mother wipe her eyes. "Everything okay?"

My mother pushed herself away from me and embraced Matteo, kissing both of his cheeks. "Everything is perfect. It's good to see you." She glanced over her shoulder. "Where are Nadine and the kids?"

"They're home watching movies. I wanted to come check on you and see if you needed anything. I was going to shovel the driveway, but I see the good son already took care of that."

"Yeah, right." I rolled my eyes. Like he would lift a goddamn finger. "Let's pretend that you didn't time this perfectly."

"Oh, please. You're looking a little weak there, little brother. I figured you could use the exercise."

"How did your driveway get cleared this morning?" I cupped my ear and leaned forward. I was being a wiseass, but I wouldn't be a good little brother if I didn't give him shit. "That's right, you pay your eighty-year-old neighbor down the street to plow yours."

He grunted. "I'm helping Earl out. Do you know how hard it is to live off of social security?"

"Yeah, you're really helping the old man out," I teased. Earl Hennington lived next door in an in-law apartment on his son's property. Truth was, the old man couldn't sit still. And the arrangement worked to their mutual benefit.

"Shit, I forgot." He smirked. "You don't need to worry about saving for retirement. You have a nice state-paid pension waiting for you in about ten years. Must be nice to be able to retire when you're forty."

"Yeah, if I haven't been killed by then."

He rolled his eyes in mock amusement. "Dramatic much."

My mother slapped him in the chest. "Don't you two even think about fighting." She walked over to the stove and pointed to the kitchen table. "Sit down while I fix you a bowl of soup."

"Yes, ma'am." He complied, taking his coat off and pulling out the chair next to mine. "I see you got home okay last night. It took me almost an hour just to get off the highway. Traffic was backed up all around the city."

"I actually booked a room at the hotel." A smile tugged at my lips at the memory.

"That was probably smart. Although those rooms aren't cheap. I'm sure you weren't expecting to fork over almost three hundred dollars for a place to lay your head."

Last night took a completely unexpected turn and I have no complaints on where I ended up. Even if Amelia didn't credit me back for the room, it still would have been worth every penny.

"It wasn't bad. Work has been out of control, so it was nice to unwind and take the edge off last night."

If this were any other woman, I would be filling my brother in on all the gory details from last night. For some reason, which I couldn't explain, I didn't want to share the details this time.

"Are you guys any closer to getting that bastard that left those four dead bodies in the warehouse last week?"

I ran my hand through my hair in frustration. "My undercover guy is starting to get a little jumpy. He's been more paranoid than usual lately, but unfortunately, he's the only guy we have on the inside at the moment."

While I wanted to hammer him for answers, I knew I had to be patient. Most of the time I loved my job, but sometimes there was so much red tape in getting things done that it created more problems than it solved.

He set everything to the side and sat down. "I don't envy you, brother. I hope you catch these dirtbags soon."

"You and me both."

He broke off a piece of bread and spoke in a hushed tone. "So, what exactly did I walk in on a few minutes ago?"

"I decided to stop acting like an idiot. I told Mom not to worry about inviting Aunt Connie and her family over for Christmas. I assured her that I was okay with it." We both glanced over our shoulders as she pulled a tray of cookies out of the oven. "She needs this."

He leaned forward with his elbows on his knees. I expected him to gloat, but he surprised me when he patted my leg and said, "I'm proud of you, little brother."

"I guess I have to grow up sometime." I smirked, but he only stared.

Matteo placed his clasped hands on the table and scrutinized me from head to toe. "You're doing the right thing. I know this won't be easy on you, so you don't have to pretend with me."

I fidgeted in my seat, weighing the pros and cons to this conversation. "I'm over Sienna. I have been for a long time. I'll be fine."

He titled his head to the side, eyeing me carefully. "You seem different."

"Do I?" I wanted to be annoyed, but I had to admit my brother was on to me.

"Yeah, you've been smiling nonstop."

"I don't know what you're talking about."

Matteo was always observant. He would make a good detective. Or maybe he just knew me better than anybody.

"You've got this starry look in your eyes."

I scoffed and wadded my napkin up and threw it on the table. "Will you knock it off. You've been watching too many Disney movies with your kids."

He smirked like he knew something I didn't. "Nice try, but you are forgetting that I've known you your entire life. Something is up with you, because you're not acting like the miserable bastard that I've grown to love."

I glanced at my mom, who was rinsing a dish off in the sink. "It's a good thing you met your wife when you were fifteen. With lines like that, you would probably still be a virgin playing Call of Duty in Mom's basement."

He gave me a suspicious once-over and pursed his lips. "You're trying too hard to throw me off track. Now I know you're hiding something."

Mom strode over and draped her arms along both our shoulders. "What do you say when you're done eating that you boys get the boxes out of the basement and help me decorate the house for Christmas?"

I glanced at my brother. "Of course." I stood up quickly before he could grill me any further.

He gave me a look that said we weren't done with this conversation.

SEVEN

AMELIA

I TOOK A DEEP BREATH AS I STOOD IN FRONT OF MY grandfather's desk. My nervous fingers gripped the tablet in my hand. "I reviewed the numbers in our proposal and looked over the win rates in the past year for the convention business, and as your chief marketing officer, I have to say that I have a few concerns."

My grandfather's blue eyes assessed me as he leaned back into his leather chair. He pushed a stack of papers aside and steepled his fingers under his chin. "No need to dress it all up, Amelia. What are your concerns?"

I shifted on my high-heels. "If we are going to win the bid, we will need to come down with our pricing. I was told our numbers were way off and we are in jeopardy of being disqualified."

"Owen was confident that those numbers would win the bid." He sat back and watched me. "So why are his numbers so much higher than what the customer is expecting?"

"Owen believed that we could start high and work our way down to a mutually agreed number. I warned him that this would blow up in our face and look where we are now."

He pulled his glasses away from his face so he could rub

his eyes. "Amelia, you've always had good instincts when it comes to business. It's things like this that have me supporting this merger, if you want to call it that, between you and Owen. So, here we are. What do you propose we do now?"

I pushed my iPad in his direction. "I believe this is in line with the customer's expectations. I was able to make some changes that improved our margins and still decreased the proposed event cost to make us more competitive."

My grandfather dragged his eyes over the documents. Once he was done skimming through the details, he looked up at me. "Well done, my dear. As always. I will look at this more thoroughly when I get home, but this is exactly why this company needs you. Having you slip into my role after I retire gives me great peace of mind. It gives me the opportunity to spend more time with your grandmother without worrying about all this." His voice wobbled. "Her Alzheimer's is getting worse, I'm afraid I don't have much time left with her."

I swallowed a lump in my throat and pasted a smile on my face. That queasy feeling in my stomach started to form. "I'm glad I could help."

"Amelia, tell me what's going on?" He looked at me with so much tenderness and I couldn't bear the thought of disappointing him. "I thought this is what you wanted. I can tell this decision is weighing on your mind."

I tipped my head back. It felt like the walls were closing in on me. I didn't have any expectations outside of my career. Running this company was all I ever wished for. It is what I was groomed for, but marrying someone I didn't love felt like I was losing something I'd never be able to get back. "I do want this, Grandfather, but I don't want to marry him."

He cocked his head to the side and caught my eyes. "Are you dating anyone?"

I shook my head with sadness. "No."

In one heavy breath, I saw all the stress and worry leave his eyes. "Then what's the problem? I know this isn't the perfect situation, but you've said many times that business is your true love. This way, you'll have everything you've ever wanted, along with all the money and success you could ever dream of having."

My eyes fell shut. I didn't give a damn about the money and the status, but I did care about the business. It angered me that I was being railroaded into a fake marriage just to keep the two families happy.

Every bone in my body was screaming at me to tell him no, but the last thing I wanted to do was disappoint the one person who has supported me my entire life. But marrying Owen? God. I'm not sure I could do it. He was a walking, talking cliché. Selfish. Arrogant. Obnoxious. Womanizer. You name it.

"Can I please have more time to think about it?" I pleaded, trying to reach the soft spot I knew he still had for me.

"My dear, as your grandfather, I can see you have some serious doubts. You know better than anybody that I wholly believe in the institution of marriage. The last thing I want is for you to end up alone. I told myself that if you didn't find anyone by the time you turned thirty that I wouldn't even consider asking this of you. You and Owen have history, even if it wasn't prefect. I always felt that with a little time and effort the two of you could make it work. I meant what I said, and I want you to be comfortable with this decision. So, yes, I can hold off Jeffery for a few more weeks while you think it over." His expression grew serious. "Now, as the partner in this business, I need to remind you that I cannot keep stalling on your behalf. The sooner you get past the issues you have about this arrangement, the better. Have I made myself clear?"

I pushed off the chair and grabbed the iPad off his desk. "Crystal."

I gave my grandfather a fake smile before walking to the door. Something told me that there would never be a day where I would be happy about this decision. Instead of going straight to my office, I decided to pay Owen a visit. I couldn't keep putting this conversation off.

I rolled my shoulders back and knocked softly on the door as I pushed it open. "Hey, I was wondering if we could..." The sight in front of me stopped me mid-sentence.

Owen was seated in his high back leather chair with his hands placed behind his head. I couldn't ignore the red-haired ponytail bobbing up and down on his lap. He tapped the young woman on her shoulder to get her attention. She froze when she saw me in the doorway and sprang her knees off the floor.

"Amelia?" Owen stood up and turned so he could adjust his fly. I did my best to shield my eyes but there were some things that could not be unseen.

The redhead straightened her skirt, snatched her oversized purse off the desk, and raced out of the room without a backward glance. She was in such a hurry she didn't even realize that her shirt was still hanging open.

I walked over to the upholstered chair that sat in front of his desk and curled my hands along the back. "You need to be more discrete around the office. At least lock the fucking door next time."

"Well, hello to you too." He pushed back his hair and acted like I just didn't walk in on him getting a blow job.

"Owen..." I warned. "Don't act like nothing just happened."

"We aren't even married yet and you're already trying to tell me what to do." He smirked. "I can't believe you're this jealous?"

I probably should have been upset that my soon to be

fiancé was just caught with his pants down, but I felt nothing. I simply didn't feel a thing.

"If we are going to make this work, you will need to cut this shit out."

He rolled his sleeves up to his forearms. "Come on, Amelia." He cocked his head to the side. "Are you trying to tell me that you're not sleeping with anybody?"

Thoughts of Marco popped into my head, but I kept my face blank. "What you and I do behind closed doors is no one's business. However, this"—I pointed to his lap—"is unacceptable. You need to be more careful."

He loosened his tie from around his neck and walked over to the cart to pour himself a scotch. "Yes, wife."

"Owen, be serious. We may not be engaged yet, but when the time comes, it will be easier to convince everyone that we are a real couple, if you don't flaunt your whores around the office for everyone to see."

He took a long swig of his drink. "I'm not staying celibate, Amelia. Not when I can still have a little fun."

I fully expected him to sneak around and break every marriage vow there was once we were married. But we couldn't risk him being so careless and open with his flings. This was the exact reason why his grandfather was so insistent that he needed to change his reputation. People would not want to do business with an unstable leader who could not be taken seriously.

"All I ask is that you please exercise some discretion."

He raised his glass to me. "I'll do my best." He walked around his desk and relaxed back in his chair. "Can I ask you a question?" His tone completely changed. He went from sarcastic to serious.

I perched myself in my seat and ran my hands down the front of my skirt. "Of course."

He leaned forward. "When did you start hating me?"

His question caught me off guard, so it took my brain a minute to catch up. "Why do you think I hate you?"

He stared back at me with an expression on his face that I couldn't quite read. "Maybe hate was too strong of a word, but I can feel the resentment every time you look at me. You're not very good at hiding it."

While his observation wasn't entirely true, it wasn't completely false either.

"I'm sorry you feel that way," I said, trying to dance around his assumption. "I'm just frustrated with this entire situation."

He angled his head to the side. "Speaking of 'the situation,' we probably should clear a few things up."

"Like what?" I turned my attention to the window. Could he sense that I was having second thoughts?

He tapped his fingers along his knee. "If you want this to work and for things to be believable, then you're going to have to start acting like you at least like me."

"I don't think you need to worry about that. This company is way too important to me." I did my best to reassure him, even though I had no idea how I was going to pull this off.

"See." He pointed his finger at me. "That right there is the problem. You're all business." A smugness that I didn't like darkened his eyes. "You weren't always this uptight. What happened to you? When did you become so high-and-mighty?"

I stared at him for a long minute. Once upon a time, those blue eyes and handsome face had charmed me into thinking that I was special. Yet even back then, I never felt anything other than attraction to him. He acted like he knew me. As is if what we had in the past was something special.

I pushed to my feet. "I'm not playing this game with you. If you want to have an adult conversation then let's have one, otherwise we are done here."

Of course, in true Owen fashion, he ignored my request. "We were good together once."

A bitter laugh flew from my mouth. "We most certainly were not."

He flexed his jaw. "You need to let go of that animosity that you're still carrying around from when I cheated on you. I think it's time to let it go."

Sometimes, I wondered how I ever saw him as anything other than the arrogant blockhead that he was. "You took me as your date to prom and hooked up with the head cheerleader and her best friend in the parking lot later that night."

He rolled his eyes. "I was eighteen. Are you going to hold that against me forever?"

Owen would forever be a perpetual man-child. He will never take responsibility for anything. He will disappoint those closest to him at every turn. Sometimes on purpose. He didn't put effort into anything, least of all his relationships.

My cheeks burned with frustration. "Some men go off to war at eighteen."

It wasn't just the prom incident. It was the boat incident where I caught him making out with Maggie Regan under the swim deck. Or the mall incident, where he snuck off to one of the fitting rooms with a sales associate at Victoria's Secret while I was looking in the fragrance section. Or the best one, when I found our young student teacher walking out of the side door of his guesthouse.

"I am not going to apologize for being a hormonal teenager."

I wanted to yank my hair out. I could not handle this man right now. "You humiliated me."

I wasn't sure why I even tried explaining this to him; he wasn't mature enough to understand. Owen couldn't handle being in a relationship back then and quite frankly not much has changed since.

He checked his watch and looked bored with this conversation. "Look, I'm not going to let you make me feel guilty for something I did years ago. You are either in or you are out."

"I told you. I am in." God, it sounded like I had just made my decision. Had I? It wasn't like I had any other choice, not if I wanted to take this company into the next generation. I haven't invested the last ten years of my life to this business just to hand it over to some faceless buyer. Sure, I could move on and find something else to do. I had plenty of money, but where would that leave me?

"Good, I know you don't want to let down the old man. And quite frankly, I'm sick of my grandfather calling the shots. The old bastard thinks he can dictate my life. I can't wait to be free of him and make my own decisions."

"We both have a lot to lose," I reminded him. Owen didn't want to marry me anymore than I wanted to marry him, but we were in a no-win situation. I found it ironic that he was worried about me screwing things up for him. My job was way too important to me to let that happen.

He arched back and folded his leg across his knee. "All we need to do is play house and try to get along. Maybe we should start working on developing a physical connection."

"You're kidding," I said in disbelief.

He better not be suggesting what I think he was.

"Nope. If you want people to believe us, we will need to brush up on our physical chemistry. You know, kissing and hand holding in public." His eyes moved from my legs up to my chest. "You'll need to get used to having my hands on you."

"Owen." I shivered at the thought. "I think it's time we discuss boundaries."

"I don't want it to feel like I'm twisting your arm to be with me. I think you are forgetting everything that I am giving up. You can't expect me to be all work and no play."

My palms started to sweat. "I'm not having sex with you."

"No one is going to believe that we are passionately in love if we aren't physically familiar with each other."

Pretending to be in love with him was going to be hard. Letting him touch and kiss me without throwing up would be virtually impossible.

"Are we done?" I asked impatiently.

He took a sip of his drink and licked his lips. "For now."

I turned on my heel and strode out of his office. I needed a damn drink and it wasn't even noon yet.

EIGHT

MARCO

I pulled my car into Quinn's driveway and grabbed the bottle of wine. Quinn and I met in the academy years ago and our friendship just clicked. Both of us worked our way up to the rank of Detective around the same time and we've been close ever since.

Other than the rare times we crossed paths at work, Quinn and I haven't spent much time together lately. We used to go out after a shift and catch a ball game or a beer, but that stopped when Quinn got married and started his family. It seemed like all my friends were settling down lately, so I didn't get invited to couples' nights all that often, which was okay with me. I was comfortable being on my own most of the time. Staying single was my choice, so I wasn't crying into my beer wondering if I was ever going to catch a garter belt. If I was being honest, hanging out with my friends wasn't always a lot of fun. Eventually, the group conversation would turn to PTA fundraisers, inner family squabbles created by young friendships, and kid-themed birthday parties. So, there wasn't much I had to contribute to the conversations. On the plus side, I didn't have to worry about missing an anniversary or arguing over chores and finances.

The door opened before I even had a chance to ring the bell. Quinn stood there with Charlotte at his side, he had one arm wrapped around his wife and the other was holding his six-month-old son. Their daughter Emery came skidding to a stop in front of me, completing the perfect picture.

"Hi, Uncle Marco." Emery smiled, reaching out and pulling me inside. "It's cold out. Get in here, silly."

I laughed at how grown-up she seemed. It was just shy of two years since I met the little thing for the first time. Gone were the missing teeth, soon she'd have a mouth full of braces. The girl was full of life, and I loved how her face brightened whenever she saw me. I had a niece and nephew of my own, but I loved Emery just the same. Quinn was like a brother to me, so his family was my family.

"I'm glad you came." Charlotte stepped forward and threw her arms around my waist.

"I wouldn't miss it." I kissed the top of her head and flashed her that dimple that I knew she loved. I could feel Quinn glare at me, but to be honest, I didn't give a shit. Charlotte and I bonded when I was the lead investigator on the case involving her ex-husband. He was a crooked district attorney and a wanted fugitive who killed a family of five while driving drunk and high on coke. I was just thankful that he was off the streets and out of Charlotte and Emery's life.

After taking off my coat and boots, Emery ushered me into the house. Christmas music and boisterous laughter filled the downstairs level. When we reached the kitchen, Charlotte's two closest friends, Erica and Mackenzie, were settled around the kitchen table enjoying what looked like a couple bottles of wine. I noticed Mackenzie brought her boyfriend, so I introduced myself and exchanged pleasantries while we all got comfortable.

"Something smells good," I said, noticing the smell of fresh garlic and spices filling the room.

"Mom and I made lasagna," Emery said, while helping her brother into his little bouncy seat. Tyler was kicking and punching his hands in the air, clearly not happy about where he was being placed.

"You did?" I rubbed my hands together while Quinn went to the cabinet to grab a stack of plates. "Well, I'll have you know that I've been craving pasta all week. I hope you made extra because I'm really hungry."

"We did." Emery smiled proudly. "We made brownies too."

I glanced at Quinn. "Looks like I'll have to double my cardio tomorrow."

"Please," Erica said with her gaze slowly moving over my chest. "Looks to me like you can more than afford a cheat day here and there." She winked and chewed the inside of her cheek as she continued to trail her eyes down the rest of my body.

Charlotte covered her face in embarrassment, while I managed a polite chuckle. It was then that I noticed that Erica and I were the only single ones at the table. I've been around Charlotte's friends a few times, but this kind of felt like a setup. Her comment also reminded me of the night where I met Amelia. She had said something similar, which came off as cute. Erica's straight-forward advances, however, were not having the same impact.

"So, Marco, how are things going?" Charlotte picked up the wine bottle and gestured toward me. "Are you still charming your way through the ladies of Philadelphia?"

I held up my glass and smirked. "Believe it or not, I've been so busy with work, that my social life hasn't been very active lately." I wiggled my eyebrows for fun because she loved it when I acted goofy.

"What a coincidence." Erica arched a dark eyebrow. "Mine has been boring lately too. Maybe we should get together sometime."

I blinked and put the pieces together pretty quickly. Erica was trouble with a capital *T*. She was gorgeous with shoulder-length dark hair and dark eyes surrounded by thick lashes. Normally, I would flirt right back with her, especially in social situations like this, but instead, I found myself giving her comment a dismissive smile and shrugging it off.

Quinn watched me closely; everyone else pretended not to pay attention. I tugged on the collar of my shirt and sipped my wine, feeling like the center of attention.

"How's the home improvement project coming along?" Quinn asked, swirling his wine around in his glass.

My shoulders relaxed and I was thankful for the subject change. "Very slowly. I may need to borrow you for a few hours."

"I'm sure I can make that happen."

"Just don't let him touch any electrical wires." Charlotte smirked and stood up to go mix the salad.

"Don't worry, I'll make sure to give him the easy projects," I teased, and he gave me the finger.

The girls hopped up out of their chairs to help Charlotte put the meal on the table. We spent the next hour talking, laughing, and eating way too much food. The evening was light and fun and just what I needed. I was feeling more relaxed than I have been in a long time.

Erica and Mackenzie told Charlotte to sit down and take a break while they cleaned up. Quinn and I went downstairs in the playroom while Mackenzie's date went outside to take a phone call. We were in charge of watching Tyler while the girls sat upstairs drinking and gossiping.

Quinn set Tyler down in his bassinet and rested his hand on his back to make sure he was asleep. "So, want to tell me what's going on with you?"

I rubbed my jaw and played dumb. "I don't know what you're talking about." First my brother and now my best friend.

"Erica is an attractive woman. She is obviously interested in you and you embarrassingly shot her down."

"What, am I supposed to jump whenever a woman shows a little interest? I'm not a manwhore, Quinn."

"Hey." Emery's voice caught me off guard. "You shouldn't talk like that." She scrunched her nose up and I winced. I totally forgot she was within earshot.

"I'm sorry, Emery."

"I've heard worse." Her father sliced his gaze to her as she sat at the desk playing on the computer. She whirled around in her chair and rolled her eyes when she noticed Quinn's expression. "Don't worry, Dad. I know better than to repeat some of the stuff I hear."

Soft footsteps descended down the stairs. "Sorry to interrupt." Charlotte poked her head in the room. "Everyone said their goodbyes and the kitchen has been cleaned up. There are leftovers on the counter for you, Marco."

"Come here, sweetheart," Quinn called her over. "You did a good job with dinner tonight." He craned his neck to give her a kiss. "Now go upstairs and relax. I'll be up soon."

Jealousy swirled inside me from such an innocent kiss. It was a reminder of everything I didn't have. What would it be like to just be able to reach out and touch someone whenever I wanted? To have someone waiting for me at home.

She stared at him affectionately and caressed his cheek. "Thank you for putting this all together. It was great having everyone in one place." He squeezed her ass as she turned away and she grinned over her shoulder. "Come on, Emery, let's go upstairs."

"I don't want to," she whined.

Quinn mentioned that she was starting to go through mood swings. The teenage years were slowly approaching and I couldn't wait to grab a bowl of popcorn and a front row seat.

"If you want to go to Olivia's house for a sleepover next

Saturday, you'll go upstairs like your mother asked you to." Quinn's voice was stern and one he didn't have to use very often.

"Can I at least have an extra hour on my iPad seeing that I helped with Tyler tonight?" Emery asked with pleading eyes. I don't know how he did it, but there was no way I would be able to say no to her.

He reached out and tapped her nose. "Let's see how well you picked up your room earlier when I asked you to and then we will negotiate screen time."

That didn't look like the answer she wanted to hear, but she was old enough to know that challenging her parents anymore wasn't going to help.

She folded her arms and sighed. "Fine." She turned to me. "Good night, Uncle Marco."

"Come here, kiddo." I kissed the top of her head. "I'll see you soon."

Charlotte and Emery headed upstairs while I settled into the leather recliner in the corner. Quinn walked over to the bar he had set up in the back and brought me a Corona. I looked over to the bookcases straddling the seventy-two-inch flat-screen TV. Every shelf was lined with family photos. There were a few pieces of school artwork that Emery had made over the years, but the rest were of family vacations and happy moments they shared together.

"Thanks," I said as he passed me the bottle. "I never thought I would say this, but you're a good dad, Quinn. Emery and Tyler are very lucky to have you."

He leaned back in the couch and put his feet up on the table. "Thanks. It's not always easy, but I wouldn't trade this life for anything."

I closed my eyes and tried to imagine a life like this. "You don't miss the single days at all?"

He looked at the ceiling like he was thinking it over. "There are days when I miss the freedom, but no, I don't miss being single. I like having someone to come home to. Knowing that I don't have to go through the highs and lows of life alone makes life more bearable." He took a sip of his beer and set it down. "Would you like some advice?"

I rubbed a hand over my face. "I have a feeling you're going to give it to me no matter what I say."

"The timing has to right. Most people will say it's all about meeting the right person, but I'm not convinced that's true. Look at me and Charlotte. She was always my person, but when we fell in love all those years ago, our timing was off. You have to be ready otherwise it won't work."

"I met somebody." I let the words slip without intending to.

He picked up the remote and paused the basketball game that we were watching. "I figured," he said, moving one of the million throw pillows that were laying around.

"We hit it off and the chemistry was off the charts."

It's been a while since I've been smitten with a woman. On the brief occasions it did happen, it was short-lived. However, this high I've been riding didn't seem to be coming down anytime soon.

He angled his head to look at me. "So, what's the problem?"

"I don't know if I'll ever see her again." I squeezed my eyes shut, trying to figure out a way to gloss over last night. I was so damn conflicted about how I felt. "We hooked up and she left while I was still sleeping."

I tried my best to hide the fact that my ego was more than a little bruised by that move. She could have at least left a note or stuck around long enough to maybe get breakfast or a cup of coffee before we parted ways. But then I reminded myself that I was the one who gave her "the rules" which was probably for the best anyway.

"Ahh..." I expected him to look smug, but instead

understanding filled his features. "That sucks, you don't have any clue on how to contact her?"

I didn't want to admit that I looked her up on the hotel website. I thought about calling her, but then what would I say? *Hey, sorry to bother you at work, but would you want to meet up sometime?* Pestering her at work just didn't seem right. Besides, if she wanted to see me again, she would have at least left me her number, right?

I pulled on the back of my neck. "I'm not sure that would be a good idea. She is out of my league and I'm… you know."

He sat forward and propped his elbows on his long legs. "You have boundaries and create rules before you even have a chance to get close to someone. It's frustrating as hell watching you go through woman after woman, sabotaging your chance at any kind of meaningful relationship."

I glared at him. "You act like I sleep with thousands of women." While I do like to have my fun, that number isn't nearly as high as he thinks it is.

"You avoid relationships like the plague, which is a pity because you are missing out on a hell of a lot of good things in life."

"Are you forgetting that the last relationship I had left a big hole in my heart?"

He put his arm along the back of the couch like he didn't have a care in the world. "No, I didn't forget, but that organ inside your chest still works, right?"

I rolled my eyes. "Fuck off."

"Stop being an idiot. Do you want to be alone and miserable for the rest of your life? Don't you want more?"

My shoulders sagged. I wasn't sure what I wanted. There was a time where I thought I would want a family like this someday, but that all changed. Over the years I've lived my life on my terms and it worked for me. Now, after one night with Amelia, I found myself wrestling with feelings I hadn't thought about in years.

"I'm not looking for anything, Quinn. If it happens, it happens. I'm not afraid to put myself out there and try again. I'm just not interested in having my heart stomped on like before."

He inched forward and suddenly this leather recliner grew uncomfortable. "I understand that better than anybody. We can't go back and change the past, but it's never too late to get your shit together. Look, if you're still thinking about her, you obviously have some feelings that are worth exploring."

He was right. I did like her, but Amelia West was out of my league. She would eventually marry a trust fund baby or some rich CEO that shared the same power and pedigree as her. Either way, she'd never end up with a practical guy like me.

"It doesn't matter." I took a sip of my beer that tasted piss warm. "It would never work out with her anyway. Like you said, I'll be ready when the time is right."

I needed to stop thinking about this insane connection I felt with her. Even if I wanted to see what was on the other side of that door that she had cracked open, I wasn't sure I would be ready for what was on the other side.

So, why did the thought of never seeing her again suck so much? And why was I thinking more about our conversations than what happened between the sheets? I wasn't normally this confused, which was why I needed to move on and leave what happened between us back in the hotel room.

NINE

AMELIA

"Hello, Sophia," I greeted my eighty-year-old friend who was resting comfortably in her recliner.

Her little one-bedroom apartment was across the courtyard from the memory care building where my grandmother was living out the rest of her life. We met one day when I was wandering the grounds. Sofia walked over and sat next to me on the bench and offered me an orange Tic Tac. We ended up talking for hours and she ended up being a great distraction. We discussed everything from her obsession of Frank Sinatra to her current frustration with the Philadelphia Eagles quarterback. Sophia was a hoot and a breath of fresh air. I made a habit of stopping by every Sunday morning after my weekly visit with my grandmother.

"It's about time you got here. Sit down, *caro*." She pointed to the chair next to her by the window. "I just woke up from my nap. How's your nonna?"

I glanced outside where there was a dusting of snow sitting along the top of the Welcome to Tranquility Farms sign. I wish my grandmother could live in the independent living complex like Sophia instead of needing around-the-clock care in the other building.

I threw myself into the recliner. "Alzheimer's sucks."

"Not a good day, huh?" she asked, setting her teacup onto the saucer. I noticed that her breakfast looked untouched. Sophia always complained about the food and I've come to realize that unless she made it herself from scratch, nothing would ever please her. The chef never used enough salt, the bread was always soggy, and the sauce never had enough garlic. She was so damn stubborn that she barely touched what was served.

"She became too agitated and didn't recognize me, so I cut my visit short."

My grandmother's condition was getting worse, and it was painful watching her get lost inside her own head. As much as I didn't want to lose her, I didn't want her to stay on this planet like this either.

She reached her freckled hand out along the little round table that separated our two chairs and patted my leg. "I'm sorry, honey. That's a pretty tough thing to watch happen to someone you love."

"Thank you," I said, fighting the urge to cry. We sat in silence for a few minutes before I switched conversation topics. "What are you watching?"

"I didn't get a chance to watch *The Young and the Restless* yesterday, so Kristina recorded it for me," she said, pointing to the weekend nurse who was in the other room going through her prescription bottles.

"I didn't realize those soap operas were still on the air. I thought they got rid of all the daytime programs," I teased her playfully.

Sophia had an obsession with drama. Although I didn't watch them myself, I loved hearing about all the ridiculous plots and storylines that played out every day.

She pointed her long bony finger at me. "Don't you even start, young lady. You know if I don't get my Victor Newman fix a couple times a week, I get grumpy."

I couldn't help but smile. "So, what's the latest gossip going on around here?"

She pushed back in her recliner and started to fill me in on how George from the second floor got kicked out of his unit, because his wife Helen caught him down in the laundry room with another female resident when he was supposed to be at the barber shop getting a haircut.

Her eyes sparkled, Sophia lived to air everyone's dirty laundry and she wasn't a fan of Helen's. "Apparently, they were sneaking in these visits a couple times a week. I didn't think old George had it in him."

"Oh my God." I laughed while holding onto my stomach.

We spent the next few minutes watching her soap opera as she caught me up to speed on the current storylines. Who knew that baby switching and coming back from the dead three times could be so entertaining?

While Kristina was getting Sophia's order ready for the pharmacy, I stood up to check her fridge. She was so tiny and I could never tell if she was eating or not. I wanted to make sure she had what she needed.

A tap at the door drew my attention, it slowly opened, and I inhaled a sharp breath at the tall figured hovering in the doorway.

"Marco," I said, feeling my mouth hang open. It was taking my brain way too long to catch up with what the hell was happening. It had been exactly one week since I left him in that hotel room. Surely this had to be some kind of joke.

"Amelia?" he said, palming the wood along the doorframe as I waited on bated breath for the shock to fade.

"What are you doing here?" I stammered as he stepped into the room and closed the door behind him.

It was ridiculous how good he looked in a simple pair of jeans; and don't even get me started on that sliver of skin that peeked out from the open top of his collared shirt.

His eyes darted around the room before he pulled his brows together. "I was going to ask you the same question."

"Well, I'll be damned." We turned to Sophia, who was watching us with a mixture of curiosity and delight. "Tell me, how do you know my grandson, Amelia?"

"Um…" I took a calming breath and looked to Marco for help. I tried to find a resemblance or a few similarities between the two. Sophia had talked about her "single" grandson many times, dropping hints here and there like little breadcrumbs. Maybe if she would have mentioned his name, I would have been able to put two and two together.

He carried a plastic Macy's bag over to the counter and took out a small, round Tupperware container. "I met Amelia while I was on the job. She needed help, and I was happy to provide it." He winked at me, the cheeky bastard. He clearly didn't give a shit that he was embarrassing me. "How are you feeling, Nonna?" He strolled over and kissed her on the cheek while I took a deep breath, hoping to calm my racing heart. Funny, how I was chilly just a few minutes ago and now my body felt like it was overheating.

Sophia picked up the remote to pause her show. Apparently, what was going on in this room was more interesting than her soap opera. "What kind of help would that be?"

Marco smiled mischievously. "She lost a set of keys and I was able to help her out of a jam." I pinched my lips together, hoping to keep my facial expression blank. I could tell Sophia was growing suspicious and the last thing I wanted to do was give her a reaction. The woman didn't miss a thing, and I would never be able to look her in the eye again. He put his hand on his hips and looked between us. "I didn't realize you two had formed a friendship or that you even knew each other, for that matter."

"Amelia's grandmother is in the other building," Sophia

explained. "We met one day when she was wandering around. She's very *bella*. Wouldn't you agree?"

I'm pretty sure that meant cute or pretty. I glared at her. "Sophia—" I started to say when Kristina poked her head through the bathroom door and rounded the corner.

"Hey, handsome. This is a surprise." She beamed at him and adjusted her pink scrubs to give him enough of a preview of her chest.

Marco quickly averted his gaze to mine. He seemed guilty for some reason, and I didn't know what to make of his reaction to her.

"Kristina." He gave her a small smile that showed off his dimples. Irritation made its way through me. He wasn't doing anything wrong, but her stare lingered on him longer than necessary. Her tone was also way too friendly for my liking. It seemed like she knew him personally. Up until today, she never bothered me, but now I was hoping she would get reassigned to another floor, or hell, another building would be better.

"I didn't know you were stopping by today."

Marco dropped his head and rubbed the back of his neck. "Yeah, I was supposed to stop by with this soup last weekend but time got away from me."

His eyes floated to mine, the insinuation in his gaze was clear. He was with me last weekend and I was suddenly transported back in time. I bit down on my bottom lip and had to look away. I could feel the blush creeping up my neck.

"So," Sofia said brightly. "How's my favorite grandson?"

He laughed. "I'll pretend you don't say the same thing to Matteo."

"You bring my food over a week late again and you won't have to pretend to hear nothing." Her voice was threatening, but the crinkles around her eyes deepened with affection.

"Easy there, tiger. I've been working twelve-hour shifts for the last five days. This is the first opportunity I've had to visit. And don't worry, Mom made a fresh batch."

"Oh, you poor thing." Kristina reached out and ran her hand along his shoulder like she was looking for an excuse to touch him. My eyes did an internal roll in the back of my head. She inched closer, confirming my suspicion from earlier. "A few friends of mine are going out tonight. We would love to have you join us. It sounds like you could use a night out."

Annoyed, I stood to go fetch a bottle of water out of the fridge. "Kristina." I crossed my arms and leaned up against the counter. I leveled my eyes on hers and gave her a pointed look. "Do you have everything you need to send over to the pharmacy?"

My behavior was petty and I was acting like a possessive girlfriend when I had no right to.

She shifted on her feet and looked down at her notepad. Did she finally remember that she was here to take care of her patient and not hit on the guests? "Yeah, I am all set."

"Great." I slammed the fridge door shut with a little more force than necessary. Marco squinted at me. "I'm going to be here for a few more hours, so if the pharmacy doesn't have what she needs, let me know and I'll run out and grab it for her."

I unscrewed my cap and took a huge sip of my water. Since when did water taste so damn sour? A bit of guilt bubbled up inside me. I wasn't a family member; I was just a friend who stopped by once a week. I didn't have any authority over Sophia's care, but I'd already shown my claws, so it was too late to bring them back in now.

Kristina's teeth sunk into her bottom lip. She blinked her big doe eyes at Marco, and I really didn't like the way she looked at him.

When he didn't say anything, she clutched the notepad in her hand and moved toward the door. "Stop by and see me before you leave," she said over her shoulder on the way out. Clearly, I hadn't intimidated her at all.

Marco plowed his hand through his thick, dark hair, messing it up perfectly. His remorseful eyes met mine. Confusion and something else mixed together, reminding me why I didn't do one-night stands.

How was I supposed to explain this to Sophia?

Feeling her eyes on me, I turned my head. My elderly friend's lips curled up slowly. I braced myself because you never knew what was going to come out of that woman's mouth.

"Amelia, why don't you come over and sit with me and Marco?"

"Nonna, as much as I would love to stay." He smiled, but I could still hear the disappointment in his voice. "I'm on a quick break. I really need to get back to the station."

I looked around the room, trying to ignore the blow to my self-esteem that he seemed pretty eager to get the hell out of here.

"You work too much." She frowned. "Please tell me you're being safe."

Marco's eyes softened. "You worry too much."

"Excuse me, but my grandson has a dangerous job that sometimes requires him to use a gun. So, don't tell me not to worry."

He wrapped his arm around her shoulder and pulled her into his side. "I'm always careful. I promise."

"You are such a good boy." Her expression melted into an adorable smile. "Come back when you can stay longer. I need more than just a few minutes, okay?" She patted his cheek gently.

He stood up, zipped his jacket and turned to me. "I can't believe you and I have never run into each other before."

"Amelia visits me every Sunday morning if you ever want to stop by," his matchmaking grandmother offered up.

"I'll keep that in mind." He chuckled and backed away, but still kept his eyes on me. "Amelia. It was great running into you again."

"You too, Detective. Be safe." His eyes softened and moved down to my mouth where they lingered long enough to make me squirm. He shook his head and walked to the door.

"You ladies have fun and try to stay out of trouble. I don't want to have to break out those handcuffs." He flashed us both a wide grin and I wanted to slink inside the walls and hide.

A minute passed before Sophia stood up to grab her bingo bag. "You have some explaining to do, young lady."

"Sophia…" I didn't want to lie to her, but I didn't want to tell her the truth either.

Joan, one of the older nurses, popped her head in. "Hey, I'm here to see if you want me to walk you downstairs."

"You know what?" I stood up and ran my hands down the front of my legs. "I'll take her." The thought of going home to an empty townhouse wasn't all that appealing. I grabbed my purse off the chair and held my hand out. "You ready to be my bingo partner, Sophia?"

"She cheats," Joan said, as Sofia was slipping her shoes on.

"How the hell do you cheat at bingo?" I asked, locking the door behind me.

Joan adjusted her stethoscope around her neck as she fell into step beside us. "She tips the bingo caller twenty bucks."

I stopped and looked down at Sophia. "Are you kidding me?"

Sophia adjusted her cardigan and continued to walk ahead of me. "Don't listen to Joan. She loves to spread rumors. She's just upset because she wanted today off and they wouldn't give it to her."

Joan turned down the other hallway; her shoulders were shaking with laughter. "You two ladies have fun."

Residents and staff greeted us along the way. You could tell Sophia was a Tranquility Farms favorite.

We walked to the back of the room as she was greeted by a man named Archie who offered her a seat on his lap as he buzzed by in his wheelchair. She refused and told me that he offered all the ladies a "ride" and she turned him down every time because he had coffee stains on his pants and horrible breath.

We finally found two seats at one of the long rectangular tables and sat down in between Dolores and Shirly. I smiled and offered them a warm hello, noticing the dozen bingo cards taking up the entire table.

Sophia pulled out her blue and purple bingo dabbers and a bottle of what looked like lemonade. Shirly slid a Styrofoam coffee cup her way. Sophia looked over her shoulder and poured it into the cup. I picked up the bottle and smelled inside.

I leaned over and whispered so no one else could hear us. "Sophia, what is this?"

"It's limoncello, but we can't have booze here so keep it down." She leaned over and asked Shirly, "do you have the brownies in your bag?"

Shirly adjusted the rollers in her hair. "No, last time Archie tattled on me and almost got me thrown out of the bingo hall. I tried to tell them I ate them for medical reasons due to my arthritis, but they said I didn't have a medical marijuana card."

Dolores smirked. "Maybe you should explain to Amelia how you got out of it."

Shirly looked at Dolores. "Stop acting like you haven't taken a ride on Archie's wheelchair before."

My mouth hung open as I looked around the room to see if anyone was paying attention.

Dolores adjusted her dentures. "Please, everyone knows

that he can't get his equipment to work right, even with the help of that little blue pill."

"Will you two knock it off," Sophia scolded. "I have a guest and you two need to stop acting like *puttana's*."

I would have to look that word up later in my translator app, but I was going to take a wild guess that it wasn't very flattering.

The room went quiet when the announcer started to call out the numbers. Everyone picked up their markers and started dabbing away.

"So, how long have you and my grandson been involved?" Sophia's question jolted my eyes away from my bingo board.

I knew this conversation was coming, but I still wasn't prepared for it. "Marco and I aren't involved."

"Then what are you kids calling it today? Shagging, bumping uglies? I'm not sure what the terms are because you can't always trust the closed caption on the TV."

I laughed. "Marco and I met a couple times. There isn't anything between us, so get your mind out of the gutter. Besides," I said, staring at the bingo cards like I was checking them over, "you know my situation."

I had confessed to Sophia during my last visit that I was considering marrying Owen. There was something about our friendship that had me spilling my whole life story. Every messy detail. That was, of course, before I had slept with her grandson.

She shook her head in disappointment. "I saw how red your cheeks got when you saw him, and I saw the way his eyes lit up when he recognized you. The only thing I see on your face when you mention this Owen person is sadness. You are marrying a man that you don't love."

I opened my mouth to argue, but she was right. "You're not going to let this go are you?"

"*Caro*, you don't love that man. Take a piece of advice from a little old Italian lady. Don't live your life for anyone else but you." Her eyes glistened with tears. "I loved my Giovanni." She looked up at the ceiling and made a sign of the cross. "He was my beloved and I was his. If it's one thing us Italians are good at, it is love. You marry for love not business, *capire*?"

The words caught in my throat. "What if I never find love?"

"You will, you just need to open up your heart." She twisted her lips. "My grandson is a lot like you. A nanna knows these things. Give him a chance. If anyone can win your heart, it is my Marco. He is such a good boy. And handsome too, yes?"

I laughed. "He is. He must get his looks from Giovanni."

She smiled. "My Giovanni was dapper and smooth with the ladies too. They all loved him, but it was me he loved."

I pulled her in for a side hug, so grateful this woman came into my life when I needed her most. "Of course, he did. You're a beautiful lady, Sophia. Both inside and out."

"Now, I'm going to give you one more piece of advice. Food is the way to that man's heart. Never forget that."

I shifted in my chair and had a feeling she was referring to one man in particular. The one that was supposed to be just a hookup. Something in my gut told me I would be seeing him again.

TEN

MARCO

The past few days have been a complete blur. Whatever little free time I've had has been spent at the gym de-stressing or at home working on my addition. Regardless of what I've been doing, thoughts of Amelia have been creeping around in my conscience. What were the odds that she was the woman my nonna has been speaking so highly of? The young friend who paid her weekly visits.

I was just stopping by the other day to drop off her meal, say a quick hello, and get back to work. The last thing I expected to find was Amelia, chatting it up with nonna.

She looked as shocked and as surprised as I was. If this wasn't a sign, I didn't know what was. Normally, I didn't give women a second thought, but lately Amelia is all I've thought about. I've never been one of those soul mate guys—especially after my last "soul mate" hooked up with my cousin. Was it possible to forge such a strong connection just after one night together? I never would have questioned it until recently. Something about this woman had captured my attention in a serious way. I ran my hand through my hair and looked at the townhouse from the windshield of my car.

Looking up her name and address in our database was a new low for me. It was borderline stalking.

I made my way up her short walkway leading to her door. The neighborhood was upscale, which didn't surprise me given the family wealth she was born into. It was also unnervingly quiet, something I didn't get to experience much thanks to my profession.

I knocked on the door decorated with an evergreen Christmas wreath with tiny little fairy lights, and a red velvet bow. I had a speech prepared in my head, but the second the door swung open, her beauty had me at a complete loss for words. Her face was soft and free of makeup. The sweater falling off her one shoulder was showing enough skin to tease me. I remembered the way she tasted, the way she smelled, and I wanted to reacquaint myself with her all over again.

"Marco." She blinked those big blue eyes up at me.

"Hey." I cleared my throat and stuffed my hands into my coat pockets. "I apologize for just stopping by unannounced like this. May I come in?"

I could only imagine what she must have been thinking. I realized that I was breaking one of my rules. It was the first time I had chased down a woman. Normally, they did the chasing. That's not me being conceited either, it was the truth. Once I made it clear that I was only available for one night, it made women want me more.

"Sure." She nodded with her long, blond hair falling forward. I had a sudden urge to push it back with my fingers.

She stepped aside, and I inhaled that smell that I've been craving since the second I woke up alone in that hotel room. I did my best not to draw too much attention to how nervous I was, but having her this close to me made that almost impossible. When I noticed a blush spreading across her cheeks, I took that as a good sign.

She took my coat and put it in a small closet next to the door. "Can I get you something to drink?" She walked into the kitchen and opened the fridge. "Unfortunately, all I have is water and wine. Unless you want coffee."

"I'll have a glass of wine if you'll join me," I said, because I was feeling out of my element here and needed something stronger than a glass of ice water.

"Is white okay?" she asked, holding up a bottle of Cakebread. I recognized the label because it was my mother's favorite.

"I'm Italian, so I drink any kind of wine."

While Amelia was in the kitchen, I took the opportunity to glance around. Her living room was warm and rich with a cream-colored sectional with gray throw pillows everywhere. I walked over to the fireplace in the center of the room and studied the pictures on the mantel.

There was a graduation photo with her in a cap and gown, an older couple on either side of her. The couple beamed at her with pride, but it was her smile that captivated my attention.

"This is a surprise," she said, coming up behind me and handing me the glass of wine. She pointed to the frame. "That is one of the few pictures I have of me and my grandparents."

I nodded. "You're pretty close with them, right?" I remembered that little detail from our conversation that night.

"Very." Her eyes got misty as she glanced at the picture. "My grandmother is in the later stages of Alzheimer's."

"I'm sorry. I can't even imagine how tough that is." I could tell she didn't want to talk about it, so I skillfully steered the conversation in a different direction. "So, you and my nonna are pretty tight, huh?"

She let out a small laugh. "Sophia and I bonded instantly. Although," she pointed a finger at me, "she cheats at everything, and her friends at the nursing home are a bad influence on her."

I coughed on my wine. "Yeah, she's pretty slick, so don't

buy into her innocent act. She taught me everything I know so don't be fooled, or she'll swindle you out of everything you own."

She titled her head to the side. "Oh, it's like that, huh?"

"Want a tip for next time? Check her pockets for extra scrabble tiles next time you play."

She threw her head back, giving me a perfect view of that neck that my mouth spent a lot of time on. I was certain that I left a mark there, but she was gone that morning before I could confirm.

"So..." She gestured for me to sit down on the couch. I was disappointed when she took the seat opposite of me. "How did you know where I lived?"

I cleared my throat and sat up straighter. There was no sense in lying, so I told her the truth. "I looked up your information from the police report."

"Ahh," was all she said, and I was grateful she didn't seem too bothered by that.

I pulled on the back of my neck, trying to relieve some of the tension. "Look, I know we weren't supposed to see each other again, but I really enjoyed my time with you that night. And then when I saw you the other day," I grinned, hoping she found it just as amusing as I did, "I knew that I needed to seek you out."

She crossed her legs, and suddenly memories of them wrapped around my back had my zipper straining against my pants. "Why is that?" she asked, drawing my attention up to her face.

"Well," I coughed, "I'd like to think that we both had a good time that night, and I'd like to do that again."

She looked appalled at that suggestion. "So, you illegally gained my address, which I'm pretty sure goes against policy, and thought it would be a good idea to show up at my home unannounced and ask for a booty call?"

My eyes widened. "Shit, that came out wrong. I'm sorry,

Amelia. What I'm trying to say is that I'd like to see you again."

"With or without my clothes on?" She challenged me with a pointed look.

Was that a trick question? Judging by the way her blue eyes were turning icy, I'd say not. Okay, time for me to backpedal. This was why I preferred casual hookups who already knew the score. I had no idea how to navigate these conversations. What I did know was I didn't go to the trouble of looking her up just to come here and get shot down.

"I just want to spend some time with you," I said, trying to defend myself.

"Why? We were only supposed to be for one night."

"Yet, here I am." I smiled, trying to use my dimples to my advantage.

She grabbed a throw pillow and placed it on her lap. "I'm sorry I left that morning without saying goodbye." She looked part embarrassed and part guilty. I didn't want to admit to her how upset I was when I woke up alone.

I nodded and reached for my wineglass. "Is there any particular reason why you stole my thunder? I'm normally the one who takes off first."

She gazed at me with a look I couldn't quite decipher. "I assumed that's what you wanted." She held her glass up in the air. "And thanks for the reminder, by the way."

"I can assure you it wasn't what I wanted, and I'm sorry if I somehow implied that I did. And if it makes you feel any better, I'm not the player you think I am. I just like to keep things simple."

She seemed to read the sincerity in my eyes. "I just didn't want things to be awkward."

"You mean like now?"

She laughed. "Yeah, like now."

She seemed to be relaxing a little bit, so I decided to test the waters. "Seeing that you snuck out on me, I'll pretend that my ego isn't permanently bruised, if you'll agree to let me take you out on a date."

"Marco, you don't need to bullshit me."

Amelia had every right to question my motives. While I wasn't typically a monogamist when it came to women, I wasn't an asshole either. I just didn't like worrying about the commitment and pressure that went along with a relationship.

"I don't need to bullshit you. Just because I'm not looking for anything serious, doesn't mean that I can't take you out for a nice meal. Or go to a movie or whatever it is you like to do."

"But you told me you didn't have anything to offer me other than one night."

The one thing I hated was when people threw my words back in my face. She was obviously stuck on the word "one night" judging by how many times she used it.

My phone buzzed in my pocket. I held my hand up, signaling that I would just be a minute. "Hey, Mom."

"Hello, my boy. I hope I'm not bothering you."

"You could never bother me, but I am with a friend right now. Can I call you back?"

I looked over at Amelia, who was watching me with interest. She dropped her eyes, slipped her hair over her shoulder and started playing with her iPad.

"Oh, okay. I just wanted to tell you that Connie and her family will be flying in this Friday morning. They will only be in town for a week because Antonio needs to get back for work. So, I'm going to host an early Christmas with everyone. I hope you're still okay with it?"

My fingers tightened around the phone, and I leaned my head back. "Yeah, I'm good." I tried to be as gentle as possible because I could sense the concern in her voice.

"You sure, because you sound…"

"Mom, relax, it's fine. I love you. I will see you on Friday."

"Love you too, son. Thank you for doing this."

I ended the call and suddenly wished I had declined it. There were so many other ways I would rather spend my Friday night, but I would have to suck it up.

Amelia was reading something on her screen while savoring her wine. She looked cute, and honestly, I couldn't take my eyes off of her. Then a crazy idea popped into my head.

I leaned forward on the couch and rested my hands on my knees. "How would you like to meet my mother?"

Amelia choked on her drink. She set the glass down on the table and patted her chest. "Excuse me?"

"What's the big deal?" I grinned, hoping she didn't think I was a psychopath. "You've already met my grandmother."

She blinked at me as if I was crazy. In hindsight, I probably should have realized that this was a bad idea. If only I had more time to wrap my head around the entire plan.

"Marco," she shook her head, seeming genuinely confused, "am I missing something here?"

I leaned back, trying to get comfortable. I placed my ankle across my knee. While I really wanted to ditch this family gathering, I didn't see any another alternative. Not to mention, this was the perfect opportunity to see her again. One too good to pass up.

"I need a date for a family Christmas party." Her eyes locked on mine. We stared at each other for a full minute while I debated on how many details I wanted to share. "My ex-girlfriend is going to be there with her husband."

She drew her eyebrows together. "Why would your ex bring her husband to your family party?"

I looked at her, curious what her reaction would be. "Because her husband is my cousin."

"Oh, shit."

"Yeah."

She pulled her legs underneath her. "How did that come about?"

I stared into my glass. I needed to explain this well enough to where she wouldn't think I was looking for sympathy. I just wanted her to understand. "Sienna and I dated for years when we younger. What we had wasn't perfect, but I thought it was solid until she cheated on me with my cousin. There really isn't much more to say than that."

Her face softened. "There is obviously more to that if you need me for a buffer."

I curled my fingers around the arm of the couch. "The fallout caused a family rift."

There was a long stretch of silence.

"Do you think you'd still be together if she hadn't cheated on you?" She seemed genuinely concerned about my situation and it sent a warm fuzzy feeling to my chest.

"I'm not sure if things would have lasted with Sienna and me. What I do know is that there wouldn't be a family rift if my cousin hadn't stabbed me in the back."

She slipped the blanket off the back of the couch and laid it over her legs. "Were you and your cousin close?"

I drained the rest of my wine. "We were very close."

There was something about the softness in her voice that had me confiding all this shit. I didn't talk about this with anyone. The subject made me uncomfortable, but talking to Amelia was easy. She wasn't judging me, she just seemed interested in knowing my story.

She looked like she was thinking something over in her head. "Is she the reason why you avoid commitments?"

I cleared my throat, still trying to find the right words. "Partly. I'm just not looking for anything serious. I like my life neat, and low-maintenance." I scratched the back of my head, needing to switch topics. I felt like I shared enough of my dirty laundry. "How about you? What's your story?"

Amelia nibbled on her bottom lip and stared down at her glass of wine. "What makes you think I have a story?"

I cleared my throat and smirked. "Well, I know for a fact that you weren't a virgin. So, I'm guessing you have a past."

"A past, yes. A personal life, barely."

Her response caught me off guard and left me curious on why she seemed so closed off. My fingers drummed along the armrest of her couch. I could tell by the tension in her shoulders and the way she was avoiding eye contact that this topic made her uneasy. Her vulnerability affected me more than it should have.

"I get the impression that you don't like to talk about yourself very much. If this conversation makes you uncomfortable, we can move along. I was just curious. I didn't mean to pry."

"What do you want to know?" Her voice was so low I almost didn't hear it.

There was something in her eyes that drew me in, had me hungry for every little detail about her life she wanted to share. I found myself watching her with a careful expression.

"Whatever you feel like telling me."

She picked at the fleece blanket, seeming lost in her head. "My life isn't very exciting." She gave me a half smile. It had me wondering if it was real or if she used it for armor. "Working seven days a week doesn't really allow much time for a personal life."

"You know what I do for a living, right? You don't think I can tell when someone is leaving out important details?"

"Can't blame a girl for trying." She smirked, but it was her eyes that were smiling. "The truth is, being single is a life choice for me. The men that I work with and the one's that run in the same social circles as me, expect things to go a certain way. They are either looking for a wife that is equally as successful as them that will impress all their peers, or they want a cookie-cutter wife to stay home and raise their family, while they spend twelve hours a day at the office and all weekend on the golf course. Neither one of those options appeal to me."

"You know that there are more than those two types of relationships, right?"

"Yes, but it's exhausting trying to find someone who checks off all your boxes. It's easier for me to put all my time and effort in my work. I've had relationships in the past, so it's not like I don't believe in them, I just prefer not to have them."

I blinked back at her in surprise. I've never met a woman like Amelia before. I'm not saying there is anything wrong with her logic. When it comes to love and relationships, I've experienced first-hand what kind of damage they can do. I've loved and lost. I've watched my mother mourn my father. I've had a front row seat to Matteo and my friends tripping over themselves for their significant others. But to never experience any of that? How could a woman as beautiful as her not have broken a few hearts along the way?

"It sounds like your work is very important to you." I remember her telling me she had a very big role at the hotel. "What exactly do you do again?"

"I run all of the sales and marketing for the corporation. My grandfather is one of the founding partners. We have ten properties scattered across the US."

I sat back in my seat. "That sounds like a lot of pressure."

"I went into business because it was the logical choice. I thrived on the pressure. I knew early on what I wanted. How about you? Did you always want to be a cop?"

I coughed into my hand. "Surprisingly, no. My dad owned a construction company. His father came right off the boat from Italy. He appreciated the value of hard work, but wanted more for my brother and me. He insisted that we get a degree. I knew that I didn't want to work in business. No offense."

"None taken."

"I majored in criminal justice, not knowing what the hell I would do with the degree. I figured it would be more interesting than political science or economics. I never set out to be a cop, but after my first year of college it became more interesting to me. I do have a minor in sociology. So, I guess I have a back-up plan if this cop thing doesn't work out."

I couldn't remember the last time I did something so simple like this. Normally, my interactions with women were strictly physical. This felt different. More intimate. When was the last time I sat and had a conversation like this? A long damn time. I could talk to Amelia for hours. That thought had me checking the time on my phone.

"So, will you be my date?" I asked, trying to keep the desperation out of my voice. Maybe she picked up on my anxiety, or perhaps she felt pity for my situation. Either way, the smile she gave me took my breath away.

"When is this family dinner exactly?"

"This Friday."

She looked off to the side and shifted her eyes back to me. The fact that she was even considering it was a good sign. "You know what?" She stood up. "Why not."

I rose from the couch and grabbed my phone off the coffee table. "I love your enthusiasm. It really helps my self-esteem."

She laughed. "Something tells me your self-esteem will be fine."

She walked me to the front door. I stopped in front of her, unsure what to do. This felt like a defining moment. There was no denying my interest, and my need to kiss her was growing by the second.

"I apologize for the ambush tonight." I couldn't help but smile as she tried to act put off.

"I'm glad you stopped by." Her voice was soft and the fact that she was mere inches from me had my control ready to snap. Without giving it another thought, I pulled her in. I already spent way too much time in my head tonight.

I pressed my lips to hers, thankful that she didn't move away from me. My fingers threaded in her hair as I forced myself to keep the kiss gentle, which was difficult because what I really wanted to do was fuck her senseless right up against this door. But I didn't come here for that, so I stopped the kiss. Never in my life had I wanted anyone like this. Not even Sienna.

Her hands fell from my waist as I pressed my lips to her forehead. "Thank you for saying yes." I gently pushed her hair back. She looked disappointed that I stopped things from getting out of control and it confused me and elated me at the same time. I held my phone out. "I think we should exchange numbers."

She lifted an eyebrow. "You mean I should have yours, because I'm pretty sure you already have mine, you stalker."

I cupped her face, tipping her chin to align her lips with mine. "I'm sorry if I creeped you out. I just had to see you again."

She blinked at me. "Don't be sorry. In case you didn't notice, I kissed you back."

Oh, I noticed all right. Her little moans will be playing on repeat in my head for the rest of the night.

"I should go." I let my hand fall away. "I'll text you my digits."

The last thing I wanted to do was leave, but I knew I had to. I didn't want to get too far ahead of myself here. I made progress tonight and I wanted to leave things on a high note. I didn't trust myself not to screw everything up before we even got started.

ELEVEN

AMELIA

MARCO AND I HELD HANDS AS WE WALKED UP HIS MOTHER'S driveway. I spent over an hour debating on what to wear because what does one wear on a fake date? After trying on a dozen outfits, I settled on a conservative pair of black dress pants and my favorite cream sweater. I loved how it hung off my shoulder, but regretted putting my hair back in a ponytail because my ears were going numb from the nippy weather.

I gazed around and admired the quaint little neighborhood with snow-covered trees and various shapes of colonial homes. It reminded me of a scene you would see in the backdrop of a Hallmark movie. There was a strip of cute shops and restaurants just a few blocks away that I would love to explore. This little town would give Clark Griswold a run for his money. Christmas was still a little over three weeks away, yet almost every house was decorated in some type of holiday cheer.

Marco's hand moved to my lower back as we approached the front door. "Four things to remember. Don't worry about remembering everybody's name, don't forget to kiss on both sides of the cheek, be prepared to be hugged a million times, and watch out for the grabby hands of some of my older uncles and cousins."

I looked over my shoulder, silently counting the number of cars filling up both sides of the street. "Exactly how many people are inside?"

"Not really sure. I have a big Italian family." His answer did nothing to calm my nerves, and I wondered if this was a good idea.

He was about to turn the handle when the door opened. A man who looked just like Marco hovered in the doorway. A smile stretched across his handsome face. "You must be the mystery girl. I'm Matteo, this ugly guy's brother."

I laughed, loving his humor. He had an easy way about him that reminded me so much of Marco. "It's nice to meet you. I'm Amelia."

"The pleasure is all mine." He extended his hand. "Come on in and let me take your coats."

We entered through the mudroom and I couldn't help but notice what looked like fifty pairs of shoes. What the hell did I get myself into?

After taking off my boots and setting them on the mat, I handed Matteo my coat and followed both men into the living room. "Don't be nervous, you'll charm the pants off of all of them," Marco whispered in my ear.

That was easy for him to say. As soon as we entered the family room, everyone stopped talking and turned to stare. Apparently, seeing Marco with a date on his arm was enough to silence a crowd.

Every inch of the house was decorated with either multiple nativity scenes or commercial Christmas decorations. The tree sat in the big bay window and had more wrapped presents sitting underneath than I'd ever seen in my life. As my eyes moved around the room, I noticed food and groups of people congregated everywhere. Kids of all ages ran through the room, laughing and squealing as they chased each other.

Marco pulled on my hand, stopping in front of a small petite woman with shoulder-length black hair. The stunning older woman was at his side in an instant. She smiled and touched his cheek. Marco let go of my hand and drew the woman against him.

"Mamma, this is Amelia." He smiled proudly while keeping his mom tucked under his arm.

I fidgeted off to the side. "It's nice to finally meet you, Ms. Rubintino."

She stepped forward and planted a kiss on both cheeks. "Please, call me Marietta." She reached for my hand and held it in between hers. "I'm so glad you're here. You are absolutely lovely. My mother has not stopped talking about you and your visits. I can't you tell how you much she enjoys your time together."

I stepped back and ran my hands down my pants. "Thank you. I love spending time with Sophia. I'm sorry she isn't feeling well."

She shook her head. "She did her best to convince the nurses that she was well enough to come tonight, but we couldn't risk it. Not in this cold weather. She's a stubborn one."

I laughed. "She certainly is."

Marco handed her the foil covered dish we brought. "It's nothing fancy," I said. "Just a small charcuterie board. I didn't want to show up empty-handed."

She grabbed the tray from Marco. "It's perfect. Thank you."

"Marietta," a short, stocky woman with short gray hair called from the kitchen. "The food needs to come out of the oven."

"I'll be right there." She held out her hand and waved the woman off.

"Is there anything I can do to help?" I asked, hoping she would give me something easy enough to do.

She patted my arm. "You are my guest. Have a glass of wine and relax before the crazy starts."

Just then, a young boy came running toward us. "Uncle Marco."

"Hey there, buddy." Marco grinned, placing both his hands on his little shoulders. "I have someone I want you to meet." The little boy tilted his head back to look at me. He couldn't have been older than six or seven. "Nicky, this is my friend, Amelia. Can you say hello?" The little boy waved and buried his face in Marco's leg. "I think somebody is shy around the ladies."

I bent over so we were at eye level. "Hi, Nicky. It's nice to meet you. I like your baby Yoda shirt. Are you a Star Wars fan?"

Nicky's eyes widened, and he shook his head excitedly. "Me too. Do you know who my favorite character is?" I leaned in and whispered in his ear, "Chewbacca."

"He... he gets chased by stormtroopers all the time."

"Have you seen the new movie yet?"

Nicky started moving his hand animatedly. "I've seen everything. My parents are taking me and my sister to Disney. We are going to Galaxy's Edge and my sister wants to go on the new Frozen ride."

"Wow, that sounds like fun."

"My dad is going to help me build my own lightsaber. Maybe you could come with me? We are going to stay in a hotel with a swimming pool and me and Isabella are going to have our own room. You can even sleep in my bed with me."

Oh my God. I brought my hand up to my heart. This kid was so adorable.

"Easy there, my little Casanova." Marco laughed while running his hands through his nephew's wavy hair. "Don't go trying to steal my girl."

His girl? Even though this was pretend, I really liked the sound of that.

"Why don't go you find your sister and tell her that I have someone I want her to meet." Nicky started to run away but Marco stopped him. "Did your mom make her chocolate-pistachio biscotti?"

"Yeah, but she told me not to tell you where they are because you'll eat them all."

Marco feigned shocked while I stood off to the side watching this adorable exchange. He leaned in and whispered something in his nephew's ear before he took off down the hall.

"Come on." He reached for my hand. "It's showtime."

Right. That's what I was here for, so he wouldn't have to face his cousin and his ex-girlfriend alone. Not because I was actually his "girl."

After introducing me to a few cousins, aunts and uncles, we settled into the comfortable loveseat in the main family room. I noticed that Marco's mom and his aunts stayed busy in the kitchen while everyone else sat around drinking and socializing. The tables were littered with veggie trays, chips and dips, and every kind of homemade dessert you could imagine.

"So, how did you guys meet?" his cousin Peter asked while passing around pictures of his granddaughter who lived in Tampa with his son and daughter-in-law. Peter was a corrections officer at a local penitentiary, and I noticed that he and Marco liked to sit around and talk shop.

Marco grinned in amusement. "I guess you could say I was at the right place at the wrong time."

His sister-in-law, Nadine's, forehead wrinkled in confusion. "What does that mean?"

I shifted in my seat. Talk about an awkward moment.

"We were stranded together in the middle of a snowstorm." He stroked his thumb over my palm gently. I'd been so distracted that I hadn't realized that he had kept his hand over my knee the entire time. As a matter of fact, he hasn't been able to keep his hands off of me since he picked me up. "We bonded over drinks and nachos." Those brown playful eyes came back to me again. I wasn't sure if I wanted to kiss him for teasing me or strangle him. Oh, who was I kidding? It was the former.

"That's so sweet," Nadine gushed like she was clearly happy for him. He told me that his family was going to make a big deal out of him bringing someone home. I'm sure they were probably getting all kinds of crazy ideas about me. I felt guilty for tricking these nice people into thinking we were something more. What was even scarier was that I was wishing that we actually were.

"You'll have to excuse us for being so nosy," his brother, Matteo cut in. "We're just curious about the woman who caught Marco's eye." He winked and sipped his wine. "Speaking of eye, I need to stop by and look at the renovations." He turned his focus back to me. "What do you think, Amelia? How does everything look so far?"

I smiled, having no clue what the hell he was talking about. "I think it looks great."

"That's an interesting way of putting it. When I was there the other day, it didn't look much different from when he first started. As a matter of fact, you were still framing the room. How much progress have you made, bro?" He looked between us suspiciously.

Marco's hand spread out along my knee, giving it a tight squeeze. "Great. The drywall is up and sanded down, just needs some primer and paint."

"I wish you would have let me send a crew over to at least do the rough work," his uncle Frank added as he sipped his beer. "You know I wouldn't charge you a cent."

"I told you, Uncle Frank, I won't let your guys do the work for free and you refused to accept my money. Don't forget, before you bought my dad's business, I worked there every summer during high school. I'm perfectly capable of hanging a few sheets of drywall and nailing a few boards. Now if you want to come over and have a beer with me when it's finished, I'd loved to have the company."

Frank clinked his drink with Marco's. "Sounds good, just make sure it's on a Sunday, you know I save Friday and Saturday nights for the ladies."

Everyone around us laughed and Marco bumped my arm and whispered in my ear, "Uncle Frank is a serial dater."

I looked at his uncle who had to be in his mid-fifties; he was handsome and certainly didn't act his age. He was dressed in a Harley Davidson long-sleeve Henley, with a pair of faded jeans with a hole in the knee. He had the bad boy vibe with a baby face written all over him. Marco's family was an interesting bunch for sure, and I was surprised by how much I found myself enjoying their company.

Matteo tilted his head to the side; he had been watching me and Marco very closely. "So, Amelia, what color did my brother end up going with?"

My back went rigid. I felt Marco's stare out of the corner of my eye. I didn't dare look at him because it would be too obvious. My heart starting racing and palms started to sweat. I didn't have time to think this through, so I blurted out the first color I could think of. "Dark blue."

"Blue?" Matteo's eyebrows went up.

"Yes, blue," I repeated. Didn't every guy like blue? It felt like I was flying by the seat of my pants here. We should have prepared better for these kinds of questions.

"You decided to paint the kitchen cabinets blue?"

Oh, hell!

"Yeah," Marco answered, lifting his beer to his lips, trying to suppress a laugh. "You'll have to stop by next week when it's finished."

I felt terrible, especially when the questions started

coming at us like machine gun fire. Some were random, some were simple, and a few caught me off guard. I tackled the simple ones, and Marco would sweep in and save me from answering the tough ones. One thing I learned about Italian men was there was no bullshitting them. I could see why mob bosses were so intimidating. They knew how to throw you off with their charming smiles and innocent questions right before going in for the kill. Luckily, Marco was good at playing along.

When they were done, and seemed satisfied with our answers, Marco leaned over and closed the deal with a sweet, appropriate kiss. It was small and innocent, but it was enough for me to feel the cracks in the strong wall around my heart.

The house started to fill up with so many people that I lost track of who I met and who was new.

The doorbell rang and every head in the room turned to see who it was. Instead of the usual shouts of ciao or hello, the chatter in the room turned to complete silence.

I recognized Antonio and his wife even before I knew it was them. They made their way through the crowd, and I felt Marco stiffen next to me as they headed our way. Their two small children ran over to greet a few cousins they recognized, oblivious to the tension growing in the room.

I didn't know what I was supposed to do in this situation, so I acted on instinct when Marco stood up. I went to his side and slid my hand across his back. He needed comfort and I wanted to be the one to give it to him.

This was the first time he would come face-to-face with his past. The woman who cheated on him and the cousin who betrayed him.

I got a really good look at Antonio. He had the same dark hair as Marco and the same chiseled features, but he seemed like a cheap imitation copy of the original. Don't get me wrong, he was good looking, but he didn't have the same effect on me as the man standing at my side.

"Antonio." Marco nodded and drew in a breath as his eyes landed on his ex. "Sienna."

As much as I didn't want to admit it, Sienna was beautiful. She was tall and slim with long, dark silky hair, and high bronzed cheekbones that looked almost sculpted. She wore a tight green dress that highlighted every curve she had to offer. It struck me how jealous I was.

"Can we talk in private, *cugino*?" Antonio asked. I guess he wanted to get this out of the way. Then again, it's been ten years, so how much longer could this be put off.

Together, the four of us walked into a small sitting room at the back of the house, easing past the crowd of people who were doing their best not to stare. There were so many relatives and Marco was right, there was no way I would remember all their names. There were a few people sitting at a folding table but they quickly stood up, grabbed their paper plates, and scurried out of the room as soon as they saw us.

Marco wrapped an arm along my waist, pulling me tight against him.

"First," his cousin cleared his throat, "thank you for meeting with us. I know that it's because of you that our family is able to share the holiday season together. It really means a lot."

Marco curled his free hand into a fist. "I didn't do it for you. I did it for my mother."

Antonio didn't seem surprised by Marco's reaction. "I understand. I still appreciate you giving us this chance." Antonio coughed into his hand and shifted uncomfortably on his feet. "I am deeply sorry for what I did to you. I'm not going to give you any bullshit excuses because there is no excuse for what I did. I was wrong and I hope that you can forgive me someday."

I remember Marco told me they used to be close. How they were practically inseparable growing up. Well, until his cousin screwed his girlfriend.

"How have you been, Marco?" Sienna asked in a soft voice. His face was stoic, showing no sign of emotion. I squeezed his hand in a silent show of support.

"Does it really matter how I've been?"

"Of course, it does." There was a hint of sadness in her eyes. "I had hoped that you were going to be okay with us being here. It bothers me that you still seem so upset."

"Upset?" He let out a condescending laugh. "You don't need to worry about me. I'm doing just fine."

"Marco." Antonio sighed. "There have been many times where I've wanted to reach out to you. To apologize for what happened. To explain…"

He cut him off by raising his hand in the air. "There is nothing to explain." He alternated his stare between the two. "It's pretty fucking clear what happened."

Antonio shoved his hands in his pockets and looked down at the floor. "I still want to apologize to you. I didn't expect for things to happen between us, but they did. It's important for you to know that I regret hurting you. I acted selfishly, I was careless, I let you down and disappointed our family. But I don't regret falling in love with Sienna, I'm just sorry how it happened."

"You mean you're sorry that you couldn't keep your dick in your pants?"

"Jesus Christ." Antonio shoved his hand through his hair and shook his head. "I guess I deserved that. I know you need to get everything off your chest, so let's have it so we can move the fuck on."

"You may find this hard to believe, but I'm not still stuck in my past. I'm not in love with your wife anymore." I saw Sienna wince and look away. "I have nothing to move on from."

Sienna crossed her arms. "Then why are you acting like this?"

"Acting like what?" He tilted his head to the side and squinted. "I'm just giving it to you straight."

She moved her hair off her shoulders, her eyes were building up with tears. "You're acting cold and indifferent. This isn't you, Marco."

"This isn't me?" he said with a coldness in his voice. "You don't fucking know me, so don't act like you do."

Pain flashed in her eyes. "I'm so sorry."

Antonio wrapped his arm along her shoulder. I didn't miss the fact that she didn't lean into him when he tried to comfort her.

"What are you sorry for?" Marco drew his eyebrows in, giving her his full attention. I wanted to tear his eyes off her. She didn't deserve it, but what choice did I have other than to stand there and let him say his peace.

"For what I did to you. We were so young, and I know it's not an excuse," she swallowed, "we were in a bad spot. I had no idea what I wanted, but I did love you." Her eyes misted over and I saw the pain and the regret. I also saw something I wasn't expecting, longing.

An uneasy feeling grew in the pit of my stomach. When the hell did the lines between real and make-believe begin to blur? When did all this pretending turn into something real? Because there was no mistaking the very real jealousy running through my veins.

"You know what, Sienna? I wish I could be a different kind of man. One that could say, don't worry about it." He let go of my hand and placed his behind his head, trying to keep calm. "What you and Antonio did was fucked up. I know we've all grown, matured, and moved on, but that doesn't mean I have to sit here and shoot the shit and act like I enjoy being around you both. I'm doing this for my mother." He rubbed his forehead and looked to his cousin. "I appreciate you manning up and apologizing, but I'm not ready to go out back and have a beer with you. And please, don't mistake that as me still torn up about what went down. My mother needs to repair the relationship with your mom, so I'm going to put my big boy pants on and act like an adult. I've said all I have to say," he told them both, officially shutting this conversation down. I was so proud of him.

"Dad," a small voice floated across the room. We all turned our heads to see Antonio's little boy staring at us with curious eyes. "Grandma said she needs your help lifting something."

He squeezed his wife's shoulder. "I'll be right back."

Once he disappeared, a tense, heavy silence dropped over us. Sienna turned to Marco. "I'd like to speak to you in private, please."

"No."

She drew back. "I hate the way we left things, can't you just hear me out?"

"If I haven't responded to any of the letters you've sent me over the years, what makes you think I want to hear what you have to say to my face."

Tears trickled down her cheeks, and she bowed her head, giving it a slight shake. "I miss you, Marco." She wiped at her face. "I was young and foolish. I thought I could replace you, but I can't."

"Shut up. Shut up. Shut up." He glared at her; he could barely control his anger. "Your husband and your kids are in the other room. My girlfriend is standing right here."

"You don't love her. I know what you look like when you're in love, and this isn't it. You don't look at her like you used to look at me."

I took in a deep, shaky breath, hoping it would stop me from saying something I'd regret. But I was too angry, and I've had enough. "You're a piece of work, you know that?" I could not wrap my head around how pathetic this woman was. "You cheated on him and threw his love away. Marco has moved on, built a life for himself, and he clearly doesn't want you anymore. Why would you do this? Why would you say these things?"

Marco looked at me with raised eyebrows. I expected him to be upset that I stepped in, because truthfully, I had no right to do so. We were just pretending. We weren't a real couple, even though in my heart it felt like we were. Yet, instead of him looking angry, he looked impressed, if not pleased.

She smacked her hands on her hips. "Excuse me, but I don't have to answer to you."

"What about your husband? You have to answer to him, right?" I couldn't keep the irritation out of my voice. "What do you think he'd say if he knew that you've been writing Marco letters all these years?"

I had no idea if Antonio knew, but I was going to take a wild guess and say no. I was so angry on Marco's behalf, and I found myself wanting to stand up for him, which was ridiculous because the man could clearly take care of himself.

Her eyes grew stormy. "That's none of your business."

"Wrong answer. Marco is my business. You lost your chance with him. He doesn't want you. If I were you, I'd go back out there to your husband… where you belong. You both deserve each other."

The rage in my voice shocked us all. If I wasn't sure about coming here before tonight, I was damn glad I did now.

Sienna's nose flared with anger. The way she regarded me with hostility was supposed to be intimidating, but instead, I squared my shoulders, not feeling the least bit bothered.

"I don't give a shit what you think. You might have caught his attention for the moment, but you are only temporary. There has only been one woman he has ever committed to and you're looking at her."

As his woman or his pretending to be woman, I felt it was

my duty to put this bitch in her place. I could not seem to tamp down on the feeling of disgust I had for her.

"Are you sure about that? It seems to me that you're still living in the past. That's your first mistake. Your second is that you think that you still have a hold on him and you don't. And your last mistake was to think for one hot second that you have a shot in hell of getting him back."

Her upper lip curled in disgust. "I'm not going to stand here a minute longer and take these insults from you." She turned her attention to Marco. "This isn't over."

"Sienna." His voice was stern. "I want you to stop writing me letters. There is nothing you can say that will change my mind. If you continue to reach out to me after this conversation, I will tell your husband about them." She wiped her eyes and moved toward the door. "One more thing. If you ever disrespect Amelia like that again, we are going to have problems."

As soon as she stormed out of the room, I placed my hand on his arm. "Are you okay?"

Marco looked down at me and did the last thing I expected him to do. He threw his head back and laughed.

TWELVE

MARCO

"WHAT'S SO FUNNY?" MY LITTLE SPITFIRE ASKED. SHE DIDN'T look amused.

My hands instinctively went to her waist. "You. That was pretty damned hot."

She pushed on my shoulders; a playful laugh escaped. "I'm so disappointed in you."

"For what?" I pulled on her hand so I could bring her close. I gazed down at her creamy white skin against my tan. Her fingers were soft to the touch where mine were rough and calloused. We were opposites in almost every way possible, yet I've never been more drawn to anyone in my life.

"That's the girl you were hung up on?" She shook her head in disappointment. "I expected more from you. I mean don': get me wrong, she's beautiful and all, but you could do so much better."

Amelia handled tonight like a champ. I was afraid my family would put her under a microscope, but after all the wet kisses to the cheeks, and constant hugs, it was obvious my family loved her. Which kind of sucked too, because they were going to be pissed at me when they found out we weren't really together. Yet, the fact that she went along with the charade and stood up for me, had me seeing her in a different light.

And let me tell you, I was really noticing her. Her long blond hair was tossed back into a shiny ponytail and her lips were coated a shimmery gloss that made it hard to look away. I could not stop staring at her.

She might have been a corporate powerhouse outside of these walls, but it was impossible not to see the sweet woman who visited my grandmother every Sunday. I couldn't ignore the kind, caring girl who connected with my family tonight as if she belonged in my life. If there was ever a picture of a perfect woman, I was looking at it.

It was becoming clear that Amelia West was going to be my downfall. I was a fool to believe that I could keep things with her simple.

"Will you come home with me tonight?" I asked, trying to keep the desperation out of my voice. I wanted more time with her, but I didn't want her to think that I planned this out.

Her eyes softened; she seemed surprised that I would ask that. "You mean spend the night?"

"Yeah." The idea of having her in my bed didn't scare me as much as I thought it would. "Your standoff with my ex kinda turned me on." I winked, playing off the seriousness of the conversation. Truth was, I had no idea what I was doing. I just wanted to spend more time with her tonight. And if that included touching and kissing, then that was even better.

"Marco." She placed her hands on my shoulders and stared into my eyes. Her gaze was searching, and I had no idea what she was looking for, but I hoped whatever it was, she found it. "What are we doing here?"

That was a good question. One I didn't know how to answer.

I squeezed her hip. "I don't really know, let's just roll with it."

She looked unsure and I was reconsidering my offer. It made no sense why she seemed so guarded.

She shook her head and glanced up at me. "You are a hard man to say no to."

"Then don't. Just say yes."

Her eyes flashed down to the carpet, and I couldn't help but wonder if maybe she really didn't want to come home with me. Maybe she just wanted me to drop her off at her door tonight and part ways. Maybe that scene in the other room was all an act. Maybe the drama with my ex was more than she bargained for. I suppose I could have read the situation wrong, but I don't think I did.

"I didn't mean to put you on the spot. I'm sorry. It was just a suggestion. I can bring you home."

I swear when it came to my professional life, I could solve some of the hardest cases. I was good at listening and paying attention. However, when it came to reading women, sometimes I felt clueless.

She shook her head. "No, I want to. I'm just surprised you asked me that's all."

"Does that mean you want to come home with me?" I asked, feeling my palms sweat with nerves. Why did it seem like I never knew where I stood with this woman?

"I do, but I didn't pack an overnight bag with me."

I pulled my eyebrows together. "Is there anything you need? Any medicine you take that can't wait until morning?"

"No, but I don't have a change of clothes handy."

I leaned in and kissed her lips. "You can borrow something of mine. Come on." I pulled on her hand before she could change her mind. "Let's go say our goodbyes."

The drive back to my place was quiet, and by the time we pulled into my driveway, I was feeling self-conscience. There was nothing special about my neighborhood. It was a typical middle-class suburb with single-family homes. But as I stared at the ranch that I purchased a few years ago through the windshield of my car, I was starting to wonder if this was a good idea.

I didn't bring women back here. I was a cop, so I needed my privacy. I couldn't risk the chance of some crazy hookup finding me. I pressed the remote for the garage door opener and pulled my jeep inside. I pushed the button to turn the car off and straightened in my seat.

"Are you ready for the tour? Just keep in mind that I'm in the middle of renovations."

She cringed. "Oh, that's right. I'm so sorry about that. We probably should have prepared better for those questions."

I ran my hand through my hair at the reminder. I was going to have to take a couple days off and recruit a few of my buddies to help move things along. If my brother stopped by before everything was finished, I would never hear the end of it. "I hope you know how to use a drill and hang up drywall. I'm going to need all the help I can get."

She unbuckled her seat belt and hopped out. "Let's see what I have to work with."

I led her into the mudroom, and we hung our coats up on the hook next to the door. I turned on the kitchen light and held my hands out. "What do you think?"

She stepped into the kitchen and looked around intently. "Marco, is that a breakfast nook?"

"Yeah," I said, moving around the paint cans and the ladder that were up against the wall. "This place was a real fixer-upper when I bought it. I tore out the dining room and opened it all up. I bumped this room out and put the long windows in last fall. A buddy of mine is going to make the bench seats and wooden table for me to fit inside the space."

"I love it," she said, walking around the island in the middle of the room. "How long have you been working on this place?" I noticed that her eyes were still on the breakfast nook, and I was surprised at how excited she was about it.

"A couple of years. I started with outside and now, I'm

focusing on the inside. I just finished renovating the master bedroom and bathroom this summer."

She moved around the room, running her fingers along everything. She tapped her chin in deep thought. "Are you looking to do dark or light?"

I placed my hands on my hips and thought it over. "Well, seeing that the kitchen flows into the rest of the house, I was hoping to keep it neutral."

She walked through the house moving her head in every direction. My living room was a mess. There were tools and leftover scraps of material scattered all around. I wanted to curse myself for not having everything cleaned up. "I have a few ideas," she said, biting the inside of her cheek. "What if you did a soft gray paint and mixed tile backsplash underneath the kitchen cabinets? I think you could do a lot with that color palette?"

"That's not a bad suggestion," I said as she walked over to the slider and stared out into the backyard.

"Is that a hot tub?" She pointed to the deck.

"It sure is. Why don't we go for a dip and brainstorm some ideas?"

She looked down at her cream blouse and black pants. "I don't have a bathing suit."

I rolled my eyes. "Amelia, I've already seen the goods."

She picked up a throw pillow from my couch and threw it at me. "You're such an ass."

"The only ass I'm interested in is yours. You can leave your bra and underwear on if you want. I'll go pour us a glass of wine and get the hot tub ready. Let me show you to my room. There is a robe hanging on the back of my door. Just strip and come out when you're ready." I winked and walked away before she could protest any further.

I poured us both a glass of wine and went out back and lifted the heavy cover off the hot tub. After grabbing a few towels out of the cabinet and stripping down, the bitter cold had me sinking into the water immediately. I picked my phone off the ledge and connected to Spotify as Thomas Rhett's voice floated from the Bluetooth speakers.

I tilted my head back and allowed my muscles to relax. Seeing Antonio and Sienna was awkward and uncomfortable. It felt like opening up an old wound. Even though it no longer hurt, you still had the scar as a reminder. But if tonight proved anything, it proved that I was completely over her.

The sound of the slider opening had me tilting my head to the door. Amelia was wrapped up in my flannel robe; she looked absolutely adorable. She slid the material down her arms, set it down on the chair and tiptoed across the cold, wooden deck.

"Oh my God, the boards are freezing," she said, sinking into the hot water.

I spread my hands out along the edge and lifted my eyebrow. "You're awfully far away."

She swam over, carefully keeping her head above the water. I swooped her up in my lap. Her breasts were partially visible through the lace bra that she insisted on wearing. I dragged my fingertips down the back of her neck. She shivered at the contact.

"I like having you here," I admitted, pulling her against my chest, but our bodies were slippery, so she had to tighten her arms around me.

"I like being here. This is really nice." Her blue eyes roamed along my deck, taking in the string of white lights I had decorating the posts. "Is this where you bring all your conquests?"

My arms stiffened at her teasing. "Actually, I don't bring women back here because of my job. I try to stay private."

She drew back and stared at me. The steam from the water had me closing my eyes. Her soft fingers traced along my eyebrow. "Well, don't I feel special."

I spread my hands along her back. "You are special, Amelia."

Yes, I was physically attracted to her, but this was beyond physical. It was turning into something I hadn't planned on. She wasn't just a fling, but was I really ready to put my feelings on the line again? After all, that hadn't worked out so well for me in the past. I had to remind myself that Amelia wasn't Sienna.

Her slender arms wrapped around my neck, and her eyes were smiling. "I feel the same way about you."

The way she looked at me was definitely something I could get used to. I brought the pad of my index finger up to trace the few freckles that dotted along her small nose and ran a path down to her neck, which was now exposed. Being with her was easy, and it seemed every time we were together, it just kept getting better and better.

Her eyes darted over to the Bluetooth speaker. "I never took you for a country music fan."

I reached for my phone and handed to her. "I like a variety. Here, pick something."

She scrolled through my playlists with interest. "Sinatra, Beyoncé, Maroon Five, and Zac Brown. Wow, that's quite the selection."

My lips brushed against hers. "What kind of music did you expect to find?"

"I don't know, rock, heavy metal, maybe?"

I rolled my eyes. "Do they even make heavy metal anymore?"

She shrugged her shoulders. "No clue."

I traced her lower lip with the pad of my thumb. "What kind of music will I find on your phone?"

"You're never going to find out."

I arched an eyebrow. "That bad, huh?" She laughed, and I pulled on her ponytail, bringing us nose to nose. "What's so funny?"

She drew in a ragged breath. "Don't do that."

"Don't do what?" Every nerve in my body was aware of our close proximity.

"Give me that detective stare. The one that has me squirming in my seat and ready to confess to crimes I never committed." She demonstrated by purposely rubbing against my stiff cock. All it would take is one little skilled maneuver and I'd be able to dive right in.

"Are you trying to distract me?" I asked as her mouth moved along my neck. My fingers dug into her side. She was addicting, and my erection wasn't the only thing growing. My attachment to her was building by the minute. The last thing I wanted was to make myself vulnerable again, but the attraction was something I couldn't deny.

Her hips moved in a slow circle. "Amelia," I groaned. My voice was rough, it practically rumbled. My fingers found her nipples, they puckered under my thumb. She pushed against my groin, and it was like a live wire was ready to go off. Her movements were slow and gentle. I was desperate to glide inside her and never leave.

I dragged her mouth to mine; our tongues moved in slow, lazy strokes. Her taste was becoming familiar. There was something growing between us, planting roots in places that haven't been touched in a while. I kissed her slow and deep, making promises with my tongue that I couldn't with my words.

My fingers gripped her hair, and I didn't know what was happening to me or why this woman felt so different than anyone else before her. All I knew was it's been this way right from the beginning.

Her lips trailed long my shoulder; the sensation caused every cell in my body to tighten. Her body continued to rock into me as my slick fingers found her clit, adding just the right amount of pressure.

"Oh my God." Her voice broke on a plea.

I twisted her nipples and pinched just enough for her to hiss out a breath. If she kept making those sounds, there was a good chance I'd embarrass myself like an inexperienced teenager. Jesus. What was this woman doing to me?

"Wait." She pulled back, her eyes looked crazed. "We shouldn't do this here."

"What are you talking about?" I asked in disbelief. She couldn't be serious.

She swam to the other side of the hot tub, as far away from me as she could go. "I don't want to… you know…" She looked at the water and cringed. "Dirty your water, because then you'll have to change it."

My mouth hung open for a full minute before I threw my head back, laughing so hard my stomach hurt. She splashed water on my face. "Why are you laughing? We could get an infection."

My body was shaking with laughter as I advanced toward her. "People have sex all the time in hot tubs," I teased, which caused her to glare at me. "Besides, the water temperature would kill any bacteria we left behind. And if you're worried about if I've had other woman in here before you, the answer is no."

"But you'd still have to empty the water and clean it out."

I could feel my eyes smiling at her cuteness. "That's correct, but I change the water pretty frequently, so that's not an issue."

Her shoulders deflated. "Oh, well, I guess I killed that moment, huh?"

I reached over and handed her a glass of wine. "Here, drink this."

She brought the glass to her lips and took a huge sip. "I'm so sorry. First, I go all nuclear on your ex-girlfriend, and then I'm acting like a dumb blonde around you as usual. You have this weird effect on me, and it drives me crazy."

My lips curled into a smile. I liked knowing that little

piece of information. "You have nothing to be sorry about. Tonight, would have been a lot worse if you weren't around. And like I said earlier, I like having you here."

She slowly sipped from her glass and averted her gaze.

"Amelia, look at me." I lifted her chin. "You made what should have been a lousy night for me totally enjoyable. I should be the one thanking you."

Which I planned on doing later, I thought to myself.

She swallowed her wine, looking unsure of herself. "How did you feel when Sienna confessed her feelings for you?"

Talk about officially killing the mood. "Surprised, I guess. I wasn't expecting her to unload all that with her husband in the next room." Seeing Sienna tonight brought up a lot of different emotions, but in the end all I felt was pissed off. "She needs to get it through her head that I don't want anything to do with her. I guess you could say that I'm the kind of guy where once you cross the line there is no going back. I don't forgive and forget easily."

Her wineglass froze halfway to her lips. Something dark passed across her features. "That's understandable." Her words said one thing, but her eyes said another.

Thanks to my line of work and years of training, I was very good at reading people. And my gut told me that Amelia was hiding something from me. Now I needed to figure out what I was going to do about it.

THIRTEEN

AMELIA

A GENTLE HAND TOUCHED MY SHOULDER. "HEY, AMELIA, IT'S almost ten o'clock, you have to get up."

My eyes slowly opened as I shifted my body to the side. Marco was staring down at me, a soft smile on his lips. "Did I really sleep that late?" I yawned as the sheet moved down my chest while stretching my arms out.

"Well, we didn't get to sleep until almost four a.m., so I wouldn't really call it sleeping in."

Our conversations from last night played over and over in my head. I don't think I'd laughed so hard in my life. Marco was not only handsome, but he was sweet, playful, and attentive. Everything about him was infectious and addictive.

"I'm sorry for passing out on you."

He stretched his long legs out over the gray comforter. "Truthfully, I wasn't too far behind you, although your snoring kept waking me up."

I laughed and playfully smacked his shoulder. "Shut up. I do not snore."

. . .

"Are you kidding me? I almost pushed you off the bed just to quiet you down. And I'm pretty sure my neighbors heard you next door."

"Please tell me you're kidding?" I didn't snore, did I? I haven't slept in a bed with anyone for a long time, so I really wouldn't know.

He smirked, curling his palm along my hip. "You did let out a few soft snores, but I'm just playing around." His hold tightened around my skin as he lifted me onto his chest. My mind was at ease and my body felt relaxed. I brushed my fingers along his tattoo. It ran from his shoulder down the length of his arm. The Lord's Prayer was written in delicate cursive font with rosary beads surrounding the text. There was a crucifix and angel wings that flowed from his elbow, stopping just a few inches from his wrist. It was all black with no color, but it was still beautiful.

"You got a thing for ink, Amelia?"

"I got a thing for yours," I said, unable to stop tracing the image on his arm.

"Do you now?" His hand moved to my face. I lowered my lips, anticipating his kiss. Desire and lust were building inside me, but that wasn't all I was feeling. This wasn't just about us enjoying each other's company physically, it was much more than that. He pressed kisses to my throat and my chest. "I can't keep my hands off of you."

I knew this thing between us was new, but would it always be like this? Eventually, the spark would burn out. It had to, right? Because it was crazy how much I cared for him in such a short time. How right and perfect my world felt when we were together. He was everything I hoped and feared. He was my strength and my weakness.

My eyes slid shut at the feeling of his hand sliding up my leg. "Marco." I moaned, feeling his erection straining against the thin sheet.

"Tell me what you want, sweetheart."

I tilted my head to the side as his hands continued to worship my skin as if that's what they were made to do. I was about to tell him it was him I wanted, but the sound of his phone buzzing on the nightstand had the words dying on my tongue.

"Damn it," he growled and dropped his forehead to mine. "I'm sorry, but it may be a call for work. I have to answer that."

"It's okay," I said weakly, cupping his cheek with my palm.

He kissed me tenderly before rolling over the top of me to reach his phone. "Yeah, Quinn." I strained to hear the voice on the other side and wanted to laugh at how flustered he sounded. He turned to me and mouthed the word "sorry" before going back to his conversation. I leaned back against the headboard and listened to him talk to his friend who was coming over later today to help him with his renovations.

My lips were still tingling and my head was spinning, but surprisingly, it wasn't on my work, or my never-ending list of things to do. I was stuck on the idea of how comfortable and relaxed I felt and how I never wanted to leave this bed. I was trying to decide if that was a good thing or a bad thing.

Up until now, I never allowed myself to entertain the idea of having a life outside of my career, which was so unlike me. I've had the same goals since I was a teenager, and now I wondered what would happen if I abandoned them all. Which was crazy because Marco made it clear that he was against relationships. So, what the hell was I doing? I couldn't just push my approaching responsibilities aside and let things between us run their course, could I?

I sat forward and reached for his shirt on the end of the bed. He was still in deep discussion with his friend, so I decided to give him some privacy. I pulled the white shirt over my head and did my best to wiggle out of his grasp. He smiled at me while they went over measurements and the different tools they were going to need for the project.

My feet hit the cold floor and I hustled across the room and picked up my clothes that were strewn around. I slid into the bathroom with my undergarments in my hand and made quick work with getting dressed. Once I finished, I smoothed my hair back into a ponytail, brushed my teeth with my fingers, and rinsed my mouth out with a bottle of Listerine he had sitting out on the counter. Nothing kills a mood faster than nasty morning breath. After washing my face, I quietly padded back into the room just in case he was still on the phone.

Marco's head popped up; he looked like every fantasy I'd ever had come to life. His dark hair was pointing up in every direction and there was a dusting of whiskers along his strong jawline. My attention was drawn to his tan chest and down to the bed sheet barely covering his waist. That fluttering in my belly picked up when my eyes reached that dimple poking out. Damn, my stupid, foolish heart started to palpitate.

I was in so much trouble.

"Don't you look cute," he said, pushing himself up to a sitting position.

I glanced down at my wrinkled blouse, cringing that I was in the same clothes as yesterday. "I'm not cute. I'm a hot mess."

"Yeah, but you're my hot mess. Now, get over here."

I tiptoed to the bed, not sure how I was supposed to act. My head was in a weird place all of a sudden. He pulled me into him and pressed a kiss to my mouth. "You taste like toothpaste. Did you use my toothbrush?"

"Ew… no. That's a line I don't cross."

He arched an eyebrow. "You do know that my tongue has been inside your mouth before, right?"

"It's not the same," I pointed out.

His grin sent my heart skipping, and I really wish he would stop doing that. "You're right, because not only has my tongue been inside your mouth, but in your vag—" I covered his mouth with my palm before the word could escape. His shoulders vibrated with laughter.

"Stop. Your point has been made. I get it."

He flipped me over on the mattress, his body hovered over mine. "Oh, you're going to get it all right." He tucked a piece of hair behind my ear and I couldn't help but notice the tenderness in his eyes. "Why does it feel like I can't get enough of you? All I want to do is kiss you, touch you, and get lost in you."

I parted my lips as he pressed a kiss to my mouth. No one has ever brought me this close to happiness before. With Marco, I could be myself. There were no empty words or hidden meanings. Everything with him was real and honest. I never experienced a kiss like this, one that made me feel so much without a single word spoken.

"You always say the perfect things," I whispered against his mouth.

His warm gaze stared down at me. "That's because it's you." He brought his lips back to mine, and I held on tight and kissed him. I kissed him for all the years I wouldn't be able to. I kissed him for all the times I wouldn't get to be with him. I kissed him, hoping to stop thinking about the pain that I was going to cause him.

When this was over, he would move on and give his heart to someone more deserving, and I would have to live with myself, knowing that no apology would ever get him back. So, for now, I would pretend he was mine, even though I knew our time together was running out.

FOURTEEN

MARCO

"So, it looks like you've finally caught the dating bug." Quinn smirked over the saw table I had set up in my living room. I had called him and Logan to help hang and tape a few pieces of drywall. Of course, I had to go into the details on why I needed to speed things up on this renovation.

"If that's what you old folks are calling it these days." I cocked an eyebrow and spun the screwdriver around in my hand.

"Are you kidding me?" Logan said, pulling the pencil out from behind my ear and writing down a few measurements. "The poor sap has been walking around with hearts in his eyes all week."

"Christ," I said, glancing over his shoulder to where Amelia and Emery were singing along to Christmas carols while swiping their paintbrushes along my kitchen cabinets. Fucking blue. I let out a chuckle. I couldn't believe I was actually going through with this.

"I like her," Quinn said at my side. "She's good with Emery too."

"She's great." I smiled, watching them make a mess as

they poured the paint into the trays. It hit me how right she looked in my kitchen. How I liked seeing her with Emery. How perfectly she fit everywhere in my life.

"Does she know how you feel about her?" There was a long pause, and I knew from his expression that he knew what she meant to me. Even if Amelia didn't. Even if I hadn't fully admitted it to myself yet.

"I want to be smart about this." I glanced over at Quinn who gave me a strange, yet not so subtle smile. "Besides, things are still new, and we barely know each other, so don't go getting ahead of yourself." My friends weren't used to seeing me with a woman outside a bar, and they have been trying to pair me up with random people for as long as I've known them. I haven't had a relationship in over a decade, and it annoyed me that I was being so transparent with my feelings.

Logan took out a utility knife and made the last cut so we could hang the final sheet of drywall. "I think this is it." Once we had it secured, we stood back and looked at our handiwork.

"Not bad." I grabbed the Gatorade off the sawhorse and took a huge sip.

"How did things go with Antonio and Sienna last night?" Quinn asked, handing me the measuring tape so I could put it back in my toolbox.

My eyes moved over his shoulder. "Well…" I laughed. "It was fine until Sienna tried to make a play for me the second her husband left the room. That did not go over well with Amelia. Remind me never to piss her off."

Quinn smirked. "Sounds like she was defending her territory."

I shook my head and ran my hands down my dust covered jeans. "We were just pretending, remember?"

Logan chuckled next to me. "I hate to break it to you, pal,

you might have been pretending last night, but there is nothing fake about the way you two keep glancing at each other. Mark my words, you'll be married with a baby on the way this time next year."

I glared at him, hating that he was partly right. Even though Amelia and I were still getting to know each other, our chemistry was undeniable. Just watching how sweet she was being with Emery caused something in my chest to shift. As if she could sense me staring at her, she turned her head and caught my gaze. Christ, she was gorgeous. This woman had knocked me on my ass before I even knew what happened.

I pulled my eyes away from her when I felt my friends grinning at me. I turned to Logan. "Speaking of kids," I said, in an attempt to steer this conversation in a different direction. "I thought you were bringing Sabrina with you."

He threw his hands on his hips and blew out a breath. "Vanessa figured Brina would be bored while I was over here working, so she told me it would be best to keep her home."

Logan and his ex-wife shared custody of his young daughter. If you asked me, that woman was going to end up on the evening news one night. She was half a step away from crazy town. Vanessa caught Logan's eye when she was busing tables at a local sports bar. They dated for six months before she got pregnant with Sabrina. Logan, being the man he was, did the right thing and married her. I gave him so much credit. He tried and held on as long as he could for his daughter's sake, but that woman sucked all the patience and love right out of him.

"Didn't you tell her that Emery was here?" Quinn asked, even though we both already knew the answer.

"I didn't want to argue with her and say anything to set her off." He looked embarrassed. "You know how she gets."

"Dad," Emery called with Amelia following her in from

the kitchen. They both had blue paint staining their clothes along with matching smiles.

"Sorry," Amelia said softly, rubbing her fingers along Emery's cheek. "I swear the paint will come off." She looked up at Quinn with an apology in her eyes.

Quinn stepped in front of his daughter and knelt down. "It looks like you had fun painting. Did you happen to get any on the cabinets?"

"It was so much fun. Can Amelia, Uncle Marco, and Logan come over for dinner later?"

Quinn's eyes softened, just like they always did with his daughter. "Your brother isn't feeling well, kiddo, remember?" He leaned in and kissed the tip of her nose. You would never know that Emery wasn't Quinn's biological daughter with how much he loved that little girl.

I stepped toward Amelia and wrapped my one arm around her waist. "You've got a little paint on you too," I said, picking the dried blue paint out of her hair.

She tipped her head back and looked at me. "What do you think?"

I let her go and surveyed the open room. Thanks to my family's construction business, I scored a good deal on materials. I upgraded things that I normally wouldn't. Amelia and I went to Home Depot this morning and picked out the backsplash and brushed nickel knobs for the drawers. I was surprised with how great everything looked with the stainless-steel appliances.

"It actually looks better than I thought it would."

"I can't believe you pulled this off in such a short period of time," Logan said, swinging a rag over his shoulder. I couldn't agree more. I was grateful that these guys could come over and lend me a hand on such short notice. It would have taken me weeks on my own.

I threw my arm around Amelia and pulled her tight

against me. "She's a great helper. Even though she uses an obnoxious amount of tape along the edges."

She elbowed me in the stomach. "Sorry, we can't all be perfect painters like you."

I grinned down at her, and she grinned back. "I'm impressed. You did a good job."

"Thanks. I just want to add another coat with the roller and then I'll clean up."

My cell phone started ringing on the table where it was charging. I walked over and picked it up, noticing it was my sergeant. "What's up, Sarg?"

"We have a situation, they just pulled your informant from the river."

"Fuck." I quickly walked into my bedroom and closed the door behind me. "What the hell happened?"

"You're not going to like it, but he jumped."

"Damn it." I've been working around the clock on this investigation. Could things possibly get any worse? I rubbed my temples, feeling frustration snake through me. His cover must have been blown somehow, because Luis Becerra was not suicidal. He had a baby on the way and did everything he could to protect his family. If he jumped, he must have felt that was the only way to keep them safe.

"Are you sure?"

"You know better than to ask that, but yes, I'm positive."

There was a knock on the door, and a second later, Logan stepped into the room. He held his phone up, obviously already up to speed. "I can be there in thirty, Logan is with me, so hang tight."

I hung up the phone and bit back a groan of annoyance. I had no idea where to go from here. The only name I had to connect to this mess was my good old friend Benny, and he was serving twenty-five to life.

Logan sat on the edge of my bed and clasped his hands together. "I was not expecting this."

"I sense a shitstorm brewing."

"You and me both, brother." He stood up and tucked his phone in his back pocket. "You ready to head out?"

"Yeah, I just need a few minutes," I said as he backed away for the door. I walked into my closet and grabbed my work clothes to change into.

Amelia stepped into my room. "Logan said you guys have an emergency at work."

I scrubbed my hands down my face. "I'm sorry. I know we had plans for later…"

"That's okay." She placed her hand on my shoulder and peered up at me. "Why don't you go, I'll clean up and show myself out."

I brushed a stray hair from her face. "You don't have to do that."

"I don't mind. How long will you be?"

I covered her hand that was still holding on to my shirt. "A few hours. I'm sorry, I know we had dinner reservations later."

I promised her that I would take her out on a date tonight. Something that surprised the hell out of me when I asked, but the second she accepted, I knew I made the right decision.

She pulled on my neck, putting us nose to nose. "Why don't you just swing by my place when you're done. I'll grab some takeout and we'll heat it up when you're finished with work. I don't need to go to a fancy restaurant, I just want you to be safe."

My eyes gentled on her. When was the last time a woman other than my mother worried about me? A long fucking time. I leaned in and gave her a kiss. "I don't deserve you."

"Funny, because I was thinking the same thing about you."

I cupped her face in my hands. "Thank you for being so understanding."

"You don't need to thank me." She looked me up and down. "But you might want to clean up before you go."

I squeezed her hand, and her smile made my heart constrict. "I'll text you when I'm done."

"Sounds like a plan." She kissed me one last time, patted my chest and walked out.

I didn't understand what was happening between us, but I was done questioning it.

FIFTEEN

AMELIA

I stared at my grandfather's estate as I pulled into the main house, a place that had once felt like a home to me. I looked to my left and noticed an unfamiliar Lexus parked at the top of the long winding driveway. I sighed, hoping he didn't have company because what I needed to say really needed to be said in private.

I leaned my head back against the seat and prayed that I was doing the right thing by telling him about my relationship. During the car ride over, I played with a few different ideas in my head and tried to come up with a way to convince him I needed more time.

It became clear after spending the entire weekend with Marco, that this conversation was unavoidable. I was already in deep and my feelings were becoming too hard to ignore.

Now, as I placed my shifter in park and ran my hand along the steering wheel, the queasiness in my stomach had me questioning if I was ready to have this conversation after all. I hesitated a bit and glanced at my phone, wondering if I should have called and told him I was coming.

I adjusted the strap along my purse and then rang the doorbell. The heavy wooden door swung open.

I furrowed my brows in confusion. "Mom? What are you doing here?"

"Amelia." She stepped forward and wrapped me up in her arms. "Your grandfather just left to visit your grandmother. I was just dropping off some paperwork before I headed over to the hotel."

"I didn't know you were coming into town," I said, feeling thrown off from her presence. "You could have stayed with me."

She shook her head. "Don't be offended, dear, I wouldn't want to bother you."

I nodded, pretending to understand when, in reality, it hurt when she refused to stay with me. It always felt like she went out of her way to keep her distance. Deep down I knew she cared about me in her own way, but it still stung, and a part of me felt foolish for even wanting more of a relationship to begin with.

"You would never bother me, but I understand why you would want your own space."

I stepped inside and followed her into the foyer. She waved her free hand toward my grandfather's sitting room as if this were still her house. This was the home I was raised in. Even after my dad died, my grandparents insisted that we stay here. They claimed it was because they didn't want my life disrupted any more than it was. As I got older, I suspected it was because they didn't trust my mother to raise me.

She moved over to the loveseat and patted the cushion. "Let's talk. It's been so long. How are you?"

"I've been well. How about you?"

She slid her hands along the armrest of the leather chair and filled me in on all the charity events she'd attended and the trip she was planning to take to the South of France right after the new year.

My phone pinged with a text, interrupting her prattling on about a friend who just bought a property in Belize. I pulled it out of my bag; my heart swelled when Marco's name flashed across the screen. I clicked on the message. It was a picture of him and his nephew.

Marco: Hey, your little admirer stopped by with my brother. Matteo was impressed with how much work was done. Thanks for saving my ass.

Me: You're welcome. Give Nicky a kiss for me.

His reply was instant.

Marco: You could kiss him yourself. How much longer are you going to be? They brought leftovers from Moms'.

My lips lifted up into a smile. This would be our third straight night in a row together. Not that I was complaining.

Me: I shouldn't be too long. My mother is in town and we are just catching up. I'll text you when I'm on my way.

Marco: The roads are getting slick. Please drive safe.

"Is that Owen?" my mom asked as I tucked my phone away, back in my purse.

"No," I told her, not wanting to get into it.

"Are you sure?" she asked hopefully. "Because you were smiling pretty hard while reading what was on that screen."

"Did grandfather say when he would be back?" I asked, trying to change the subject. The last thing I wanted to do was tell her why I was actually here. My mother adored Owen and has been pushing us together since we were in diapers.

She sat up in her chair and folded her hands in her lap. "Amelia, what's going on?"

I rolled my lips together and silently wondered if I could confide in her without her judging me. "I have something I need to talk to him about."

Her gaze narrowed. "Why do I not like the sound of this?"

I ignored her tone. "I wanted to talk to him about the contract."

"What about it?"

I closed my eyes and swallowed the ball of nerves in my throat. "I'm having a change of heart and I need more time."

She stared off into the distance. "I thought this was all settled. What's brought on this sudden change?"

"I feel like I'm rushing headfirst into something that I'm not sure I'm even ready for. I just wish it didn't have to be like this."

Her gaze finally shifted back to mine. "Amelia, you are strong and loyal, and have enough drive to take the family name further than your grandfather ever could. Your dream has always been to run the company and I know this isn't the path you wanted to take to get there, but you need to accept that this is your destiny."

"You honestly want your only daughter to marry out of obligation instead of love?" I was taken aback by her directness. "Please make me understand why it has to be this way?"

She visibly swallowed. "You're young. You need to understand that relationships take time to build and develop."

"Why don't you understand that there isn't a 'relationship' to build on with Owen?"

She shot up from her seat. For the life of me, I couldn't understand why she was so upset. "This is the life that you wanted. Owen is the perfect man for you. You used to be crazy about him. I know he can be a bit unpredictable, but deep down he cares for you. If you marry him, you will never have to worry about anything ever again."

"If I marry him, it feels like I'll be making the biggest mistake of my life."

It felt like my head and my heart were at war with each other. This thing with Marco was still new. I could see myself falling in love with him in a way I would never come back from, yet it didn't stop me from wanting to be with him.

"Amelia." She reached out and squeezed my hand. "You are so close to having everything you've ever wanted. Let Owen be the man that can give you the life you deserve."

I laughed out loud. "Owen is the man you want me to marry. The life you are referring to is the 'life' you want me to live."

"I know this is complicated, but Owen will rise to the occasion and things will work out for the best."

That's where she was wrong. Owen would never come around. He would never be the husband I would want or need. He was too busy being the center of his own universe. That's why I felt so strongly about pursuing things with Marco, because these feelings, no matter how hard I tried to ignore, weren't going away.

I might as well just throw the grenade and get it over with.

"I've met someone," I said, rushing the words out before I could take them back.

"Is it serious?" she asked without any show of emotion. Her lack of curiosity surprised me.

I blinked at her in confusion. "We are just getting to know each other." That was a massive understatement. This weekend was the best I ever had. I haven't smiled or laughed so hard in my life.

She eyed me warily. "Good."

I cocked my head and stared at her. I swear, this woman was testing both my patience and my sanity. "You don't understand. I care for him. Yes, it's new, but it feels like things are changing. I look at the world differently and I'm not sure what I want anymore."

She closed her eyes, looking defeated. "Who is this man that has you questioning everything? How well do you know him?"

"His name is Marco. He's a detective. We've only known each other for a few weeks, but he makes me feel alive when we're together. He makes me…"

"What you're feeling is fleeting. It will pass. Trust me," she said cool and indifferently, her words cutting me off at the knees.

"Why are you being like this?"

"I'm looking out for you and your interests. You need to put a stop to whatever you have going on. Put some distance between you and this man. This isn't just about you, Amelia, there are people counting on you."

My eyes stung with unshed tears and I looked away. "Give me one good reason why I would walk away from the only man who has shown me what real happiness looks like."

"Amelia." She closed her eyes and looked up at the ceiling. She was taking way too long to answer me and suddenly the hairs on the back of my neck prickled. "Your dad wasn't you're biological father."

My head jerked back like she physically struck me. "Excuse me?" I said, shocked that I could even find my voice. What the hell was she talking about?

"There was a boy I dated when I was younger." She wiped the moisture from her eyes. "Your father and I were going through a rough patch and I ran into Marcus at a friend's wedding. We were both married, but that didn't matter because I was head over heels in love with the man."

"You had a husband!" I reminded her, wondering how she could be so calm when it felt like my entire world was crumbling around me. "What about your husband?"

"I loved Greg, but not the way I loved Marcus. For those few weeks we were together, I was happy, but his wife found out about our affair and he left me." She took a few deep breaths like she was wrestling with regret, but I couldn't bring myself to care. "Your father agreed to raise you as his own. He loved and cared for you in every way that mattered."

Tears ran down my face as I tried to hold myself together. I brought my hand up to my heart; it felt like there was a crushing weight sitting on top of my chest.

I was young when my father passed away, but I was old enough to remember him. My grandparents always made a point to tell me stories and keep him alive in my memories. He's been gone for twenty years, so why did it feel like I was losing him all over again?

"You kept this from me all these years?"

"I know this is a lot to take in, but I hope you understand why when I tell you the full story."

My stomach dropped. "There's more?" It felt like things were falling apart around me, and I had no idea how to stop it. I had a million questions because none of this made sense.

She reached for my hand, but I pulled it back. "I know you're hurt and you have every right to be."

"I'm not just hurt. I'm confused. I'm devastated." I tried to keep my voice even. "Are you sure that this man is my biological father?"

"Listen to me. Greg never wanted you to know. He swore me to secrecy and made me promise that I would never tell you. He wanted to protect you."

"Why would he do that and what would he need to protect me from?"

"You know he survived a bout of cancer in his youth?" She looked at me for confirmation and all I could do was shake my head. "He always believed that he wasn't going to live a long life. He loved you from the second you were born and wanted to make sure you were always provided for."

I pushed to my feet and started to pace. Never had my life felt so out of control. Never had I felt so lost. All these years I believed that Greg West was my biological father, and if he wasn't my father… then that meant that I wasn't the sole heir of Jeffery West. OH. MY. GOD! The pieces of this bizarre fucked-up puzzle were falling into place.

My head snapped to hers with that realization. The grandparents I loved and adored… the two people I admired my entire life, weren't my blood relatives.

"Greg was left sterile by the chemotherapy he had when he was treated for cancer as a teenager." I knew that he was diagnosed with leukemia at fifteen and after chemotherapy, he had a successful bone marrow transplant, he was in full remission until his mid-thirties. The disease is what ultimately took his life. "He knew that you weren't his. When I found out I was pregnant, he took it hard, but then we talked it through and made the decision to raise you together. He always wanted a child of his own." She cleared her throat and looked away. "The problem was, your grandparents were also aware of his infertility."

I stopped pacing so I could stare at her. "So, you all lied to me?"

"No, we loved you and tried to give you the best life possible." She shook her head. "Your grandfather was angry as hell when he found out and wanted your father to divorce me. But your father would hear nothing of the sort and gave his parents an ultimatum. They either accepted you as their own flesh and blood or he would cut them out of his life forever. Your father was an only child, and your grandparents nearly lost him once, they weren't going to risk it again." She turned her eyes away briefly, as if she were trying to control her emotions. "Over time, your grandparents grew to love and accept you. When Greg passed away, you were all they had left of him."

I hung my head. My chest hurt with a pain like I'd never felt before. "I don't understand. I'm not sure how I feel about all this. How do I know what's true and what's a lie?" I glanced around the room; there were so many memories in this house. My eyes got misty as they landed on the chair and small table near the window where my grandmother and I had tea parties. We would play on the stairs, and I would dress up in her fur coats and pearls, and we would eat finger sandwiches and do crafts. My gaze moved over to the desk in front of the fireplace where my grandfather used to read me stories before bedtime. Most of the time, he would end up falling asleep before me because he was so tired after a long day. But he never missed story time, no matter how busy or exhausted he was. So many damn memories. I was struggling with so much. So many lies on top of lies.

My mom stood from the couch. She stepped closer and looked ready to reach for me again but thought better of it and wrung her hands together. "Don't ever doubt your grandparents' love for you. You might not have Greg's blood running through your veins, but you are an extension of his heart. You were a part of him, and your grandparents loved you without conditions."

I shook my head, trying to process what this meant. "What does all this have to do with you pushing me into marrying Owen?"

"You can't tell your grandfather this or I will lose everything. He made me promise to never tell you or I would be cut off financially." She rubbed her hand over her forehead. "Can you promise me that?"

"You are in no position to ask that of me right now."

I always wondered how she could afford her lifestyle. My father left her a little bit of money, but most of it was left in a trust for me. I guess now I know.

"Marrying Owen is the only way to ensure that you can hang on to your shares of the company. Edward Eastan does not know that you are not Greg's biological daughter. If he found out that your grandfather lied to him, then your ownership in the company could be challenged after the transfer and your grandfather could lose everything."

I pushed my hands through my hair in frustration. "I can't believe this."

She sighed. "Sweetheart, your last name might be West, but Greg never officially adopted you. If the Eastan family were to somehow find out, they could challenge your paternity and the contract could be null and void. In the eyes of the law you are considered a stepchild and stepchildren are not considered legal heirs."

"But, I'm his beneficiary."

She nodded her head and swallowed. "You are correct, however, if for any reason, your biological father wanted to establish paternity, and it came to light that your grandfather knew that you were not his legal heir, the Eastan family could contest the contract due to fraud and misrepresentation."

My mind went back to that fucking contract that I have yet to sign. "Why didn't Dad just adopt me?"

"We weren't thinking that far ahead. This succession was planned out fifteen years ago. By that time, Greg had already passed."

I ran my hand through my hair, hoping my world would stop spinning. Up until this point I thought I was in control of my life, now I couldn't believe how wrong I was…

SIXTEEN

MARCO

Normally, I hated Monday mornings, but today was an exception. I sat on the edge of Amelia's bed, watching her get ready. Her long blond hair was pulled up on top of her head as she carefully applied a bunch of makeup she didn't even need.

"Why do you wear that stuff?" I asked.

The mascara wand paused over her lashes. "Because I have to look professional at work."

Right. I guess that made sense. Amelia didn't talk about her job much, but I knew that her grandfather owned the hotel chain and she had some big fancy title, which came with a lot of responsibility.

"Do you enjoy what you do?"

She placed the mascara wand back in the tube and stood up. "It's my dream job." Her voice got quiet as her gaze moved to the floor. "I practically grew up working at the hotel. As soon as I was old enough to get my working papers, I started that summer. My grandfather wanted me to learn every area of the business so I could someday take over for him. I've worked in housekeeping, hospitality, the back office, and human resources. But my real passion was always in marketing. I loved working with clients and bringing their ideas to life."

Listening to Amelia talk about her job and looking around at her expensive furniture in her upscale condo was a huge wake-up call for me. We came from two completely different worlds. I was a cop and even with the amount of overtime I worked, I would never make enough to where we would be evenly matched financially. In my Italian upbringing, the expectation was that the man provided for his woman. The realization that I could never give her the expensive things she was used to or be her equal in that regard bruised my ego.

"Hey." She strolled over to stand in between my legs, her eyes were filled with concern. "What's wrong?"

"I was just thinking about our differences." She frowned, making me regret even bringing it up. If we were going to continue to spend time together, we needed to talk about it. "My job is not only dangerous, but the pay is shit." I stared into her eyes. "I would never be able to give you all this."

"Stop right there." She placed her finger over my mouth. Her brows folded together and all I wanted to do was reach up and smooth them apart. But she looked pissed, so I figured it would be best to keep my thoughts and hands to myself. "Just because I have all this doesn't mean I need it. You give me the one thing that money can't buy and that's happiness."

I sighed and brought my hands to her waist so I could pull her on my lap. "Thank you for saying that, but I still feel inadequate when it comes to you."

She pulled my head back and feathered her fingers in my hair. "You're an idiot. You know that?"

"Why thank you." I rolled my eyes.

"You have more decency and respect in your pinky than any other man I've known. I don't ever want to hear you talk like that again. Do you think that I'm so shallow that I couldn't be happy with a man who makes less money than me? If I wanted to date a rich guy, I wouldn't have to look very hard. I have no interest in just being arm candy for some inflated ego in a suit. In case you haven't figured it out by now, I like you Marco. Just the way you are."

My hands moved up to frame her jaw. "I like you too."

Her fingers started tracing light patterns on my shoulder. "I'm glad we got that settled."

I leaned in and kissed her gently, teasing her lips even though my pulse was fluttering. Her mouth opened and my tongue slipped inside. I moved her head to get a better angle so I could dive in deeper. Amelia West could kiss, and it was becoming one of my favorite things to do.

"I should probably hop in the shower," I said, dragging my mouth away from hers.

She sighed reluctantly as she stood up. "It's probably a good idea. I'll go downstairs and whip up a quick breakfast." She strolled over to the closet and slipped on a pair of heels.

I picked up my bag and walked past her as she stood in front of the full-length mirror. She had on an emerald top with a black skirt that was a little too short for my liking. I squeezed my eyes tight, trying not to think about all the men that will get to look at her today. I wasn't normally the possessive type, but then again, I haven't had a girlfriend to worry about in a long time either.

Shit! Was that what she was? My girlfriend? I knew it was just a label, but why was it so hard for me to acknowledge it?

She was putting a pair of diamond studs in her ears and caught me staring. I gave her a grin and forced my feet to move toward the bathroom so I could get ready.

I made quick work with getting dressed. I had just applied a little gel in my hair and was fastening the top button of my dress shirt when I heard the doorbell ring downstairs. I stuffed my razor and my toothbrush into my toiletry bag, grabbed my keys and wallet off the nightstand, and started toward the landing. I reached the bottom step and came face-to-face with a woman I didn't recognize.

Her eyes widened when they saw me. She gave me a once-over and I did the same.

"Mom." Amelia's cheeks were flushed and not in a good way. "This is Marco," she said, voice shaking and looking more than a little uncomfortable. "Marco, meet my mother, Tamara West."

"Nice to meet you." I extended my hand, which she barely acknowledged. Her greeting was limp and probably lasted less than a second.

Tamara's eyes slanted to her daughter. "I didn't realize you would have company this early in the morning."

"Maybe because that really isn't any of your business."

I inhaled a deep breath, trying to not let on about how awkward I felt. Sensing this conversation wasn't something I should be a part of, I decided to peel out of there.

"You know what? I'm just going to swing by the drive-thru on my way to the station and grab a breakfast sandwich," I said, noticing the ingredients on the counter to make omelets.

"You don't have to rush off."

I slid my hands in the pockets of my dress slacks. "I have an early meeting anyways," I lied. "Why don't you visit with your mom. You don't get to see her very often."

I wasn't sure how long her mom was in town for, but I knew something must have gone down last night. Amelia didn't look very happy about whatever it was they talked about yesterday. It didn't take a genius to figure out things were strained between these two.

"Let me at least make you a coffee to go." She hurried over to the Keurig machine and placed a paper cup underneath.

I shoved a hand through my hair while her mother and I silently waited for the coffee machine to do its job. I could see Amelia fumbling to secure the lid on the cup. Her jumpiness had me concerned, and I worried that leaving her alone with her mother might not be a good idea.

"Here." She gave me a shaky smile and handed me the coffee.

"Thanks." My eyes bored into hers, silently asking her if she was okay.

She nodded and reached up and patted my chest. "I'll see you later tonight."

I slid my hand down her arm and threaded my fingers with hers. "Call me if you change your mind about coming over."

"I won't."

Her mother cleared her throat, reminding us that she was in the room. I bent down and kissed the top of her head. "I'll catch you later."

"It was nice meeting you, Ms. West. I hope you enjoy your visit."

Tamara pursed her lips. "Thank you." And then she turned on her heels and walked away from me.

"Well, okay then! I guess that's my cue to leave," I muttered under my breath. I grabbed my duffel bag off the floor while Amelia handed me my coat by the front door. I cupped her face and brought us nose to nose. "Have a good day, sweetheart."

"You too."

I could not leave her condo quick enough. That woman was intense and nothing at all like I had pictured her to be. While the physical resemblance was undeniable, Tamara West was as warm and friendly as Cruella De Vil. I wouldn't be surprised if she skinned puppies herself in her spare time, just for the fun of it.

———

Amelia stood over the paint tray, pouring the last of the trim paint into the foil pan. We had one more coat to add along the window and we were all done.

"So how did your visit go with your mom?"

She paused what she was doing and sighed. "I'm sorry if she seemed so cold. She's a little uptight, but her bark is worse than her bite."

"I wasn't concerned about me, I was more concerned about you. You seemed a bit agitated around her."

She groaned. "You picked up on that, huh?"

"It was like missing a hole in a doughnut."

"Our relationship is complicated. Her attitude this morning was directed toward me, not you. I'm sorry if she made you feel uncomfortable."

"Amelia, I'm not offended. I'm just concerned about you, that's all. I didn't like seeing you so upset. I couldn't give a shit what she thinks about me."

I hoped I wasn't out of line, but her mother obviously had issues with us being together. I didn't even attempt to start a conversation with her this morning. Given the tension in the room and her silent treatment, I worried that anything I said wouldn't be very nice.

Her eyes lowered before looking back up, I couldn't help but notice how sad she seemed. Maybe I shouldn't have even brought the topic up.

"She isn't happy with me at the moment, but she'll get over it."

I couldn't imagine having a mother like that, she was the exact opposite of mine. Amelia was sweet and caring, which made it hard to believe a woman like Tamara West could give birth to something so perfect.

We spent the next half hour finishing up and I couldn't have been more relieved when I took the final swipe of the paintbrush.

"What do you think?" she asked, stepping back with her hands on her hips, surveying our collective efforts.

I stepped into her space and wiped a splatter of white paint from her cheek. "I think I might have to keep you around." Her breath hitched and I watched a blush take over her face. "You were a big help. Thank you."

She smiled against my lips. "It's the least I could do seeing I got you into this mess."

"Very true," I said, spanking her ass playfully.

She yelped. "Was that necessary?"

I lifted an eyebrow and wrapped my arm along her waist. "Don't act like you didn't enjoy that."

Her eyes flared, just like they always did. My heart pounded in my chest. A flood of emotion hit me, and instead of saying things I wasn't ready to say yet, I flipped her over my shoulder and carried her to my bedroom. She was still laughing as I tossed her onto the center of my mattress. I stripped my jeans down and ripped off my shirt. She leaned up on her elbows and stared at me. Her eyes traced over my skin, causing my erection to grow and peek outside of my boxers.

"Take off your clothes," I instructed as I slipped my hand inside my waistband and fisted myself, working my hard-on up and down.

Amelia dragged down her leggings and thong and threw them on the floor. My eyelids felt heavy as I fought to keep them open. It was torture watching her and being so close to her. But there was something I wanted to try and I needed her to be ready. I stepped over to my nightstand and reached in the top drawer to find what I was looking for. My grin grew wide when she noticed what I had in my hand.

"Handcuffs." She swallowed.

"I thought you'd like to try these with a professional this time. With someone who knows what he's doing."

She took in a sharp breath. "Okay."

Placing my knee on the bed, I leaned in and brushed her hair to the side so I could kiss her neck. "Do you trust me?" I asked, sucking on her earlobe.

She wiggled against me, rolling her hips into my growing erection. "Yes."

My cock twitched from the contact. "Good, because I'm going to fuck you. Hard and however I want. And you're going to love every second of it."

She grabbed my hips and pulled me closer. "What are you waiting for, Officer?"

I pressed my lips to hers briefly before pushing off the bed.

After I secured the cuffs around her wrists, I looked down. I envisioned this. Fantasized about it even, but nothing I pictured was as good as the real thing. "You're perfect for me."

Her eyes grew heavy as I pulled my cock out of my boxers. "First." I crawled over the top of her and positioned myself at her mouth. "I want to feel your tongue on me. I want you to take me nice and slow."

Amelia stuck her tongue out and worked it around my shaft smoothly and carefully. I slid my cock in painfully slow until her mouth was full. "Fuck, that feels good." I groaned and picked up the pace. I moved in and out, sliding my tip over every inch of her face before I traced my crown around her waiting lips. She opened her mouth and I pushed back inside. Her tongue swept over me as I fought to keep my rhythm slow and controlled. But that only lasted for less than a minute because her mouth was wet and hot and it felt too good. I fucked the back of her throat, feeling my calves tighten with each powerful stroke. Watching my cock move in and out of her mouth was the most beautiful sight I've ever seen. I was trying to hold back, to make this feeling last, but everything inside me tightened and I was ready to snap. I glanced down to make sure she was okay before pushing back in. I was careful not to get too carried away because I didn't want to hurt her.

I felt my legs shake and the cords in my neck grew tight. I was unbearably deep and I couldn't even think straight. "Amelia." I pulled out again before I lost control. She looked at me with a stare that spoke volumes. Her tongue came out, and she licked me from the base to the tip and swirled her tongue along the glistening cum. I groaned. "Are you sure?"

She nodded, giving me permission, and I wasted no time. I shoved myself down her throat, going as deep as I could go. My hips had a mind of their own and no matter how much I wanted this to last, I was done. The visual and the sensation she caused would be burned in my brain forever. My balls tightened right before I came quick and fast, feeling the most intense orgasm rush from my body.

I pulled out and leaned back and just stared at the gorgeous woman in my bed. Her hair was wild and everywhere, her face was flushed, and her mouth hung open as her chest rose with heavy breaths. "You are so beautiful," I said, brushing soft, sweet kisses to her lips. My legs were still shaking, but I slid off the bed and unhooked the cuffs and did the same thing with her wrists.

"Are you okay? I didn't hurt you, did I?"

"No, you didn't hurt me. I think I enjoyed that as much as you did."

I busted out laughing and dropped my head into her neck. Her delicate fingers splayed in my hair. "I highly doubt that."

I spent the next hour making love to her. Every touch, every caress, and every kiss were an unspoken vow. A promise and a declaration. We might have set out with no rules or expectations, but that was changing.

For the first time in my life, I felt content. Like this is where I was supposed to be. With her, here in this moment. Now I knew what all my friends have been talking about. This feeling, it all finally made sense. There wasn't a doubt in my mind that I was ready for her. Ready to bring her into my world. Ready to take the next step. I didn't want to be with anyone else. I just wanted her, and I hoped with everything I had that she wanted me like that too.

Her fingers came up and played with the gold rope chain along my neck. "You're not going to be mad if I fall asleep on you, right?" She yawned as I pulled the comforter up to her chin.

I kissed her cheek softy. "Go to sleep, beautiful. I'll make sure your phone is charged." I rolled off the bed and reached for her phone so I could plug it in. There was a new message on the screen. "Who's Owen?"

"What?" She jerked up in panic.

"Whoa." I pushed her back down and fixed the blanket over her chest. "You got a text message from some guy named Owen."

She got quiet for a minute. "Oh, sorry. You startled me. I was just about ready to drift off to sleep."

I handed her the phone, expecting her to read the message. Instead, she just shook her head and placed it back down on the nightstand.

"Is everything okay?"

"Yeah." She waved her hands in the air without making eye contact with me. "I'll just deal with him tomorrow."

That was an interesting choice of words, I thought to myself. I was curious and wanted to ask her more but didn't want to pry. The last thing I wanted was to come across as the jealous boyfriend. Still, the hairs on the back of my neck prickled. My cop instincts were telling me that there was something going on.

After setting the alarm on my phone, Amelia settled into my side and kissed my chest. I refused to let any nagging feelings kicking around in my stomach ruin this moment.

I kissed her temple and waited for a few minutes before she drifted off to sleep.

SEVENTEEN

AMELIA

"I can't believe Tamara dumped all that shit on you," Ava said over the rim of her cosmo.

I picked up my own martini and held it up in the air. "I should be used to it by now."

It was Friday night, and Ava and I were having cocktails after work. I have spent every night for the past two weeks in Marco's bed and I really needed her advice. Our days and nights have blended together, consisting of shared meals, late night cuddling, and texting sweet nothings every chance we got. Things were changing, and with everything going on with my mother and the fucking arrangement, I was feeling overwhelmed.

She waved her finger in my face. "Fuck that. And you know what? I hope your grandfather does cut her off. I would pay money to see her shopping at Walmart with her Gucci bag and Jimmy Choos."

My fingers tightened around the stem of my glass and I looked around to make sure no one heard her.

"Fuck!" Ava craned her neck to look over my shoulder.

I turned around in my seat to see what had her all

agitated. "Double fuck," I said, and grabbed my phone to make sure Marco was still running late.

With Owen walking our way, I was hit with a very unfriendly reminder that the happy little bubble I was living in was about to pop.

"Relax. Don't let him see you panic," Ava whispered, trying to get the look of unease off my face.

"Hello, ladies." He slid up next to me and draped his arm along the back of my stool.

He looked so put together, with his blond hair styled perfectly and his clean-shaven jaw. It just went to show you that looks could be deceiving.

"What are you still doing here? I thought you'd be long gone by now." I tried to sound happy to see him, which was always a challenge.

Ava snorted and tried to hide her smirk behind her glass. She was well aware of what a slacker he was at the office. It was six o'clock at night and normally he would have been gone two hours ago.

He tucked his free hand in his pants pocket. "I have a Christmas party just a few short blocks away. I figured I'd hang out at the office until then."

"Ahh." That made sense, although I still wished he were already gone. I fiddled with the cocktail napkin on the bar and tried to think of something I could say to get him moving along. "Well, don't let us hold you up. Wouldn't want you to get last dibs on all the single ladies at the party." I smiled cheeky. He thought I was being playful, but I was dead serious.

He rested his arms on the bar and leaned forward. "Don't worry about that, they'll wait for me. I have time for a quick drink."

Ava gave me a sideways glance filled with concern. I squirmed in my seat while Owen ordered his Macallan and soda. The last thing I wanted to do was sit and chitchat with the source of all my frustrations. I wanted him to be long gone before Marco got here.

"So, Amelia, I'm glad I ran into you. Is there a reason why you've been avoiding me these past few weeks?"

"Avoiding you?" I acted shocked. Owen had tried to reach me all week. Silly me thought if I'd ignored him then I wouldn't have to deal with him.

He unbuttoned his coat and leaned sideways. "I wanted to invite you to dinner next week, but with the way you've been dodging my calls, I haven't been able to make that happen."

I drained the remainder of my vodka, hoping it would settle my nerves a little bit. "I apologize. I've been so swamped, but I have been meaning to return your messages."

His brows pulled together. I could see it in his eyes that he knew I was full of shit. Owen might have been lazy when it came to business, but he wasn't a dummy. He knew something was up. I was also a terrible liar.

"Why don't you pick the day and the time, and I'll pick the place?" he said, swirling the frozen sphere of ice in his drink around before bringing it to his lips.

"Sure, let me take a look at my calendar and I'll get back to you."

"How about Wednesday? I'll pick you up at seven."

"You just said that you'd let me pick the day and the time."

He leaned back against the bar and adjusted his tie. "If I left things up to you, this ball would never get rolling. We can't keep putting this off. How are we supposed to sell ourselves as the perfect couple if we don't start acting like one?"

His gaze was creepy and I didn't like it. My suspicion was confirmed when his eyes dropped to the scoop neckline of my black sweater. The one I wore for Marco tonight.

"We are not a couple," I reminded him through gritted teeth.

"Yet." He stared while I blinked back at him. "Something is going on with you. I sure hope you're not having second thoughts, because if you are, you need to find a way to get over them."

Was I having second thoughts? Yes, I was. But I was also at a loss on how to get out of this mess without risking everything that I'd worked for over my lifetime. Things between Marco and I were moving faster than I expected, and Owen's ill-timed visit tonight was a reminder that I couldn't keep this secret for much longer.

"I don't know what you want me to say, Owen. We both verbally agreed to the deal, but now that it's quickly approaching, it's getting more real."

"Amelia, I'm willing to do my part. Things would be a lot easier for both of us if you stopped acting like this is the worst thing that could possibly happen to you. Marrying me won't be the end of the world. Who knows, you might actually end up liking me once you stop hating me. And once you do, it will be easier to convince everyone that you're in love with me."

"You know what, Owen?" Ava cut in with a forced smile. "Maybe you should save this conversation for another time. Amelia and I are trying to have a girls' night out and you're cramping our style."

He tilted his lip and smiled at her, but there was nothing friendly about it. "Maybe you could be a good friend and convince her she needs to get on board and take one for the team. Going through with this doesn't have to feel like a funeral dirge." He looked between us. "Do you know how many women would love to be in your shoes?"

Ava rolled her eyes. "Owen, while I'm sure your privileged, entitled ass is convinced that any woman would be fortunate enough to get a piece of you, what your conceited head doesn't understand is you are a dime a dozen. Amelia is the catch here, not you."

The two of them have never gotten along. Ava's sharp tongue and Owen's arrogance never meshed well. They have tolerated each over the years at best. If I had to score this round, it would go to Ava, but I felt slightly bad for her laying Owen out flat.

He narrowed his eyes on my friend. "For a girl whose mother used to clean houses in my neighborhood, you sure learned how to use a lot of big words."

She slammed her drink down. "For a guy who spent his entire youth in expensive prep schools, you sure are a brainless fuckwad."

He clicked his tongue. "Always so classy."

"All right, you two." I held up my hands. "Enough." I looked around the crowded bar and was thankful that no one was paying attention. Ava was always insecure about her upbringing, and he knew exactly what buttons to push.

Owen ran his hand across his chin, looking annoyed. "This company needs us, Amelia. We can take Eastan West in a direction and really make a name for ourselves." He reached for his phone to check the time and tapped his knuckles on the bar. "I'm going to head out. I'll see you on Wednesday. We have important things to discuss, so please don't reschedule or blow me off."

I watched him finish his drink and walk away. Just as he was winding his way around the crowded pub tables, he bumped into Marco as he was entering the lounge. Owen didn't even look up or apologize as he continued to make his way toward the front of the lobby. Marco shook his head and spotted me across the room.

I stood up on shaky legs to greet him, because, Jesus Christ, that was close. "Hey there."

He dipped his head toward mine and wrapped his arm along my waist. "Sorry I'm late."

"Better later than never." I smiled.

He looked down at my outfit and grinned. "You look

nice." Unlike when Owen's eyes took me in, this was different.

"You got a little more scruff than usual," I pointed out, running my fingers across his stubble.

"I'll shave."

"Please don't." I slid my hands up his chest and folded them around his neck. "I love it."

He quirked an eyebrow. "Then it stays."

I was laughing against his mouth at how accommodating he was being when Ava cleared her throat.

I pulled away and shook my head. "Sorry, Marco, this is my friend, Ava."

She extended her hand; she was practically glowing in excitement. "It's a pleasure."

He accepted her offering while draping his free arm along my shoulder, tucking me into his side. I should have been nervous that someone from the office would see me, but I was so happy that he was here that I couldn't care less.

"I apologize for being late. I was following up on a lead at the airport and I got stuck in traffic."

Ava waved him off. "Amelia and I don't get a chance to see each other as much as we like, so this worked out perfect. Plus, I'm glad I finally got to meet you."

Marco held his hand out, signaling for the bartender to bring us a round of drinks.

"So, is this your first time here?" she asked, with a teasing smile. "Oh, that's right. I just remembered you've actually stayed here in one of the rooms before."

Marco coughed in his hand and I narrowed my eyes on my best friend. Our freshly poured drinks were placed in front of us.

She waved her hands through the air, smirking at me. "Don't look at me like that."

I rolled my eyes. "Will you stop embarrassing me?" Leave it to her to bring up our first night together.

"How am I embarrassing you? If I wanted to do that, I would bring up the night when you 'technically' first met. The night you were handcuff—" I leaned forward and kicked her in the knee to prevent her from finishing that sentence. "Ow." She winced and reached down to rub her leg.

I picked up my martini and took a generous sip while Marco laughed beside me. I bumped him with my shoulder. "Whose side are you on?"

"If I were you, I would pick her side." Ava waggled her eyebrow suggestively. "She's the one you're taking home tonight."

I buried my face in my hands and groaned, feeling mortified beyond words.

Marco held his beer out, trying to hide the twitching at the corners of his mouth. "I think we should do this more often."

"I disagree," I mumbled.

Ava spent the next thirty minutes entertaining Marco with embarrassing stories about me. I sat back while he held my hand in his lap as they both laughed at my expense and teased me every chance they could. I chuckled when she told the story about how we stumbled upon a group of naked guys running around in a farmer's field that were pledging for their fraternity. They explained as we drove them back to campus that their clothes were taken and they had to find their way back in their birthday suits without being captured. They never forgot how we helped them from getting caught and we ended up with open invites to all their parties, and free beer for the rest of college. Best freshman year memory.

Ava's phone buzzed on top of the countertop. She held the screen up, showing Marco a picture of a smiling Madison. "Excuse me for a second." She slid off the stool and walked to a quiet part of the room.

"Have you figured out what you want to do for dinner?" he asked before taking a sip of his beer.

We had plans to grab a quick bite to eat downtown and

then head back to his house to decorate the tree we picked out last night. I might have gone a little overboard on decorations at Macy's today during my lunch hour.

"I wouldn't mind just grabbing a couple cheesesteaks from Jim's to-go."

He shook his head with a smirk. "You and those damn cheesesteaks."

"I eat healthy all week, so I can treat myself on the weekends."

I worked out at the hotel gym every morning before work and ate clean Monday through Friday. The weekends were a different story.

He held his hands up in surrender. "Hey, you won't hear me complain. Besides, you're a cheap date."

"I also want to bring your grandmother a Christmas gift when we visit her on Sunday. Would you mind if we made a quick stop before we leave the city?"

He brushed a piece of hair off my shoulder. "Of course not. I think it's sweet that you're thinking of her."

"I'm sad that we won't get to see each other on Christmas."

Christmas was less than a week away. Marco and his mom were bringing Sophia to celebrate the holidays at Matteo's in-law's house in Delaware. My mom was here until the new year and I was expected to spend Christmas day with my family. Marco and I were celebrating this weekend. His gifts, along with all the decorations I bought for the tree, were stashed in the trunk of my car.

Ava made her way over and slid her phone into her purse. "It looks like my adult time is over." She drained the rest of her drink. "Drew and Madison are outside waiting for me."

I grabbed my coat from the back of my stool and Marco helped me slide my arms through the sleeves. He signaled for the bartender's attention. "We have to get going anyway. We'll walk you out. Let me just pay the tab really quick."

Marco signed the bill and placed his credit card in his wallet. He laced his fingers with mine as we followed Ava outside. Marco, being the gentleman he was, walked her to her waiting car where we said our goodbyes.

Holiday lights decorated the buildings as we walked through the Christmas market outside city hall. The sidewalks were crowded with people of all ages, some carrying their shopping bags, others just taking in the storefront windows while sipping hot chocolate and enjoying the street performers providing entertainment. Marco put his arm around my shoulder for warmth, but I really loved how comfortable he felt. The more time I spent with him, the easier and natural it became.

"Tell me again what you're looking for?" he asked as we sidestepped over a patch of ice.

"I'm buying your grandmother a scarf. She's always wrapped up in a blanket every time I visit her."

We moved around the little white tents and spent the next fifteen minutes laughing our asses off as we talked about everything from favorite holiday movies to the worst gifts we ever received growing up. Marco told me that he and Matteo always got more clothes than toys when they were younger. And of course, he teased me about how spoiled I was growing up.

"Let me get this straight." He pulled me to a stop in the middle of the crowded sidewalk. "You had a Tiffany necklace replaced three times because your housekeeper kept throwing it out?"

"Yes, but it wasn't her fault. The instructions said to wrap the necklace in tissue paper to prevent the chain from tangling up. She would find rolled up toilet paper on my vanity and throw it out thinking it was garbage."

His mouth fell open. "You really were a spoiled little brat growing up, weren't you?"

My hands flew to my hips. "You have one second to take that back."

He shook his head. "Sorry, but I speak the truth."

I playfully punched him in the chest. "That's not nice. Just because I had nice things growing up doesn't make me a bad person."

He smiled down at me. "I didn't say you were a bad person, just that your life was just a little bit different than mine."

"Opposites attract, right?" I teased, kissing the corner of his mouth.

His gloved hand slid behind my neck, holding me in place. "They sure do."

He took my lips in a soft caress. There was something about this kiss that felt different. It wasn't hurried or heavy. It was sweet and slow, and I wanted to cherish it, because I never felt anything so perfect before.

My heart stilled in my chest as the realization hit me. I was in love with him. Here under the star-filled sky, with snowflakes falling around us, I lost a piece of my heart that I would never be able to reclaim. It didn't matter that we came from different worlds, because we were making our own little world together. Despite our differences, we were compatible in all the ways that mattered.

I pulled back when I felt his grip on me loosen. I opened my eyes to find him watching me. He brought his hand up and brushed his thumb across my jaw. The look on his face was warm and tender. Funny how something so soft and gentle could have the power to break me in the end.

A little boy bumped into his leg, causing him to stumble back a bit.

"Well, I guess that moment is gone." He laughed.

I moved a lock of hair that had fallen on his forehead. "We can pick up where we left off later."

I looked over his shoulder and spotted what I was looking

for. "There it is," I said, dragging him over to the white tent. I pulled the scarf off the display shelf. "What do you think? Will she like it?" I asked, running my hands along the heavy knitted scarf.

Marco tilted his head to the side. "It looks like something the Pope would wear."

"Seriously?"

He ran his hand along the top of his hair. "It reminds me of one of those scarves they sell at the Vatican."

I glanced at it one last time. It was red and green with geometric shapes. I thought it looked festive and Christmassy.

"I wouldn't know that because I've never been to the Vatican."

"That's right. I forgot. Maybe I'll take you to Italy someday."

I sucked in a breath. He was talking about the future. A future I wasn't sure we would ever have. When he said stuff like that, it was impossible not to think about how much longer I could keep the truth about that contract buried. I would eventually have to tell him, and there was no way he wouldn't hate me in the end. As soon as that thought struck, I shook it off and refused to let it steal the joy from this moment.

I lifted my lips into a smile. "Wine, pasta, and you on the beach in a speedo. Sounds like the perfect vacation."

He narrowed his eyes at me, and I stuck my tongue out and turned toward the cashier to pay for Sophia's gift. Once it was in the bag, I grabbed Marco's arm and linked it with mine.

"Now, let's go get that cheesesteak."

EIGHTEEN

MARCO

"You seem tired," I said, getting a glass out of the cupboard. "Are you sure you want to open gifts tonight?"

We just got back from visiting with my grandmother, who was as spunky as ever. Amelia, on the other hand, was quiet on the drive home, making it seem twice as long. She's been a little off, but I chalked it up as exhaustion from all the decorating and shopping we've done over the last forty-eight hours.

She pinched her lips together and paused a beat longer than normal. "I'm sure."

Considering I interrogated people all day long for a living, it was almost impossible to ignore how distant she was being tonight.

I racked my brain trying to remember if I said or did something to piss her off. Nothing came to mind.

She leaned over the counter while I mixed my Jack and Coke. "Do you want a glass of wine?" I asked once I finished making my drink.

"I can get it." She moved toward the fridge where I kept her bottle of chardonnay. It should have felt weird how familiar she was here in my home, but it didn't. The only thing weird was the way she was acting.

With our drinks in hand, she followed me over to the loveseat that sat in front of the tree we decorated last night.

She took a tentative sip of her wine and placed it on the coaster. "Are you ready for your gift?"

"I thought you already gave me my gift earlier," I teased, and I loved watching her blush while reminding her of our quickie in the shower this morning before we hit the mall.

She chuckled and made her way over to the tree. The gifts for my family were overflowing and pushed up the lower branches, completely spreading out past the tree skirt.

"I love the look and smell of a real, fresh pine." She smiled and stood back, holding a small box in her hand.

I set my drink on the end table and picked up the two boxes I wrapped for her. We both sat on the floor with our legs out. I held the bigger box out for her to open first.

We both agreed not to go crazy on each other and to stick to two gifts each. Which was fine with me, because one… I hated shopping, and two… what the hell do you buy a woman who has everything anyway?

"Ladies first," I insisted and watched her tear into the red and white tissue paper. She tore the lid off the rectangular box and pulled out her gift. She held up the gray hoodie that said "Property of the Philadelphia Police Department" on the front and turned it around. Once she saw the back, she broke out in a fit of laughter.

"Really?" she said, still shaking her head at my last name on the back of the sweatshirt in big blue letters. "You just had to get me a sweatshirt with your name on it, didn't you? You even put your full last name on there instead of the shortened version you use for work."

I shrugged, playing coy. "I couldn't resist. There's more."

My last name was Rubintino, but I went by Detective Rubin for work. I protected my privacy and the last thing I needed was for some psycho with a grudge trying to look me up.

She reached inside and pulled out a ridiculously overpriced pair of leggings. "I'm impressed. How did you know these were my favorite?" She held them out in front of her for inspection.

I rolled my eyes. "They are the first thing you change into when you get home from work. Although, don't expect to get another pair from me anytime soon. Do you know how many pairs of sweatpants I could buy for the same amount I paid for those?"

"Hey, they are super comfy, and they last forever."

"They should for what they charge. I only had to take out a small mortgage to pay for them."

"Oh my God." She nudged my foot playfully. "Just shut up and open your gift."

I laughed at her teasing, but truthfully, I was glad to see that she was in a better mood from earlier. I ripped the paper off the small square box to find a bottle of Armani Cologne. I held it up. "Thanks, I already have a full bottle, but this is the only stuff I use."

"I know. I love it, so I wanted to make sure you never run out."

I lifted my eyebrow and picked up the medium-sized gift bag that held a small box inside. It had a fancy jewelry store logo on the front that I recognized. I flipped the lid off and pulled out a gold, Italian horn charm. "The Corncillo," I said, admiring the twisted horn.

She looked uncertain while looking down at her feet. "It's supposed to protect and ward off evil. I figured it was appropriate considering your job and the kinds of people you have to chase down for a living."

I leaned over and fanned my hand along the back of her neck. "I love it," I said, leaning in for a kiss. "Thank you."

She swallowed and I felt my heart constrict. She really did

worry about me and my safety. The only women who cared this much were my mom and nonna.

"I have one more gift for you. Come here." I pulled her off the floor and walked her toward my bedroom.

"What are you doing?" she asked, looking confused as I stepped up to my dresser and stretched my hand into the back of the top drawer.

I pulled out a small box and handed it to her.

She tilted her head to the side. "What did you do?" She looked at me with amazement while I felt my heart beat wildly in my chest.

I stuffed my hands inside the front pockets of my jeans and met her eyes. "Open it."

She looked up at me, and I hoped like hell that she liked it. She was careful as she opened the box and when she finally saw what was inside, she sucked in a breath. "An infinity bracelet." She ran her fingers along the symbol and rubbed her thumb across the blue sea glass charm. I added that to the bracelet because it reminded me of the color of her eyes. "It's beautiful."

I would have given her anything at that moment just to see the smile on her face. That was until I saw the tear leak out of the corner of her eye. I brought my hands to her shoulders and pulled her to my chest. "Hey, what's wrong? Do you not like it?"

When I saw the bracelet in the window, I knew it was simple, but it reminded me so much of her... and of us. Even though I haven't promised her a future yet, this was my way of showing her that I didn't see this ending anytime soon. I wasn't ready to get down on one knee, but I was warming up to the idea of more with her.

She wrapped her arms around my waist, bringing us closer. "I love it. Did you know that I always wanted to get an infinity tattoo on the inside of my wrist?" I shook my head, because that was the first I had heard of it. "I never got one because I assumed it wouldn't look very professional."

"Amelia, almost everyone has a tattoo nowadays. If you want to get one, then get one."

"I know and I may still do that," she sniffed, "but now I can wear this and every time I look at it, I will think of you. This is the best gift I've ever received."

I inhaled deeply and took a step back. "If you're happy with it then what's wrong?"

She placed a hand on my chest while holding the bracelet out with the other. "Nothing." She shook her head, but I didn't believe her. "Will you put this on me?" She held her arm out while I tightened the clasp and pressed a kiss to the inside of her wrist.

There was a smile on her face as she stared at the bracelet, but I could tell there was something still bothering her. "Why don't we get changed and pick something to watch on Netflix?" I suggested, placing my hand on her shoulders. "Does that sound good?"

She nodded her head and that uneasy feeling I had all day was really starting to settle in deeper.

Amelia went into the bathroom while I pulled a couple mugs out of the cabinet for hot chocolate. I was just about to grab a bag of microwave popcorn when I spotted her out of the corner of my eye. The sound of her sniffling caught my attention.

"Everything okay?"

Her voice was shaky as she patted the seat next to her on the couch. "Come sit with me. We need to talk." She picked up the remote and turned the TV off.

I set her cup down and paused when I confirmed that she was, in fact, crying. "What's going on?"

She pulled her legs underneath her and twisted her hands in her lap. "This is harder than I thought it would be."

Every worst-case scenario ran through my mind. Patience

wasn't my strong suit, and there was nothing more unnerving than a man hearing the words "we need to talk" from his girlfriend. Fuck, was she breaking up with me? Right before Christmas?

"Please, just say what you have to say," I said as calmly as I could.

She nervously adjusted the throw blanket around her shoulders. "I need to know where you see things going between us?"

I sat back and tilted my head to the side. "I'm not sure what you mean?"

"Do you see a future with me?"

I shoved a hand through my hair, wondering where she was going with this question. "I think we are off to a great start, but where is this coming from?"

"When we first met, I never imagined us getting this far." Her words came out choppy while she fidgeted with the charm that dangled along her bracelet. "It was only supposed to be for one night, but I think we can both agree that somewhere along the way things became more serious."

I scratched the back of my neck and felt my jaw tighten. "You don't sound very happy about that. Am I missing something?"

She swallowed. "Yes… No… Let me explain. Before I met you, I agreed to an arrangement."

My head came up in surprise. "Arrangement? What the hell does that mean?"

"I wanted more time to figure things out between us, but I'm not sure how much longer I have." My hand tightened around the armrest. "My grandfather and his business partner are retiring early next year. There is an agreement in place that was drawn up years ago, that basically states that I will inherit fifty percent of the business. Edward Eastan, who is the other half of Eastan and West Corporation, is leaving his share to his grandson, Owen. There is one condition." She looked down at the floor and made a show of stalling for time before bringing her tear-filled eyes back to mine. "Owen and I have to marry."

It took a minute for everything to sink in. I was trying really hard not to freak out, but that lasted all of sixty seconds before I flew off the chair. "I'm sorry, did I miss the part where you were raised in a foreign country or something? Because I don't know," I threw my hands out, "last I checked you lived in the good ole US of A where you married whoever the hell you wanted."

"I have a choice. No one is forcing me to do anything."

I looked at her like she had lost her mind. I stared at her, trying to hold in my shock and anger. There were so many thoughts and emotions flowing through my brain that it was impossible to think straight. I've dealt with a lot of fucked-up shit in my profession, but this… this was unreal. And the fact that it was personal and I let my guard down made it ten times worse.

"So, let me get this straight. You knew from the very beginning that this was only temporary? The entire time we spent together you thought it would be best to lie to me?"

There was always a feeling in my gut telling me she was hiding something, but I rationalized it away instead of confronting her. I was a cop and I let myself get distracted. I worked off of intuition, so maybe I shouldn't put all the blame on her. I should have seen the signs. Maybe if I was thinking with my big head instead of my little one, I wouldn't be so blindsided.

"Technically, I never lied to you, Marco." My name was a plea on her lips, she was practically begging for my understanding or forgiveness, I couldn't tell which one, and I was too exasperated to care. "I can't tell you how much I agonized over this. There were plenty of times where I wanted to tell you, but I got scared."

I swallowed hard, wishing my voice didn't sound as lethal

as it did, but I didn't have the energy to try to control it. "A lie of omission is still a lie. I warned you. I told you what I needed from you. At least I thought I did. You knew my hesitation on starting a relationship, and here we fucking are. You've had weeks to tell me. You didn't do that though, did you?" I stepped forward, refusing to let her look away from me. "You lied to me. You let me develop feelings for you. All the while, you've kept your little marriage secret to yourself. Are you fucking him too?"

She shook her head. "Of course not. There is nothing romantic about this arrangement. Owen and I are not a couple."

"Yet," I added, because according to her there was a piece of paper that was going to change that.

"I deserve your anger, and I'm sorry." Her voice was heavy with regret. "If I could go back and tell you sooner, I would."

"Why are you telling me this now?"

"Because you deserve to know the truth."

"Then why the fuck did you wait so damn long?"

"Because things have been going so good between us, and I didn't want to ruin that. I was afraid of how you would react."

I was so caught off guard that I couldn't even process anything other than my own outrage. "Is this what you want?"

Please say no. Please say no.

My eyes held hers for a second; this was fucked up in so many ways. Every part of me was begging her to tell me she wouldn't go through with it. Not in a million years did I imagine this conversation happening when she asked me to sit down a few minutes ago. How did we go from blissfully happy to fucked up so quickly?

"No, I don't want this marriage. I want my job, but this

isn't just about me. This is a complicated situation with a lot of moving parts."

This was such bullshit, and to add insult to my already open wound, she had the nerve to act like she was a victim.

I could see the hurt in her eyes, hear it in her voice, but I wasn't sure what I was supposed to do with it. How was I supposed to feel? Because right now, I could barely stomach to look at her.

"Why the hell did you agree to that?"

"I agreed to it before we met, but I never anticipated falling in love with you. It was never part of the rules."

"Don't you dare," I bit out. She was tearing my heart into a million pieces. She might as well have struck my chest with a knife. How dare she throw the rules we discussed on our first date, like they were still applicable.

"Marco, please." Tears slipped from her eyes, but my body was numb. So damn numb. I couldn't believe this was happening. She just dumped a fucking grenade in my life. Every doubt and insecurity I had packed away started revealing themselves again. "Let's talk this out. I know you're upset, but we can figure this out. I can't lose you. I just can't. Just the thought of it hurts."

My eyes narrowed. "Are you backing out of the deal?" She stayed silent, and every second that ticked by felt like hours. The longer we sat there, the more I questioned everything. When she took too long to respond, I knew I had my answer. "Then we have nothing to figure out."

Her face fell. "What do you want me to do? I've worked hard my entire life to get to this point." She looked off to the side. "Up until I met you, my career is all I ever wanted. Now, for the first time in my life, I'm not sure what I want anymore."

Pain and anger tangled inside of me. "You're not sure if you want me? Is that what you're saying?"

"Marco, I'm confused. I didn't expect to feel this strongly

about us. But unless you can tell me that you see a future with me, I'm not sure I can just walk away from my obligations. If I don't sign that contract, I could lose everything."

"You expect sympathy from me?"

"No. I want a commitment from you," she shouted in frustration.

I stumbled to a stop and glared at her. "You want me to marry you?"

"No, that's not what I meant." She shook her head, looking so damned confused. Join the fucking club, sweetheart. "I mean yes, maybe someday, but right now I need to know if there is a place for me in your life. If you see a future with me at some point. If you say yes, then I will give it all up. I would risk everything just to be with you. If I have a choice, then I choose you, but I can't throw it all away unless you give me some type of guarantee. That's all I'm asking."

"Let me see if I have this straight. If I promise you a future right here on the spot then you will stay with me. And if I don't agree to your demands than you're going to turn your back on me. All for some family loyalty."

"Marco, please…"

"You are un-fucking-believable. This must be some sick joke. I know you're not a dummy, so you must be pretty damn delirious if you think I will commit to anything with you right now."

"I'm trying to explain my actions and my decisions."

My fingers curled into my hair, tugging hard enough for a sharp pain to rip across my skull. Anger seeped through my veins. I was filled with so much uncontrollable rage.

"I don't want to hear about your reasons. You failed to mention that you were going to be marrying someone else. You've had weeks to tell me. Instead, you chose to lie to me. Carrying on a relationship with me under the circumstances was wrong, and you know it. And putting me on the spot and asking me to give you a guarantee is extremely unfair."

"I never knew how to tell you." Her voice was scratchy, practically raw from crying. "Marco, please, I love you."

I was about ready to lose my shit!

"Get out."

She froze. "Please don't do this."

"You know where the door is, use it."

"This isn't just about me. There are people counting on me. Things you don't understand."

My temper was raging and I needed her to leave. I paced back and forth, bracing my hands behind my neck. There was nothing to understand. No way she could spin it or explain to make this okay.

"Amelia, I have nothing else to say to you."

"Please listen to me."

"I don't trust you. We are done."

"Did you not hear me when I told you I love you? Does that not mean anything to you? I knew being with you was taking a huge risk, but you are worth it."

I slammed my fist through the freshly painted drywall. She jumped at the sound.

"Get. The. Fuck. Out."

She stood and wiped the tears from her cheeks. "I honestly thought waiting was the right thing to do. I thought if we had a little bit more time then things would figure themselves out." She picked up her purse and looked at the scattered tissue and wrapping paper lying on the floor. She covered her mouth on a sob and swiftly moved toward the door. There was a part of me that wanted to beg her not to leave. To stay so we could work things out, but my stubborn pride won out. "I'm going to give you some time to cool down. I'm walking away because that's what you need, even if it's the last thing I want to do. Believe me when I say, my feelings for you are real. I love you more than I thought possible, and will be waiting for you if you change your mind." Her hand paused on the knob. "I know we have a lot to work through, but what we have is worth fighting for. Please don't give up on us."

The second the door shut behind her, I picked up the mug of hot chocolate and threw it across the door she just walked out of. The ceramic mug, just like my life, had just shattered into a thousand pieces. I slumped to the floor and was left wondering how the hell I allowed my heart to get broken again.

NINETEEN

AMELIA

MY COMPUTER WAS TAKING FOREVER TO WARM UP, SO I BANGED on my mouse as if it were to blame for all my problems. I've done nothing but cry, and I was not the type of girl to shed tears easily.

Work was usually a good distraction for me, so once my screen turned on, I clicked on my email and tackled my inbox. I've gone over things in my head a million times and thought about what I could have done differently. If there was a way to get the job and keep the guy.

I clicked on a proposal for the National Law Enforcement and K9 Conference. Just wonderful. It seemed like the universe was working against me. So much for work being my escape.

If I was going to get through these next few hours, I needed something other than coffee. I opened the top drawer of my desk and pulled out a protein bar hiding under a stack of index cards. I was just about to skim through the documents when someone knocked on my door.

"Come in," I called, looking up from my computer screen. My department was mostly deserted due to the holiday schedule. I assumed it was the maintenance staff, because they were working different hours and trying to keep their evenings free.

The door slowly pushed open, and my mother stepped into the room. I closed my desk drawer, the protein bar no longer appealed to me.

"What can I do for you?"

After the fallout at my house the other morning, I made it abundantly clear that we didn't need to speak to each other unless it was absolutely necessary. The way she treated Marco was totally unacceptable.

"Would you like to join me in the main dining room for brunch? They have a new menu that I'm dying to try out."

"Why?" I met her gaze. "Do you have more life shattering secrets you need to reveal?"

She crossed a line the other day, and there was too much animosity between us to remain civil. Well, at least for me. She claimed she was only looking out for my best interests when in fact she was only looking out for herself. I should let my grandfather cut her off, and I should turn my back on this company because everything I've been told my entire life has been a lie. But every time I thought about it, I couldn't bring myself to do it.

She lowered herself into the seat across from my desk. "I would like the opportunity to make things right."

I looked out into the hall, thankful that it was so quiet today. "I'm not sure you can."

"I'd still like to try."

I rose from my chair and walked over to the window, overlooking the city below. Light snow still blanked the streets while people walked and talked. Their lives were going on as normal, while mine stood still.

"You got your wish." I folded my arms across my chest. "Marco and I are no longer together."

She was quiet for a moment before clearing her throat. "If

it makes you feel any better, I'm sorry. I know you cared for him."

I turned my head and glared at her. "Did you? Is that why you were so rude to him?"

She clasped her hands together in front of her. "I was caught off guard, and things are so complicated right now. I had every right to be concerned. Besides, it's for the best that you forget about him and move forward."

Her words cut deep. She wanted me to just brush my feelings aside when I've never felt so lost and sad in my life. "Forget about him?" My voice rose along with my irritation. "I am in love with him." Her eyes widened. "The kind where you don't just get over it, but with your track record, I don't expect you to understand that."

"Amelia." She shook her head. "I had no idea it was that serious."

How would she know? She wasn't a part of my life. We saw each other a handful of times a year, if that. That made her the last person on earth I would want to confide in.

"It doesn't matter. I told him the truth and he made it clear he wanted nothing to do with me."

I'd be damned if it didn't hurt me to admit that. It's only been two days and that aching hole in my chest only seemed to get bigger and bigger. I thought I could distract myself with mindless hours of reality TV or fill it with my work, but nothing was helping.

"How much did you tell him?" She looked over her shoulder.

"Not that," I clipped back. Although I would have told him about my paternity if the topic came up. I would have told him anything if that meant he could forgive me.

She tapped her red manicured nail along the armrest of the chair. "You're obviously still angry with me, so I'm just going to cut to the chase here. I never should have put that burden on you. I'm ashamed of how I've treated you. I'd like the chance to fix things."

She actually sounded genuine, which surprised me. Yet, old habits and her history of manipulation had me on guard. After all, she wanted me to marry dipshit just so she could keep her stuffy little country club membership and not have to give up her personal shopper at Neiman Marcus.

"Why now? Why all of a sudden?"

"I know I lost the chance of being the mother you deserve, but I'd like to try to rectify my mistakes. I realized after I left your place the other day that I was only making things worse. I felt like I've let you down."

I shook my head, thinking about how hard that was for her to admit that. "You've got a lot riding on this deal too."

"I'm ashamed of myself." She looked up at the ceiling and back to me. "I know that I've disappointed you, but the truth is, I'm more disappointed in myself. As my daughter, you should have always come first. I've spent a lot of time thinking about how I could have handled things differently. But, Amelia, your dad and your grandparents never wanted you to find out. Regardless, Greg West will always be your father, not Marcus."

I closed my eyes, not wanting to hear that man's name. The man who knew about me but didn't want me. I was curious about him, but it felt like I was being disloyal to my father just by entertaining the idea. Yet, the desire to learn any little bits I could about the man who created me dominated my thoughts.

"Tell me about Marcus."

Her eyes slid shut. "It's not a pretty story, and I don't want to hurt you any more than I already have."

"I want to know. I deserve to know." I had to remind myself that what she said about him didn't matter. He obviously kept his distance from me all these years for a reason.

"Okay." She hung her head in defeat and patted her legs. "What questions do you have?"

So many, I thought, but I was almost too afraid to ask.

"Where does he live?"

"In Boca."

I blinked at her, almost too stunned to talk. "Is that why you moved to South Florida?"

She laughed, but there was no humor in her voice. "No, that was just pure coincidence."

I swallowed, feeling an unpleasant knot settle in my throat. "What does he do?"

"He runs a popular Irish Pub in downtown Boca, but I think that's just a little hobby, because he makes most of his money in real estate."

A pub owner didn't sound like her type, but real estate mogul did. And trust me, nobody knew my mother's type better than me.

"Does he have any other children?"

"I promised myself that I would not lie if you asked me, so yes, he has three children." The tears that slipped from her eyes caught me off guard. She reached over and grabbed a pack of Kleenex out of her purse. "When I told him I was pregnant, he was furious. He said he already had his family, and he didn't want any more kids, especially one that wasn't his wife's. He gave me an ultimatum, I either get an abortion or I never contact him again."

My mouth opened and snapped shut. I didn't know how someone I never met could hurt me so deeply. He sounded like a piece of work and if he had any redeeming qualities, I sure as hell didn't need to find out.

"I think I've heard enough." I cleared my throat and rearranged a few things on my desk. "But thank you for telling me."

She pressed her fingers to her eyes and took a deep breath.

"Of course. I'd like to work on our relationship. I know it may be too little too late, but I'd still like to try."

I stared down at the floor. "I don't know what to say." This was all so unexpected and I was unsure of what to do here. Not to mention, I still didn't trust her.

"How about we start small. Maybe lunch or dinner? Let's spend some time really getting to know each other. I know I placed a huge burden on your shoulders. Let's see if there is anything that can be done to get you out of this mess."

She seemed determined to make things right between us, and I didn't have the strength to carry this grudge any longer. I closed my laptop and decided that a good meal and a short conversation wouldn't hurt.

"I haven't had lunch yet, so if you're still interested in checking out that new menu in the main dining room, I'm free."

She pushed to her feet and picked her purse up off the ground. "I would love that."

I held my hand out. "Lead the way."

The elevator ride downstairs felt awkward, but by the time the doors opened to the lobby, I was actually looking forward to spending some time with her.

"Hello, ladies," Denzel, one of our head waiters, said as he approached our table. "Can I start you off with something other than water?" He placed our menus down in front us and filled our glasses. We were seated at a corner table that overlooked the Christmas market outside city hall. My heart deflated at the memory.

"I'll just have a Diet Coke with lime, please." I placed my napkin on my lap while my mother ordered a glass of sauvignon blanc.

"Of course." He tipped his head and moved toward the bar so he could punch in our order. I set my phone face down on the table so I wouldn't be tempted to glance at it every time I got a notification.

We both took time looking over the specials before Denzel returned with our drinks.

"Do you know what you want, Amelia?" Mom asked while taking a sip of her wine.

I pursed my lips. "I'm debating between the shrimp cocktail or the bacon wrapped dates."

"Why don't we get both," she suggested and turned to Denzel. "I'll also have the kale and apple salad."

"And how about you, Ms. West?" he asked, as my mom handed her his menu.

My eyes paused on the lobster bisque, which was Marco's favorite. I shook my head and moved my eyes over to the specials. "I'll have the spinach salad with cranberry dressing, please."

He winked. "Perfect choice. I'll be right out with your appetizers."

Silence settled over us and I looked down at my water. My mom reached for my hand. "Why don't you tell me about this Marco fella?"

I contemplated how much I wanted to get into. If someone were to tell me this morning that I would be sitting here, enjoying lunch with my mother, talking about my now ex-boyfriend, I wouldn't have believed it.

"There really isn't much to say other than, I am one hundred percent, head over heels in love with him."

"Does he know how you feel?"

"I told him." My voice was strained and with every second that ticked by, more pressure built up in my chest. The hurt on his face and the pain from his words would not leave my head. It felt like I was back in that house, reliving one of the most painful moments of my life. Tears threatened to spill from my eyes, but I forced them back. Allowing my emotions to break free wasn't going to do me an ounce of good. It wasn't going to change the outcome, and it sure as hell wasn't going to bring him back.

"You can talk to me, Amelia." She stared at me closely, sensing my internal suffering. I felt so damn mentally exhausted. "You don't have to keep everything bottled up inside. It might make you feel better if you talked about it."

Picking up my napkin, I wiped my eyes, wondering how it was possible that I even had any tears left to shed. At some point, I would be all cried out. "I can't right now, Mom. It hurts too much."

If she was disappointed, she didn't show it. "Fair enough." She placed her elbows on the table and leaned forward. "Believe it or not, I have a little experience with heartbreak myself, so if you ever change your mind I am always here to listen."

I just nodded my head, because I just wasn't quite there yet. Denzel approached the table and placed our appetizers in front of us. I took a sip of my Coke while he refilled our ice waters.

I was just about to dig in when I spotted Owen walking our way. My stomach clenched in discomfort.

"Tamara, it's good to see you." He walked around the table and kissed her cheek. "Is it just me or do you get more gorgeous every time I see you? It must be that Florida sunshine because you look radiant."

"Thank you." She smiled as he pulled out a chair to join us.

He flagged down a passing waiter. "I'll have my usual." The waiter discretely nodded his head and walked away. Owen grinned, leaning back in his chair.

"So, Owen." I gave him a tight smile. "To what do we owe this pleasure?"

"Do I really need an excuse to have a drink with the two prettiest ladies in town?" The corner of his mouth tipped up. I couldn't believe how thick he was laying it on. You would think he would get sick of his own lines after a while.

"Such a charmer." I picked up my soda and tried to sound

convincing. I had a feeling he was up to something, I just wasn't sure what. He was acting way too friendly.

"Actually." He scooted his chair closer to mine. Our legs practically brushed up against each other. "Tamara, I heard you were in town and I was hoping to run into you."

"Oh, why is that?" She put her white napkin down on the table.

"Well, I think it's time we started putting on a united front, don't you think?" He draped his arm along the back of my chair. He really needed to learn personal boundaries. "Considering I'm going to be your son-in-law in a few months."

I gritted my teeth. He was trying to rattle me, but I refused to engage. Maybe he would take the hint and move along if I just ignored him.

"Well, we should all get together after the holidays then," she suggested.

The waiter came over holding a silver tray. Owen grabbed his scotch and said, "Make sure you put it on the company account."

My eyes did an internal role in my head. He really got his rocks off acting so superior to our staff. It was obnoxious. I was certain that *please* and *thank you* were not in his vocabulary.

"Actually, Tamara." He took a generous sip of the amber liquid and twirled the glass around in his hands. "My parents are expecting the West family to celebrate Christmas Eve with us. Mother would like to meet with you to discuss the wedding preparations. She also requested that you both attend mass with us and dinner afterward."

The shrimp I was holding paused halfway to my mouth. One, Owen probably hasn't stepped foot inside a church since the day he was baptized. And two, I already had plans.

"No can do. I'm spending Christmas Eve with Ava and

her family." It was our tradition and something I looked forward to every year.

"I'm sorry for your predicament, but my mother is expecting you. Maybe you can stop by Ava's a little earlier in the day."

What in the ever-loving hell? Who does he think he is? My eyes must have spoken my thoughts because my mother set her fork down and drained the rest of her wine.

"Listen, Owen." I was just about to lay into him when a perky blonde, dressed in a short black leather skirt and a deep V-neck sweater appeared at our table.

"Owen, I thought that was you."

"Hey, Stella."

She flipped her long hair over shoulder. It's Stacey," she corrected him, but he didn't seem to care.

"Right." He leaned forward, and I watched his eyes do a predatory crawl up and down her body. "How could I forget?"

"Anyway," Stacey continued. "I just wanted to stop over and say hi." She looked between us and shifted on her feet. "And to let you know that I'm working this weekend. If you get a chance to stop by the club, make sure you ask for me." She handed him a card and I couldn't help but notice the stripper pole and silhouette logo.

"You got it." He winked, and I watched a deep blush creep up on her cheeks. Funny how some women could be so affected by so little interest. I reached across the table for my water, wishing I had something stronger to drink. "It was great seeing you." He turned around in his chair and immediately dismissed her.

My mother's phone rang in her purse, and she pulled it out of her bag. "I have to take this. I'll be right back." She pushed away from the table, leaving me and Owen alone.

He shifted closer to me. "Alone at last. Now, back to tomorrow."

"I'm sorry, but I can't make it. You'll have to give your mother my apologies."

He ran a hand through his hair, looking exasperated. "Why are you always so difficult?"

I glared at him. "I have been spending Christmas Eve with my best friend and her family for years. You expect me to just cancel on her when you've only given me twenty-four-hours' notice?"

He leaned forward; he was close enough for me to smell the alcohol on his breath. "This time next year you will be my wife and we will go to bed on Christmas Eve and wake up on Christmas Day together. Doesn't that sound wonderful?"

"It's a good thing I'm not your wife yet." I smirked.

His jaw tightened and the look in his eyes had unease crawling up my back. "I can't wait to fuck that smirk off your face. If you're trying to turn me off, sweetheart, take a good look down at my dick that's saluting you right now. It gets harder every time you speak. So, please, keep the shots coming because pretty soon you're going to hear what I sound like when I do."

"You're a pig."

He laughed and stood up. "Oh, Amelia. We are going to have so much fun together."

I watched his retreating back as he walked out of the restaurant. I don't know what prompted me to antagonize him, but what I did know was that I had reached my limit with Owen Eastan.

TWENTY

I RUMMAGED THROUGH MY DAD'S OLD WORKSHOP, LOOKING FOR nothing in particular. I used to love this place when I was a kid. I'd spent almost every Saturday morning of my young life helping my dad fix something for Mom or working on some project he had going on. There wasn't a tool in the shop that didn't get used, or a part he needed that he didn't have. He shared a lot of wisdom with me in the hours we spent together. It was times like this where I missed him the most.

I slumped down and leaned back in my dad's old recliner, wishing he were here to give me advice. I haven't seen or spoken to Amelia since I kicked her out of my house. I was so angry at her for keeping something so important from me and for violating my trust. But mostly, I was pissed at myself for being so blind. My stomach knotted at the thought of never being able to kiss her, hold her, or touch her again. She would be giving those things to someone else. And I'd never forgive her for it.

"Hey, Marco," my mom called from the spot where she had been watching me from the doorway. "Want to help me put these groceries away?"

I rubbed a hand over my scruffy jaw. "Sure."

I followed her into the kitchen and put the canned goods in the cupboard while she filled the fridge with fresh produce. She set a few leftover containers on the counter for me to take home so she could make room on her shelves for her fresh fruits and vegetables.

"Are you going to tell me what's going on with you?" she asked as she shoved a head of lettuce into the bottom drawer. She had been asking me about Amelia since I got here, insisting that she would get it out of me one way or another.

I sighed. "Mamma, I'm not ready to get into it."

As much as I loved my mother, her concern could be suffocating. No matter how old I was, she would always see me as her little boy. Sure, she would listen to me, but she would also want to fix things, and this was something she couldn't fix. She couldn't just put a Band-Aid on my broken heart.

"Okay. Why don't you tell me why you're hiding out here?" I went to open my mouth, but clamped it shut. "You don't think I can tell that you've avoiding going home?"

"Are you seriously complaining about me spending more time with you?" I joked, even though we both knew her words were true. She could always read me like a book, which made dodging her questions pointless, because I knew she wouldn't let up until she got to the bottom of things. "Or are you just worried that I'm here for the food and dry-cleaning services?" I grinned, giving her that dimple that used to get me out of trouble when I was younger.

She closed the fridge door and crossed her arms. "I don't mind the company, but you're not really here with me, your mind is somewhere else." I frowned at her. "I raised you better than this, Marco. You don't ever run from your problems. Whatever you did, you fix it."

"What makes you think I'm the one who did something wrong?" I challenged her, feeling super sensitive on this topic.

"I may be old, but I'm not stupid. I'm Italian and I can tell when two lovers are in a fight."

We both turned our heads at the sound of the front door slamming shut.

"She finally told you about that stupid arrangement, didn't she?" my grandmother said as she walked into the kitchen with Matteo following right behind her.

I stared at her in shock, momentarily speechless. My brain must have short-circuited because there is no way my nonna was talking about what I thought she was.

"She told you, and you didn't tell me?"

She casually unfolded her scarf and unbuttoned her coat. "Amelia trusted me with that information before she even met you. It wasn't my place to say anything."

My grandmother was actually taking the side of the woman who betrayed me. Does it get any more ridiculous than that? How the hell could this even happen?

My mother placed her hands on her hips and looked between us. "What is she talking about?"

I braced my body against the counter, needing something to steady my growing anger. "I can't believe you knew all this time and didn't say anything. Where is your loyalty?"

Her lack of consideration to my feelings really ticked me off.

She handed her coat to Matteo so he could hang it up for her. "Tell me, *nipote*, when is the last time you came to visit me and talk?"

I raked a frustrated hand through my hair, knowing how fond she was of her young friend. This entire exchange had me on edge, and the last thing I needed was her meddling in my business.

"Nonna, I've been busy."

She dragged her glasses down the bridge of her nose so she could narrow her eyes; her wrinkles deepened at the corners. "So you say, but so is Amelia and she still makes time for me."

I looked up at the ceiling and swore under my breath, and then my entire body went still. "Wait. Have you seen her?"

She dragged the chair out and put her purse on the kitchen table. "Yes, I've seen her. She won't tell me what happened because she said she doesn't want to put me in the middle, but I can tell she is miserable."

"You know it hasn't been a walk in the park for me these past few days either, but it's nice to see that you're so concerned about me."

She pushed away from her chair and charged toward me. Well, as fast as an eighty-year-old woman could move. She waved her bony little finger in my face. "Marco Anthony Rubintino. You may be a foot taller than me, but you are not too old to have a wooden spoon smacked across your backside."

I blanched at her threat and cut my eyes to my brother who was laughing his ass off. "Sorry, Nonna. I'm just upset. I know Amelia is your friend and you care about her."

I loved my grandmother with all my heart, but the woman drove me crazy with her need to fiddle in my business. Truth is, there wasn't anything she wouldn't do for the people she cared about. I just wasn't sure whose corner she was in right now.

She placed a gentle hand on my arm. "Yes, but never second-guess my love for you again. I worry about you, Marco. I have since the day you became a police officer. I know you are a grown man, and I don't like to interfere with matters of the heart. But I will tell you this. You need to stop using what happened to you in the past as an excuse." She patted my cheek and pinched it lightly. "If you want to be with Amelia, then let yourself be with her. Be happy, my boy. That's all I want for you."

I sighed, trying not to let everything she said bother me.

Her heart was in the right place, but the woman knew no boundaries. "Don't you think I should have been told that she was supposed to be marrying someone else?"

My mother gasped in shock. "What?"

My grandmother put her head down as my brother stepped forward. "What the hell is all this shit about?" Matteo snapped.

I rubbed the back of my neck, realizing I was not going to get out of here without talking about this. "The short version is that Amelia agreed to marry some other guy before she met me, and she just informed me about it a few days ago."

"Oh, Marco." My mother's eyes misted with tears. She really liked Amelia, and that made this entire situation ten times worse. "How could she do that to my baby?"

I grabbed her hand and hauled her toward me. "I wish I knew, Mamma." I rubbed her back as she shook her head against my chest. She seemed almost as upset as I was, so I wasn't sure who was supposed to comfort who.

Her tears hit my shirt, and Matteo placed his palm on my shoulder. "I'm sorry, bro."

My cell buzzed in my pocket. I pulled it out and glanced at the screen. "What's up, Logan?"

"I've had a shit day. Wanna meet for a few beers?"

I looked down at my mother, whose eyes were filled with worry. I felt like a goddamned disappointment to her as usual. Why couldn't I have a normal, stable life like my brother? Why couldn't I be married with two adorable kids and have a job that required me to carry a briefcase instead of a gun? Why did my personal choices always have to bring her emotional pain?

Yeah, unwinding with a few beers seemed pretty damn good right now.

———

"I was surprised you called earlier. I thought you had plans tonight?" I asked Logan as we sat in a booth at a local sports bar, sharing a pitcher of beer and a basket of wings. I couldn't get out of my mother's house fast enough when he called. She was having a hard time, and my grandmother was unusually quiet. Matteo on the other hand was just pissed on my behalf.

"I did, but I had to cut my date short. Brina had an asthma attack and Vanessa had to bring her to urgent care."

"Is she okay?"

"She's fine now, but of course, by the time I got to Vanessa's house, Brina was already in bed and Vanessa made me feel like shit that I wasn't there."

I let out a low whistle. "Don't beat yourself up. Brina is fine, and it sounds like Vanessa was just being her normal bitchy self."

"I still feel so damn guilty."

I shook my head. "That's exactly how she wants you to feel, so stop worrying about what she thinks and focus on your daughter."

"I'm trying, even though one wrong move in front of Vanessa and everything blows up in my face. It feels like I'm walking through a field filled with landmines whenever I'm with her." He reached for the pitcher and poured himself another beer. "So, what's the latest with you? Do you still have Amelia on ice?"

I swallowed hard and tried to focus on the basketball game on TV. I was too stubborn and proud to admit it out loud, but I hated that being here reminded me of what I was missing. Normally, I enjoyed getting out of the house, and having a few drinks, but looking around at all the happy couples everywhere I turned was really fucking with my head.

He squinted his eyes at me. "You really care about her, don't you?"

I didn't even bother to deny it. "Is it that obvious?"

The past few nights, I've spent tossing and turning, thinking of all the different clues and signals I missed. Replaying every conversation we had through my head, wondering if I should call her and demand answers to the questions that kept me up all night.

Logan sat forward and rested his arms on the table. "I hate to break it to you, but you've been moping around all week. I've never seen you like this. If she has you so twisted up inside, then she obviously means something to you. The question is, what are you going to do about it?"

"I'm not sure." I leaned forward and rubbed my temples, feeling a headache coming on. "She left the ball in my court. I know she wants to talk, but I'm still too damn angry at her and I'm not sure with me feeling this way if that would be a good idea."

"I get that you need more time, but you're only losing ground the longer you wait. If you're this miserable then call, text, email whatever the hell you have to do to ease your mind."

"Did you not hear me when I told you she agreed to marry some asshole, all for a fucking job?" Just the thought of it made me crazy and I would never understand. No job was worth it.

"I heard you." He smirked, seeming amused by my outburst. "I also heard the part where she offered to give up everything for you too. Or do you not remember that part of the story?"

So much for me coming out tonight and drowning out my shitty mood. I should have just stayed home, drank my own beer, and ate a frozen pizza. It would have been a lot cheaper too. "You honestly think she would walk away from a life she loved and years down the road not resent me for it?" I snapped because that was a real fear of mine. It was the same fear that pushed her away. "I'm not going to risk my heart again. Been there, done that."

"Oh, so you know what's best for Amelia now." The familiar voice had my head turning to the side in slow motion. Or at least that's what it felt like when my eyes collided with the petite brunette who was now standing at the end of our table.

"Ava," I sputtered because it was taking my brain a few seconds to catch up. I looked down at my glass and wondered if I had more to drink than I remembered. I opened my mouth to say something but hesitated, still not believing that Amelia's best friend was standing right in front of me.

Logan leaned forward and angled his neck to get a better look at the woman who was staring daggers at me.

"And while you're are so concerned with risking your own precious little heart," she continued, "you forgot to mention to your friend that you broke hers too."

I just stared and blinked, feeling completely thrown off by this ambush. There were so many things going through my head. So many questions I wanted answers to but was too chickenshit to ask. Like, was she still going through with it? Was she as torn up about this as I was? Was any of it even real? Every question led back to the same place.

"Listen." I ran a hand through my hair a couple times wondering what the hell I was supposed to say. "I understand you are Amelia's best friend, but I'm not the bad guy here."

She stood there with her arms folded over her chest. "You're also not the good guy that I thought you were either."

Anger seeped into my bones and my entire body grew tight with irritation. "Excuse me?" Why the hell was I the one getting attacked today?

"She begged you to hear her out. She was planning on turning her back on her family and her obligations. All she wanted from you was an acknowledgment that you saw a future with her. Instead, you acted like a petulant child and threw her out. I heard the vile shit you said and let me tell you something..." She poked her hand in my chest. "If you weren't a cop, and I didn't have to worry about getting arrested, I would take the sharpest set of hair scissors I have in my shop and snip off your nut sack."

I jerked my head back while Logan coughed next to me. "She lied to me. She knew we had an expiration date. I did nothing fucking wrong here."

Ava was crazy. The woman clearly had a screw loose if she thought I was in the wrong. Who the hell was she to come over and berate me like a child? I wasn't the one who lied, so I had nothing to feel guilty for. Other than being a lousy detective who missed all the clues. If Ava was angling for a fight, she was pissing me off enough to give her one.

Her hands were planted firmly on her hip now. "Did she or did she not tell you that she loved you and you told her to get the fuck out?"

Damn, she really knew how to throw a punch. When she put it like that, it did sound bad. Visions of Amelia crying flashed through my mind, especially when I sent her away right after she said the words that I wasn't brave enough to say.

I love you. More than I thought possible.

I shook my head at the memory as the waitress came by and dropped off a new pitcher. I was struggling to keep my emotions in check, but the weight of her words caused a surge of anger to sneak up in the back of my throat.

"Your goddamned right I told her to get the fuck out. You want to make me out to be some heartless bastard then go right ahead, but Amelia's not the innocent victim in all this. She jumped into my bed and kept me in the dark the entire time we were together." The pressure in my chest was building and building, ready to explode. "Then," my eyes burned into hers, "after weeks of lying to me, she had the audacity to give me an ultimatum? I don't fucking think so, sweetheart."

I watched her face soften for the first time since our little stand-off. "You have no idea how badly she wanted to tell you sooner. She never felt like there was a right time, but you're right. She probably should have said something, but that's between you two."

I rolled my eyes, oh now it's none of her business. Funny, how just a few minutes ago she was perfectly comfortable making mine and Amelia's relationship her main mission.

"Hello." Logan smiled and put his hand out. "I don't think we've met. I'm Logan."

She looked down and shook his hand. "Ava." Was all she said and turned back to me.

"Would you like to join us for a drink?" He slid further down the bench seat of the booth to make room for her. His offer had me seething, and I was about ready to choke him for suggesting it.

Thankfully, she waved him off. "No thanks. I'm good."

"You sure?" He licked his lips, making it known that he was interested. "I don't bite." The crinkles around the corner of his eyes deepened. "Unless, of course, you wanted me to."

She looked at me and back to Logan. "You might want to bite your damn tongue and learn how to talk to a lady when you meet one."

He sat forward and placed his arms on the sticky wooden table. "My apologies. It's the Irish in me. I'm actually quite shy, but I do tend to get a little tongue-tied around a beautiful woman when I see one. I promise, I'm really not a player. In fact, you can feel my shirt, it's made from boyfriend material."

She rolled her eyes, and I blew out a long breath, wondering how the hell he even scored chicks with word vomit like that. "Are all your friends so damn chatty?" she asked me.

"Actually, I've been told my personality is one of my best assets." He smirked, clearly not taking the hint that she wasn't interested. Instead, he just stared at her like a goo-goo eyed moron.

She looked him up and down. "If I wasn't a happily married woman, I would debate that fact." She shifted her attention back to me. "Now, as I was saying. I get that it feels like she dropped a bomb on you. You have every right to be upset that she waited so long to tell you, but you didn't give her a full chance to explain. Who knows whether it would have made a difference or not?"

As far as I was concerned, a lie of omission was still a lie. And I warned her I didn't forgive easily, she knew my heart was already bruised. So why was I suddenly having a brief moment of regret?

"Listen, I have to get back to my friends. I'm sorry if I came across as a bitch, I'm just frustrated because Amelia deserves to be happy and Marco," she leaned in and touched my hand, "you made her happier than I've ever seen her. So, please, I'm begging you, don't waste another day wallowing in your anger and denying yourself the chance of ever knowing the truth."

I averted my eyes as she disappeared into the crowd. Her words struck me deep.

"Damn." Logan angled his head to the side, trying to catch whatever glimpse he could.

"Dude?" I smacked my cup down on the table, the liquid spilling over. "She is married with a kid," I informed him as he shamelessly continued to search her out.

He held his hands up. "I know, but did you see those black leather pants she was wearing? If she ever leaves her husband, you need to let me know."

My eyes slid shut, not acknowledging his idiotic request. My stomach was too tied up in knots and for the first time in the past week, I was feeling confused and second-guessing everything.

TWENTY-ONE

AMELIA

Butcher & Singer was an upscale steak house in the heart of Philadelphia. It shouldn't have surprised me that this is where Owen would choose to meet. He liked to be seen and noticed. This was his crowd, not mine, and it was the last place on earth I wanted to be.

The overpriced filet that he took the liberty of ordering for me while I was in the restroom sat untouched on my plate. I asked our server to put it back on the grill, because I did not eat my steak medium rare. By the time they brought it back out, Owen had already finished off his meal.

He was a real charmer.

I sat across the table from him, playing with the stem of the wineglass and studying the way he spoke to the waiter as he cleared our dishes. It was apparent that Owen enjoyed talking about himself. I was convinced that he loved the sound of his own voice.

"Shall we get this conversation out of the way?" I suggested, brushing a few crumbs off the table so I could lean across it. I did my best, played my part, and I was ready to call it a night. I was sick of slowly sipping my wine and staring at my watch, pretending to tolerate him.

Owen held up his finger to the waiter to get his attention as he attempted to go serve another table. "We'll take a bottle of Dom Perignon please, and two glasses."

I arched an eyebrow. "Are we celebrating something?"

Between the bouncing of his leg, and the constant clearing of his throat, he'd been jittery all night. He's pulled on the collar of his dress shirt no less than twenty-five times, because yes, I counted, and straightened his tie every five minutes. I was really hoping he would just ask for the check so I could put an end to this date and go on my merry little way. All the way home to my empty townhouse where I would go to bed alone and cry myself to sleep, because that's all I seemed to do lately.

The waiter arrived and placed the ice bucket down in the center of the table. He filled the two glasses and carefully set them down in front of us.

"Thank you," I said, feeling my own nerves start to take flight.

Owen surprised me when he leaned forward across the table and reached for my hand. I froze as he slowly brushed his thumb across my knuckles. I stared down at the display of affection and tried not to make a big deal of him touching me.

"You look nice tonight." He smiled tightly while looking over at the plum colored dress that he's seen me in a dozen times. "I think it's time we make things official."

Oh. My. God.

This was it. It was really happening. My life was about to become my worst nightmare and I had no idea how I would get through this. I knew this was agreed upon, but I was already losing strength and things hadn't even started yet.

Owen pulled a ring out of the pocket of his dress shirt and held it out. "We're going to make great business partners."

His words were met with silence as I looked down at the bubbles fizzing along the top of my narrowed fluted glass.

"I know this isn't ideal." He sighed. "This whole situation

sucks and may seem unfair to the both of us." He swallowed and scratched the back of his neck with his free hand. "Regardless of how insane this seems; we have the same goals and dreams. I really think we can make this work."

My defenses were crumbling and my composure, good God, there was no way he couldn't see it slipping. "Owen, I..."

"Let's get married and take over the company."

Fuck! It felt like a Mack truck was barreling toward me, and the only thing I could do was watch it happen in slow motion. I felt powerless.

My head and my heart were struggling between knowing what I needed to do and wishing that I didn't have to do it.

I had to remind myself that this was nothing more than a business arrangement. It wasn't his fault we were in this mess. He was just as much a victim as I was, but I still resented him all the same.

I might be able to give him my hand in marriage, but my heart would forever belong to someone else.

He slid the ring on my finger and I had to close my eyes as I felt it push past my knuckle. The word *yes* would never leave my mouth. The enormous diamond was perfectly round and heavy. The surrounding stones in the band caused the candlelight to flicker across the tablecloth. My entire body shook from the inside out.

I picked up my glass and took a huge swig of my champagne and looked around. That's when I noticed people clapping and smiling while I felt like I was about to have a mental breakdown. My stomach stirred with apprehension as they all went back to their overpriced food and conversations. They thought they were witnessing a romantic moment between two lovers; they couldn't have been more wrong. If a group of strangers could have me feeling like a fraud, I could only imagine how I would feel around the people I knew.

Sucking in a breath I stared down at the ring hating everything about this charade.

Owen slid his chair back, stood up and held his hands out. I rose from my seat and allowed him to pull me into his arms. "The ring sure did cost me a mint, so make sure you always wear it. I want people to see it." My eyes bounced between him and the rock that now felt like dead weight pulling me under. A pang of guilt hit me, making my chest feel uncomfortably tight.

He reached for my chin, and I practically jerked back, but his hold was strong. My entire body cringed when his lips descended down onto mine. I kept my lips pressed closed and prayed for the seconds to pass. If he was offended that I didn't reciprocate, he didn't show it. His ego would never allow it.

"Let's sit down and go over a few things. I want to make sure we are on the same page." I was too numb to fight with him, so I slumped back in my seat feeling defeated. I just sealed my fate, and it felt like there was nothing left of my soul. Empty… that's what the feeling was. Everything I sacrificed up until now seemed pointless.

Owen rested forward on the table, completely unaware of my turmoil. "First, are there any men, past or present, that I should be concerned about?"

I swallowed and averted my gaze. "I'm not sure what you mean?"

I was acting dumb and trying to avoid giving him an answer. Truthfully, I wasn't sure. I've done everything I could to get Marco to talk to me, but he was so damned stubborn. I've called and left messages and even sat outside his house waiting for him to come home. His decision was clear, and I really should have paid attention when he told that he didn't forgive easily. If he would have just listened to me, and took the time to really understand my situation, then I wouldn't be sitting here right now.

Owen stared at me for a long, uncomfortable moment as if he were trying to figure me out. "I was just curious because you keep your private life pretty closed off."

I tipped my champagne glass to my lips and swallowed. It felt like acid rushing down my throat. "My focus has always been on my work. Something you already know. I don't have time to invest in relationships."

He nodded his head, seeming satisfied with that answer. "We should probably set a few ground rules, don't you think?"

"Such as?" I plucked the bottle out of the silver ice bucket and poured myself another glass. The champagne was pricy and tasted bitter, but there was no need to let it go to waste.

"We're going to have to live together. How attached are you to your townhouse?"

I couldn't give a shit about my house. If I learned anything about myself over the past month, it's that the house itself doesn't make it a home, it's the people in our lives that do. And I've never felt more at home than at Marco's little ranch.

"Where are you suggesting we live?" I asked, chugging the liquid down my throat, hoping it would wash away the sadness and anger I was feeling.

"Well, my condo is too small, and your place is too out of the way for me. I need to be close to the city, but still in the suburbs. A lot of my connections are made on the golf course. I need to be near a country club where I can shake hands and make connections. But I still want to be close to all the action in the city." I didn't speak, so he kept going. "Our legal team will be drafting up an NDA. No one will know about this arrangement but the people involved. I want to prove to my grandfather that I'm serious about this. I want to appear solid and show him I'm ready for this commitment."

I've heard enough and felt like it was time for me to establish a few rules of my own.

"I'm willing to hold your hand in public, and put on a front at the office, but behind closed doors, I want my space. I'll give you yours as well. I also want to make it perfectly clear that I'm not sleeping with you."

"Wrong."

I drew back in my seat. "Excuse me."

"We will share a bedroom and you will be my wife in every sense of the word. I know I have a bit of a reputation, but I'm getting it all out of my system now. One of the stipulations in the agreement is that I have to stay monogamous. I'm too young to go without sex, Amelia, so you're the only game in town now. And just so we are clear, you won't be getting it elsewhere either."

I glared at him and did my best to keep my shit together. I lowered my voice, but I was still seething. "You expect me to believe that you won't sleep around. Is that what you're saying?"

He looked everywhere but at me. "You have my word that I won't fuck anyone once we are married."

"Have you ever thought that maybe I don't want to fuck you? Not to mention, we both know that your word doesn't mean shit. It never has and it never will."

His laugh was dry, and it held no humor. "I know I've got my work cut out for me, which I might say is quite intriguing. It's actually refreshing because I'm not used to a challenge. Getting pussy comes way too easy for me. However, my darling fiancée, I'm going to enjoy touching you and learning about all the things you like. You know all the familiar things that go along with intimacy."

He reached for my hand, but I yanked it away. "The only reason why I'm agreeing to this is because I have no other choice."

"You always have a choice." He ran his hand along the back of his neck; he looked like he was getting impatient.

"Look at it this way. We are doing this with a clear head. We know what we are walking into and what to expect. This isn't about love. It's a means to an end."

I swallowed the tears that I refused to shed and grabbed my purse off the back of my chair, knowing my life was about to change.

TWENTY-TWO

MARCO

My phone vibrated on my nightstand. Without even looking I knew it was Logan calling. I was supposed to meet him at a New Year's Eve party over an hour ago. I've been sitting on the edge of my bed, showered, dressed, and stalling.

He sent me a picture of the beautiful woman he was trying to set me up with, but I wasn't even slightly interested. Normally, the only thing that would keep me from hooking up with a warm body would be if I was sick or working. I knew he was only trying to get me out of my funk, but the thought of touching someone other than Amelia had a knot of apprehension forming in my stomach.

It's been ten days since we broke up. Ten days of her calling and texting me. Giving her the silent treatment hasn't been easy. There have been a few times where I've been tempted to pick up the phone, but my stubborn pride won out. Only it didn't feel like much of a victory.

It didn't matter how much time I've had to sit and stew on everything, my mind kept replaying every conversation we had. I tried to do what I do best—search for clues and try to make sense of all this, but the outcome, no matter which way I played it, seemed the same.

My phone buzzed again. Logan was getting impatient, and I needed to put on my big boy pants and stop avoiding the inevitable. I pushed myself off the bed and walked over to my dresser and was about to spray myself with a few drops of cologne when I remembered that it was Amelia's favorite. I set it back down and looked at myself in the mirror. It didn't feel right to put effort into my appearance for someone else, but what choice did I have? I fixed a few strands of hair and forced myself out the door.

The bar was hopping by the time I walked in. There were people everywhere wearing hats, bright colored glasses, and silver and gold Mardi Gras beads. I scanned the crowd and immediately spotted Logan and a few guys from work. Everyone was standing around a small pub table, drinks in hand, and laughing over the loud music. I made the welcome round, shaking hands and clapping backs.

Logan broke into a smile when he saw me. "Hey, dude. Just in time." He looked over my shoulder and I turned my head to see two women making their way toward us. The blonde strolled over to his side and he snaked a hand along her waist. "Stephanie, this is Marco."

The woman held her hand out. "Nice to meet you, Marco." I picked up on a hint of a Jersey accent when she spoke.

I raised my hand to return the gesture. "Nice to meet you, too."

"And this is Fiona," Logan said, pointing to the redhead in a short black dress. I recognized her from the picture he sent me. Fiona was gorgeous. She was tall and thin and could pass for a model. She had legs for days and hair that went down to her waist.

"You must be my date tonight." She smiled, and I could tell by the way she stared at me she was expecting a reaction.

She crossed her legs, causing the slit that ran up the middle of her thigh to open further. I waited for my body to respond to her, but I never felt a thing.

"The one and only." I forced a smile as a beat of awkwardness played between us. I was usually good at making small talk, but for some reason, I struggled to keep the conversation moving. The old me would have welcomed the attention but tonight it felt awkward.

"I'm going to grab a drink. Can I get you another glass of wine?" I noticed she was already holding a full glass, but I was trying to be polite.

"I'm good, but I'll come with you." She linked her arm inside mine. *Bold move*, I thought, but it would be rude for me to ignore her, so I gave my head a quick shake, and went with it. If this were a couple of months ago, I would have been completely okay with this setup. Now, not so much.

Fiona slid up next to me as we inched our way to the bar. I placed an order for a Jack and Coke and another glass of pinot for her because she had already finished hers and was ready for a refill.

"So, you're a homicide detective," she said, running the tip of her finger along the center of her chest. She knew my eyes would follow, but in spite of her best efforts, there wasn't even a twitch behind my zipper.

I managed another smile. "I am."

"That sounds dangerous and kind of hot." I wanted to roll my eyes. "I bet you know how to use a set of handcuffs too."

My mind went straight to Amelia and the memory ignited a fire in my chest.

I picked up my freshly poured drink and tried to drown my frustration in my whiskey. We moved from the bar area and stepped off to the side, so the people in back could place their order. Fiona was doing nothing to hide the fact that she was expecting to go home with me tonight. As attractive as she was, I wasn't the slightest bit interested. If anything, I was annoyed.

I pulled my phone out, pretending to check my messages. I glanced at the time, noticing that there was a little under two hours left to go before the ball dropped. I was debating on whether I should push through for at least another hour or make an excuse to leave early. I slipped my phone back in my pocket and decided to give Fiona a shot. It wasn't her fault that I was still pining away for someone else.

"So, what do you do for a living, Fiona?" I asked, trying to ignore the commotion next to us. A group of young college kids were doing shots. Their cheering and chanting were distracting.

She flipped her hair over her slender shoulder. "I'm a model. I live in Manhattan, but was born and raised here in Philly. I'm home visiting for the holidays."

I sipped my drink. "Nice." I guess I called that one. I probably should have acted more interested but, this mindless conversation was going nowhere fast.

"So, why don't you tell me about yourself. Surely, a man as good-looking as yourself has a few stories to tell." Her flirty little giggle landed right on my nerves as she moved closer. "And I can't wait to hear them all."

Despite taking a step back to reclaim my personal space, I could still smell the overpowering scent of her perfume. "Oh, I have plenty of stories, but I'm not one to kiss and tell on the first date."

"Just so you know, I'm all for kissing on the first date." She brought a hand up to my shoulder and ran it down my arm. The move was meant to be sensual, but the only thing on my mind was trying to figure out a way to defuse the situation. "In fact, maybe we can finish this conversation in a more private place where you can kiss me wherever you like. I also promise to return the favor."

I removed her hand off my arm, halting her movements. I

didn't want her hands on me. Her sexy poses might work for the cameras, but the only thing I wanted was for her to back the fuck up.

"Are you always this forward?"

Her red-painted lips curved up into a smile as she inched for my mouth. "Only when I'm interested."

"Well, I'm not." Surprise flashed in her eyes as she stumbled back on her heels. "Why don't we go find our friends," I suggested, letting her know that she'd gone too far. She probably didn't get turned down very often, if ever.

She gave me a stiff smile and made a point of stalking away. Her long red hair swayed from side to side, her steps were long and angry. So much for coming out to unwind tonight. Now I wish I had listened to my gut and stayed home.

I was questioning why I even agreed to this. What I was certain of, however, was that I was going to kick Logan's ass for putting me in this position.

"What are we celebrating?" I asked the guys when we finally reached the table. Fiona went to stand next to her friend, no doubt complaining about what an asshole I was. Now that there was a little distance between us, I was finally able to relax a little bit.

"Dwayne finally asked Amanda to marry him," Logan announced loud and proud.

Dwayne worked in the vice unit and our paths crossed many times. His nickname was Stone Cold because the dude never smiled, however he had a grin as wide as the Grand Canyon as he stared down at his fiancée. "Congrats to you both. That's awesome," I said, as Amanda held her hand out, showing off her ring. She looked as happy as could be. "It's about time, considering you bought that thing two years ago," I reminded him.

Dwayne looked down at Amanda, his dark eyes sparkled

with affection. "I would have married her the day we met if I thought her parents would be okay with it."

Dwayne and Amanda were perfect for each other in every possible way. But Amanda came from a strict religious Caucasian family, her father was a pastor and Dwayne was African American. It took a while for him to win her parents over, but once they realized how happy he made their daughter, they finally saw him for the stand-up guy he was.

"Well, I'm happy for you guys." I patted him on the back and kissed Amanda on the cheek. I was sincerely elated for my friend, because he deserved all the happiness in the world, but a part of me was envious as hell. He got to be with the woman he loved, while I had to stand here, missing the one I lost a piece of my heart to.

"Thanks, man." Dwayne clinked his drink with mine, and I couldn't help but notice how much his eyes lit up just talking about it. "I'm pretty fucking thrilled myself."

"So, when's the big day?" Logan asked before chugging the rest of his beer.

"It depends." Dwayne looked to me. "We were hoping to book the ballroom at Amelia's hotel, but they book up to three years in advance. Do you think she can pull any strings and help us out?"

I pulled on the back of my neck, feeling Logan giving me a side glance. Dwayne was obviously too wrapped up in his own happiness that he didn't realize that I came here alone.

"Uh…" I paused, searching for the right words; it felt like everyone's eyes were on me. "We aren't together anymore."

"Oh, shit." He reached out and patted me on the shoulder. "I'm sorry, dude. That sucks."

"Thanks, but I'm good," I lied, keeping my eyes glued to the ground. "I'll text you her number. I'm sure she will be more than willing to help you out if she can."

"We would appreciate that," Amanda said politely, her gaze darting over to Fiona.

"Thanks." I glanced up, needing to get the hell away from this table for a minute. "I'm going to get another round. What are you guys drinking?"

I collected their orders and edged my way through the crowd. Logan and Dwayne were right behind me. I looked over at the girls who stood shoulder to shoulder in a small circle. Their conversation seemed heated. Logan's date shot me a dirty look.

"Dude." Logan nudged me. "Your attitude needs a serious adjustment. I don't know what you said to Fiona, but Stephanie looks like she wants to cut your dick off."

"Don't give me a hard time, but I just wasn't feeling it."

Dwayne's mouth hitched up to one side. "I think I know what this is about." His brown eyes lit up with playfulness, but I didn't dare smile back. The guy was sharp as a tack and the fact that he was busting my balls meant he had already had a few drinks before he got here.

I crossed my arms over my chest. "Let's drop it."

Logan leaned into Dwayne's ear and whispered, "He's too stubborn to admit that he's in love."

I turned my back, studying the bottles of alcohol along the glass shelf, not giving them any reaction to feed off of. For the first time in my career I was wishing that marijuana wasn't illegal, because chilling out with a nice big, fat joint sounded pretty damn good right now.

"You really think he's still hung up on her?" Dwayne's voice was filled with amusement.

I could see Logan nodding his head through the mirror. "Oh, I know he is, but he refuses to do anything about it."

Dwayne let out a small, sarcastic whistle. "Is that why he's over here avoiding the smoking hot redhead?"

I finally spun back around to face them. They were hitting every single one of my buttons. "Will you two idiots knock it off."

"Not until you stop lying to yourself and admit how you really feel."

My gaze moved between my two friends. "You really want to know how I feel?" I slipped my hand in the front pocket of my jeans. "I feel like you two assholes can suck my dick. How's that for a feeling?"

Logan shrugged and took a sip of his drink. "Sorry, man, but that's not really my thing."

Dwayne held up his hands and smirked. "Don't look at me. I'm already taken."

Logan set his drink down and released a heavy sigh through his nose. "Listen, we've all had our hearts broken. It sucks, but this moping shit has to stop. Either man up and go after her or get on with your life and get over her."

"Get over her," I gritted through my teeth. My chest was heaving, I've had enough of their games. "I haven't been able to sleep in my own damn bed because I reach for her in the middle of the night. I can't cook in my own damn kitchen because she occupies my every thought," I admitted, cutting right through the bullshit. "I even fucking listed my hot tub for sale because I can't sit in there anymore and relax without being assaulted with memories of her."

Logan grew silent while Dwayne stared at the dirty floor. I knew coming out tonight wasn't going to be easy, but I didn't expect it to be this bad.

My phone buzzed in my pocket. I picked it up and looked at the screen. I held the phone to one ear and covered the other with my free hand to hear better. "What's up, Quinn?"

"Where are you?"

My eyebrows drew together. "I'm at Sharkey's, why?"

"Get your ass in an Uber and get over to the Autograph. I had to drop off some security equipment to the guys and there is an engagement party going on. Want to take a guess whose it is?"

My hand tightened around the phone, so hard I thought it

might crack in half. I lifted my head, Dwyane and Logan were both watching me.

I came out tonight hoping that I could move on, but I failed miserably. Because what Amelia and I had was real, unlike that fake fucking engagement party that was taking place across town. If I was ever going to finally get my head out of my ass and make my move, now was the time.

Amelia's words rang in my head.

What we have is worth fighting for.

"I'll be there in fifteen."

"Get here sooner before it's too late," he said and hung up.

TWENTY-THREE

AMELIA

I HUFFED IN FRUSTRATION, THROWING MY RED COCKTAIL DRESS ON the never-ending pile on my bed. Every dress I pulled off the hanger felt wrong. Everything about this night felt wrong. I looked at myself in the mirror; for a girl who was getting ready to celebrate her own engagement, I sure looked miserable.

It's been ten days of trying to get Marco to talk to me. Ten days of silence. I was so tired of pretending that everything was fine. As the days ticked by, things only started to get more out of control. I felt like a beaten down woman who just wanted to have a pity party for one here in the comfort of my own home, instead of going out tonight and putting on a public appearance.

I looked at my hair and makeup and sat down on my mattress, never feeling more damn miserable in my life. The bracelet that Marco gave me for Christmas dangled along my wrist, further reminding me how messed up this was. The last thing I wanted to do was take it off, but I couldn't exactly wear it tonight of all nights either. With a heavy heart, I released the clasp and tucked it away for safekeeping. In its place was a diamond tennis bracelet that my mom had gifted me for my high school graduation.

After taking a few minutes to pull myself together, I finally decided on a silky, deep blue shimmering floor-length gown. My forehead wrinkled in irritation as I slipped my heels on. The gown was beautiful with an off the shoulder neckline and a slit that ran all the up to my thigh. The last thing I wanted was to give Owen something good to look at, but tonight wasn't just about him. It was about doing the right thing. It was about starting my new life, even though it felt more like an ending than a beginning.

After fifteen minutes of pacing in my living room, my phone buzzed with an incoming text. I set my wine down and swiped the screen.

Owen: I'm outside waiting. Come out when you're ready.

The jackass couldn't even pick me up at the door. Cursing, I slid my jacket on, stuffed my phone in my clutch, and stormed out the door.

The drive downtown was tense as Owen continuously reminded me that I would have to drop my scowl and smile a time or two. By the time we made it to the valet, I hopped out of the car and raced toward the front entrance of the hotel. He caught up to me as I reached the elevator bank and grabbed onto my elbow. "Remember, this is supposed to be the happiest night of your life, so start pretending to fucking like me."

"I don't need a reminder." I smiled tightly as an older couple walked up. Owen's hand went to my lower back, my much, much lower back. "What are you doing?" I hissed on a whispered breath.

His fingers tenderly brushed my hair off my one shoulder. He leaned his mouth under my ear and pressed a kiss that was salacious enough to draw attention. "I'm acting like a man who can't keep his hands off his fiancée."

"If you don't remove your hand from my ass, you're going

to feel the heel from my shoe spike you in the balls." I smiled sweetly while he barked out a laugh. The elevator doors pinged open and I stepped out of his hold, making a point to squeeze between a group of people, causing him to stand on the other end.

When we reached our floor, I allowed him to grab my hand and lead us toward the party. The room was already filled with guests and everyone was dressed in their best suits and cocktail dresses. There was a long line at the open bar as waiters in tuxedos circled the room, holding silver trays with hors d'oeuvres and champagne. A string quartet played classical music on the stage, but there would be a much livelier band performing after dinner that would be the main attraction.

Owen shook hands, and I said my fair share of hellos as we moved through the crowd. This was our "coming out" moment, and I could practically hear the gossip and the whispers behind our back. People turned their heads as we walked by, staring as Owen made a big show of pulling my chair out for me and kissing my cheek. He was laying it on thick and the crowd seemed to be lapping it up.

"Breathe, Amelia," my mother whispered as she took the seat next to me. "You look beautiful. Keep your chin up and don't let this get to you." She patted my hand. "Everything will work out."

I tried to appear as confident as possible as Owen's parents joined our table. How the hell was I supposed to act so happy when my entire world was falling apart?

"Hello, Susan." I forced my tone to be polite and slipped into the role that I needed to play tonight. That's exactly what this felt like. A performance. Only I was a horrible actress and it would be a miracle if I pulled this off.

"Amelia, you look lovely," she commented, but made no effort to make eye contact. In fact, she barely passed me a smile.

"Thanks, so do you." Owen's mother, Susan, had the same dirty blond hair as her son and a personality to match. She was well-dressed and exactly what you would picture a rich socialite to look like. The amount of jewelry she wore was ridiculous and was probably purchased from one of her trust fund monthly disbursements. As far as I knew, she never worked a day in her life.

"What do you think of the ring?" she asked, folding her hands in her lap. Everything about her was formal. The way she sat. The way she talked. The way she dressed. No matter how many years I've had to deal with her, I'd never feel comfortable around her.

"It's beautiful."

"See, son. I told you I picked out the right one." She winked and my back straightened. It took a minute for my brain to register.

"Your mother picked out my ring?" My eyes flickered to the massive diamond that took up a good chunk of my left finger. I was growing more and more uncomfortable by the minute.

Owen pulled on the lapels of his suit coat. "I've been busy."

I bit back my response and contemplated wringing his neck. Instead, I dug my fingers into the chair and figured it was best not to cause a scene.

Susan cleared her throat. "I've also put together a binder filled with wedding preparations," she said, seeming unfazed by the thick tension at our table. "I was able to secure one of the best florists in the city, and I'm having a photographer flown in from Paris that came highly recommended. I also met with a designer from New York who you'll need to meet with this week."

How thoughtful. Was she even going to consult with me on my own damn wedding?

"I can't wait." My tone was filled with sarcasm, but she

was too enamored with herself to pick up on it. I took a hefty sip of my drink. Was this the life I resigned myself to? A controlling mother-in-law, a loveless marriage, and stiff dinner conversations? Did she even care that her only son wasn't marrying for love? Or was she more concerned with planning the biggest social event of the year? Seeing how she got her rocks off on being the center of attention like her son, my guess would be the latter.

Mya, one of our waitstaff, extended her tray, offering me a glass of champagne. "Thank you, Mya. It's nice to see you out tonight. I take it your father is feeling better."

"Yes, he is. Thank you so much for asking about him. The doctors think it was just a UTI."

I set my fluted glass down on the table. "That's great to hear. If you need more time off, let me know and I'll arrange it for you. Family comes first."

Mya has been an employee with us for over twenty-five years. When I trained in hospitality, she was tasked with showing me the ropes. I'll never forgot how kind and patient she was with me.

Her eyes filled with gratitude. "Thank you so much, Ms. West."

"Excuse me." Susan snapped her fingers and held up her glass. "I'd like a refill, please."

I rolled my eyes and Mya's smirk told me she caught it.

"Amelia. Do you know all your employees by their first names?" asked Owen's dad as Mya made her way through the crowd.

I took a sip of my champagne and set it down. "I try my best to know every employee I come in contact with. I want them to know they are appreciated and never want them to feel that I am not approachable. There are too many corporations with toxic work environments. Our workers are the backbone to our success."

Owen draped his arm along the back of my chair. "What

do you think, Dad?" His thumb grazed the top of my shoulder. "Am I a lucky man or what?"

I bit down on my bottom lip in annoyance and fought the urge to kick his leg away that was pressed too tightly against mine.

I spotted my grandfather walking through the entrance and stood up. The sight of him had me breathing a little bit easier. He was the closest connection to home and comfort that I had left.

He took my face in his hands and gazed at me with pure affection. "You look beautiful, Amelia."

"Thank you." I pulled back slowly and watched the second his eyes caught on the huge rock on my finger.

"Sir." Owen stepped forward and slung his arm along my waist. I gave him a pointed look as he held out his free hand to my grandfather.

"Congratulations, son." His eyes came back to mine. His forehead creased as he studied me. "Is everything okay, Amelia?"

His gaze floated between me and Owen, searching for some reassurance that everything was fine. I wished I could give him one instead of a simple nod of my head. "Of course."

He didn't look like he believed me, but then again, my tone was anything but convincing. No matter how hard I tried, I sensed he could see how miserable I was. He's spent the last few weeks convincing himself that Owen and I were building on something promising. For the life of me, I never understood where he got the romantic notion in his head that Owen and I should be together.

Owen's fingers tightened around mine. "Everything is great, sir. Why don't we have a seat?"

He placed a hand on my lower back. I was about to shove it away, but then remembered where we were. "Amelia, you need to relax," Owen whispered as the waiters placed our plates on the table.

More guests filtered into the room, but it still felt like everyone was watching me. The sea bass I ordered was delicious, but I couldn't bring myself to take more than a couple bites. Thankfully, my mother made sure my wineglass never went empty. It was the only thing bringing me comfort tonight.

The servers began collecting our plates and silverware, getting ready for the dessert. I felt detached from everything and everyone around me. I participated here and there during the conversations, but my heart just wasn't into it. I was counting down the seconds until this was over with.

"Amelia, It's time." Owen held out his arm and ushered me up to the stage. He picked the microphone up out of the stand. My heart fell into the pit of my stomach.

"Ladies and gentlemen, may I please have your attention." His voice echoed through the grand ballroom.

The chatter died down and everyone stopped what they were doing. Every face in the room was now focused on us. Owen smiled big for the crowd and made a show of bringing me to his side. "I want to start out by saying thank you for coming out tonight and celebrating with us. This night represents a new year with new beginnings." A few people clapped and then a few others joined in. He reached for my hand and the room went silent. "As many as you know, Amelia and I were childhood sweethearts." He looked down at me with a big, polished smile and I wanted to puke. "She was always the one who got away, but I'm happy to tell you all I finally caught her." He paused, waiting for the canned laughter to die down. "I'm so honored to stand before you and announce that this beautiful woman at my side, who I've loved my entire life, has agreed to be my wife."

There was a mixture of applause and loud whispers. Owen grabbed my waist and drew me into him. I knew what was coming next, even if I didn't want it to. He crashed his lips to mine for what had to be the worst kiss of my life. I poured every ounce of energy I had into faking my happiness when inside my spirit was falling apart. I pulled back the second I could to catch my breath.

A tall, dark figure appeared in the back of the room. Chills peaked along my skin. Marco stood frozen in place, his face was solid as granite. Our gazes locked and my entire world started to spin.

TWENTY-FOUR

MARCO

Seeing her across the room was more painful than I could imagine. It felt like someone was chipping away at my heart, piece by piece.

I paced along the hallway, praying that I wasn't too late. I didn't want to believe it when Quinn told me, but after witnessing that kiss, there was no denying it.

Our eyes collided as she rounded the corner. "Marco?" I faltered at the sight of her. She was beautiful. So damn beautiful. "What are you doing here?"

I took a minute to look her over slowly. She looked the same, but she might as well have been a stranger. She was so close but felt so out of reach. The faint voices and music down the hall could be heard, but the only thing that mattered was standing right in front of me.

"I need to talk to you."

Her eyes darted nervously around the room as I took a cautious step toward her. "Marco, I…"

"Amelia."

She whipped her head around to the man who had just stepped into our path. This is the first time I actually laid eyes on him and suddenly all my anger had returned. His attention landed on mine and I had to bite my tongue to keep what I was really thinking about him to myself.

"Owen." Her eyes dropped closed. "Could you please give me a minute?" She looked up at me with a mixture of regret and panic on her face, but it was no match for the anger I felt.

He stepped forward and I had to hand it to the guy. He knew a threat when he saw one. I looked him over and stretched taller.

His eyes narrowed; they were cold and calculating. He took in my gray jeans and black button-down, passing silent judgment. Smug bastard. While I was dressed well enough for the party I just left, I would have been turned away by his staff at the door for not wearing a suit and tie. Thank God, Quinn snuck me in through the security entrance.

He smiled, but there was nothing friendly about it. "Are you going to introduce me to your friend, Amelia?"

Her eyes flashed with alarm as she fiddled nervously with the diamond bracelet on her wrist. Not my bracelet, it was probably one he gave her. I clenched my jaw, not wanting to show any emotion in front of the prick. "Owen, this is Marco." She swallowed. "Marco, this is Owen."

His upper lip curled, like he couldn't wait to gloat about having what I wanted. He stretched his hand out for me to shake. "I'm the fiancé."

He might as well have sucker punched me. The effect would have been the same. His point was made and it sucked balls. Still, I hated this for her and everything about this backhanded business arrangement. Seeing them together just hammered home the reality of it all.

"Congratulations." I forced the word out, feeling like I had a knife held to my throat. He looked like he wanted to tell me to fuck off and that only made me want to ruffle his feathers even more.

He snaked a hand along her waist and pulled her in.

"Thank you. As you can see, I'm a lucky man." The sight of his hands on her and his possessive tone ignited a fury inside me. "I'm afraid I'm at a loss here. How do you know *my* Amelia?"

It was taking every ounce of control I had not to surge forward. "Why don't we just cut the bullshit. We both know you're not a real couple. So why don't you go schmooze with all your country club buddies in there and let us have a private conversation."

I was no doubt fucking things up royally, but this arrogant ass was exactly what I was expecting.

"Who the hell do you think you are, coming here and insulting me?"

I knew this was wrong, but I could not stand here and continue to act calm. I might regret this stunt in the morning, but right now I couldn't imagine just standing back and doing nothing.

Amelia unpeeled his hands from around her waist and stepped between us. "The last thing you want is to cause a scene, Owen. Remember, appearances are everything."

The muscle in his jaw ticked as he seemed to weigh his options. You could tell he wasn't ready to be done with this conversation, but it wasn't worth risking his precious reputation either. He squared his shoulders, pulled down on his lapels, and straightened his jacket. "Make it quick. We have a couple's dance coming up soon."

My shoulders relaxed as I watched him spin on his heels and march off.

Amelia crossed her arms over her chest. "What is it you have to say to me?" She was close enough to where I could see the faint dusting of freckles across her nose. The same freckles I used to love to trace with my fingers while she slept.

"Why do you seem so standoffish?" I asked, wondering if I was missing something. Her anger took me by surprise. Wasn't I the one who was supposed to be pissed?

"I think the better question is, why are you doing this to me?" Her voice trembled as she looked away. "I've been calling, texting, sitting outside your house, waiting for you to come home. You shut me out, Marco. I understand that you needed space, but you pushed me away and your words hurt me. I'm not trying to stand here and make this all about me and my feelings; you have every right to feel the way you feel." She took a breath, and I stood there, feeling my heart twisting and tightening in pain. "Don't you see this is exactly what I was afraid of? This moment, right here, is exactly what I feared."

"But I'm here now."

"Why now? What changed?"

"Because the thought of losing you forever scares the shit out of me." My voice was desperate, but I was past caring about appearances. "I just needed time to think."

"No, what you needed was distance from me. You needed your anger justified." She wiped a tear from her eye. "I laid everything out on the line for you. I know you were hurt and confused, but I was ready to throw away my entire life's ambitions for a chance to be with you. But you were so pissed that you couldn't see past your own anger." She shook her head from side to side and everything inside me rattled. "I can't do this with you, Marco, no matter how much I want to be with you, I no longer have a choice in this matter."

"You said what we have is worth fighting for."

"You're right, but I can't fight for someone who gave up on me so easily. You didn't believe in us enough when I would have given up my entire world for you."

"Amelia." I took a deep breath. I've had this whole speech planned out in my head. I rehearsed it all the way over here, yet I had no idea what to say. "Before you go through with this, I want to have my say." My gaze lasered in on the big as fuck diamond around her finger. Seeing it up close was a sharp reminder of the time I wasted while wallowing in my own misery. I wanted to throw her over my shoulder, carry her out of this room and never look back.

"Okay?" She looked at me with a mixture of confusion and hope. No matter how I twisted and turned this around in my head, I needed to tear these walls down between us first and follow my heart.

"When you told me about this fucked-up arrangement, I wasn't sure how to feel." I paused, trying to keep my composure. "I know it feels like I've been ignoring you but believe me when I say, you are all I've thought about." I blew out a long breath. "Please, just put yourself in my shoes for a minute, okay? I felt betrayed and lied to."

"I hated that I hurt you." Her arms folded around her stomach. She looked like she was going to fall apart at any second. "I took my time because I was scared of what it would do to us. I felt so damn guilty about not being completely honest with you, and I will always regret how I handled things. You deserved better and I'm sorry."

I couldn't swallow down these feelings any longer. I wouldn't waste another minute, so I moved into her. My fingers reached out and trailed down her neck, every inch of her came alive under my touch. I was drawn to her in a way that I couldn't explain. Everything that mattered to me was right at my fingertips. I pulled her closer, not allowing any space between us, because this type of connection doesn't happen to everyone. What we had was special, and I wanted to show her I finally realized that. The time for talking was over. If this was my only shot, I was taking it.

I placed my hands on either side of her face and crashed my lips to hers. Where they belonged. A sense of peace settled over me. I was utterly crazy about this woman. The feelings I had for her would never go away and it was stupid of me to think that I could just get over her.

Her entire body melted into mine without any concern about what was going on around us. She belonged with me.

Not him. I didn't give a shit that she had his ring on her finger. It didn't matter that the room down the hall was filled with people that came out to celebrate an engagement that never should have happened in the first place. She didn't love him, and she never would.

I pulled back slowly and took a deep breath. I was scared to ask, but I had to know regardless of the outcome.

There was too much at stake.

My hands were on her hips, holding her in place. "Am I too late?"

She looked away, blinking back the tears. Whatever hope I was holding onto disappeared. I dropped my head because I knew when I looked up, I would have to face the truth. The pain in my chest felt like a dam that was about to break. I hated this, but I wasn't strong enough to stand here and try to convince her if her mind was already made up. Just like I couldn't go back and rewind time. If she was going to break my heart, she was going to look me in the eye when she did it.

I tilted her chin up, forcing her to look at me. "Say it," I choked out. I wanted to shake her and ask her why. Why she was doing this. Beg her not to go through it, because no job was worth a life of misery.

She wiped the tears that continued to stream down her face. "I don't want to hurt you."

"Tell me," I demanded, while keeping my voice deadly calm. "I want to hear you say it."

"Yes." The pain in her voice felt like an arrow shot straight through my heart. "You're too late."

I took a stumbling step back. She might as well have cut me off at the knees. I guess coming here and handing over my heart changed absolutely nothing for her.

"You told me you loved me. If you really meant it, then you wouldn't do this."

"Are you kidding me right now? I love you so much that

it hurts. I meant every single word I said to you. Please don't ever question that, but, Marco," her tears were thick as they trailed down her chin, "you told me to leave. I assumed you didn't want me anymore. I figured your silence was your way of telling me we were done. So, I told myself that if I couldn't have you than I might as well have my career."

"It's been a little over a fucking week." I shook my head and started pacing a small path along the hallway. She stood there, watching me as I came undone. "You told me you loved me and now I find you here—wearing another man's ring."

"I explained to you what the situation was. I can't change my decision now no matter how badly I want to."

I stepped forward. "Explain this to me. How you're going to marry him. Share a bed with him," I hissed, feeling the bite from my words. "Knowing that it's all a fucking lie!"

"Why are you doing this to me?" A violent sob ripped from her throat. "I would have chosen you a million times over this."

My chest rose and fell in heavy breaths. "Excuse me, but I didn't realize I had competition. You dropped a bomb on me, and I needed more than a fucking minute to process everything."

"Owen is not your competition. This is a marriage of convenience. Nothing else. I may be his on a piece of paper, but everything I have to give belongs to you."

My gaze was hard and unwavering. Still, I took one good long look at her face, trying to memorize it in my head because this would be the last time I would ever see it. That organ in my chest broke apart into tiny little bits because that kiss was the last one we would ever share. I would never touch her or hold her again. No, someone else would be doing that. I needed to face the truth that she no longer belonged to me, and maybe she never did.

"A lot of good that does. I came here and thought maybe if

I told you I loved you it would change your mind. But it sounds like your decision was made the second you walked out my door. Have a nice life, Amelia. I hope it's worth it."

I turned and walked out of her life forever, all the while pretending that my heart wasn't breaking at never seeing her again.

TWENTY-FIVE

AMELIA

"Amelia, do you need anything?" Julie, my grandmother's nurse, timidly asked as she moved around her bed.

"No, thank you." I closed the Danielle Steel novel I was reading to her while she slept. My grandmother had every hardback written by the author at home in her library. I remember when I was twelve, and she found one of her precious copies in my room. She sternly lectured me, saying the material was inappropriate for a girl my age. After sensing my disappointment, she brought me out for ice cream shortly after to ease her guilty conscience for being so hard on me. That's the type of grandmother she was, kind and compassionate, but firm when she needed to be.

Julie placed her hand on mine, squeezing it gently. "I know this is tough, but at least she had a good morning."

Glancing over at her bed, I sighed. Even during her best days, she still got names and dates mixed up. So, while I was glad that her memories still came and went, it made me sad to think that one day they wouldn't come at all.

I rubbed my tired eyes; sleep has been failing me this past week. All I wanted to do was settle into a peaceful dream and wake up from the nightmare that had become my life. Now that my engagement has become official, it's become harder and harder to accept.

Julie titled her head, her expression softening into a smile. "That's a beautiful ring. Congratulations."

"Thank you." I winced, realizing that my words lacked any enthusiasm.

I didn't have the energy to fake happiness that I wasn't feeling. And there wasn't a bandage big enough to cover the hole in my chest. It wasn't just my heart that hurt either, it was head, my body... everything hurt. Because I was crazy, stupid in love with a man who waited until I had a ring on my finger before telling me how he felt.

"Let me know if there is anything you need." She squeezed my arm before walking off to attend to another patient. There was commotion at the door and I turned my head.

"I heard you were here."

I was hoping to avoid Sophia this week. Not that I didn't enjoy her company, I was just feeling too raw and emotional and the last thing I wanted to do was rehash what went down with her grandson. I'm sure she knew what happened on New Year's Eve, and I wouldn't blame her if I wasn't her favorite person right now.

"Hey, Sophia. How are you?" My tone was too chipper, my smile was too tight. She raised her right eyebrow in challenge, letting me know that she was onto me. My elderly friend didn't miss a trick.

"Well, I'm glad you asked." She pulled a chair up next to me and got comfortable. "I've been wondering why you've been avoiding me?"

My shoulders deflated even though I knew I deserved it. "Please don't take it personally. I've just had a really rough week."

She continued to stare at me and it made me

uncomfortable. "I understand. Everything is complicated right now."

I reached for her hand, thankful that she was taking it easy on me. I expected some snappy comeback because Lord knew I deserved it. "I've missed you."

"I've missed you too." Her lips pinched together and she leaned forward. "I see you've got some new jewelry. That's quite a rock you got there." She frowned, staring intensely at my left hand. "It looks like you've made your decision."

I looked down at my ring and swallowed. My heart felt as heavy as my left finger. "Like you said, it's complicated."

"I hope it works out for you, *mio, caro*." I stole a glance at her face, it was filled with pity. I hated seeing that look in her eyes. And I hated how it made me feel. "I hope he at least treats you decent."

Knowing what I knew of Owen, I doubt that would be true, but I've already made peace with my decision, so there was no point in crying over spilled milk. I've already agreed to the arrangement and it's time I accepted it no matter how much I hated it.

"You think I'm crazy, don't you?" I leaned forward in my chair and rested my elbows on my knees.

She pulled the small container of orange Tic Tacs out of her pocket and popped one in her mouth. "I only know that you do not love him. You love my grandson."

I adjusted the blanket over my grandmother's shoulders; she was starting to get restless. "I love Marco with everything I have, we just weren't meant to be."

"Perhaps if you met another time then?" she said, handing me one of her breath mints.

A tear fell and I wiped it away. "If my circumstances were different, there isn't a doubt in my mind that we would be together, but that's not my reality."

She adjusted her sweater and leaned back in her chair. "The two of you never told me how you first met."

I slipped the Tic Tac in my mouth and tried to hide my smile. "It's kind of embarrassing. Why do you want to know so bad?"

"I'm an old lady." She shrugged. "I like to hear the love story."

"I'll save you all the shameful details, but I was drawn to him right from the start. We kept running into each other, and I tried to resist him, but my heart couldn't seem to stay away."

"It sounds more like fate intervened."

"Everything happened so fast, and we got too comfortable." I swallowed the emotion clogging the back of my throat. "I waited too long to tell him."

She grabbed my hand and held it. "He's angry now, but he loves you. Just like you love him. It's not too late to change your mind."

"Sophia, I begged him to hear me out, but he wouldn't give me a chance. I've been walking around these past couple weeks thinking that he didn't care about me as much as I did him. Then he showed up at my engagement dinner..." A sob broke free. I couldn't even finish my sentence.

"Amelia. My grandson has always been stubborn. He's had a lot of issues from having his heart broken before. But if I've learned anything over the years, it's that life will sometimes throw you a curveball. You can either take a swing and hope for the best, or watch it go by and wonder what if. You are both letting fear stand in your way. Do you understand what I'm saying?"

I wiped my eyes and lightly bumped her shoulder. "When did you become such a big baseball fan?"

Her eyes sparkled. "I dated some players when I was a young girl. There were lots of gigolos in old Italy."

"I didn't know you dated anyone other than Marco's grandfather."

"I dated a young man who was a catch in town, but we didn't work out."

"What happened to him?"

"He became a famous porn star and last I heard he was living with his gay lover in Florence."

I don't know why my mouth was hanging open because nothing that comes out of her mouth should surprise me at this point.

"*Tesoro*." Her tone grew serious. "I lost the man I loved. I will never get my Giovanni back. Never hear his voice. Never see him smile." Emotions bubbled inside me because I knew where she was going with this. "I know what's it like to be sad. I remember the ups and downs of young love. But, *cario*, I'm too old to give my heart away again. I would never try to replace Giovanni because he's irreplaceable. There is no more love for me in this life, and that's okay. Someday we will meet again. But for now, I like being alone. It's what I choose. But you, you are stronger than you think. You still have your whole life ahead of you. You still have choices." Big fat tears rolled down my cheeks. "I know that your grandmother loves you. She would want you to be happy. Your grandfather sounds like a decent man, he will understand. I know you have dreams, but sometimes dreams change."

I closed my eyes and sighed heavily. "I let him go. I told him it was too late."

"Do you regret it?"

"Of course, I do." Just like I knew my love for him would never go away. So, what the hell was I doing?

"My Marco is a handsome man, isn't he?" I narrowed my eyes. "A looker like that won't be on the market for long. Someday he'll meet some nice young girl, and they will settle down." The idea of him with anyone else made me angry enough to commit murder. And if this little old lady didn't stop talking, she was going to be my first victim. She winked. "I see that look in your eye."

There was no doubt that Marco was what I wanted. But the thought of losing the hotel to some private equity firm was tearing me apart, but that was nothing compared to disappointing the only family I had left. My grandfather would lose all his hard work, and my mother would lose the financial stability that she needed. I might have wanted it all, but that didn't mean I was going to get it. This was my moment of truth. Where I had to decide if I was going to risk it all for the man I loved or if I was going to stay on the path that I was on. Or maybe I had already made up my mind the second he walked away from me on New Year's Eve and I'm just realizing it.

"I think I screwed up."

Nervous energy started coursing through me. My knee started to bounce as I thought of what was at stake; I stood up and started pacing. I was so resigned to what my brain was telling me was the right thing to do that I never fully listened to my heart. I never gave it a chance, and no matter how much time passed, I would never move on from loving him. I could always get another job, but I could never replace Marco.

"Amelia." My grandmother's voice had me whirling around in surprise. She was awake! My mouth dropped open and my eyes felt like they needed to do a double take.

"If you love that man, then you go get him." Her voice was soft and familiar, and I stood there with my heart pounding in my chest, waiting for her to say something else. "If he gives you a hard time, then be persistent. Do whatever you have to do, but you don't give up. I want you to live and love, because that hole in your chest? No job will fill that."

I sucked in a deep breath and leaped across the room so I could lean over her bed. "You're awake?" I asked in amazement, not sure if I should talk or just let her talk. I knew this moment wouldn't last long. They were rare and precious.

She smiled warmly, and her weathered hand reached for

mine. Her eyes were filled with so much tenderness. "I don't know how much time I have before I slip away, so please let me say this."

Sophia's hand rubbed my back. "I'll leave you two alone," she said, before she quietly walked out of the room.

"Loving someone isn't always easy. Sometimes it's a lot of work. Lord knows I sacrificed a lot over the years with your grandfather, but I knew what I was getting into when I married him. He gave me a good life, and I wouldn't have wanted it any other way."

"Loving Marco comes at a cost," I said sadly, feeling my throat tighten. Admitting the truth dampened the happiness of her being awake.

"It always does, dear. That's how you know he's worth it."

"Oh God, I've missed you." I just wanted to hug her and never let go. Instead, I just clutched her hand and squeezed it tight.

"I'm proud of you, Amelia."

The lump in my throat grew bigger as my eyes filled with tears. "I'm not sure how proud Grandfather will be when I tell him I'm backing out of the deal."

"He will understand. He loves you, my sweet girl. We both do." She patted my hand and then I saw her eyes dart across the room. She was searching for something familiar. Her face became agitated. "What's that noise?" Her voice was loud, and I withdrew my hand. As much as her doctors tried to reassure me that this was a normal part of the disease, it never got easier. "Why are there people in the room? What do they want?"

I looked to the spot where she was focusing on. It was getting dark and the dim lights cast an eerie shadow in the corner of the room. I stood up on shaky legs and turned the light on, hoping she would calm down.

Carefully, I eased back over to her bed. "The people are

gone now. It's just us." I gentled my voice and gave her a calming touch on her shoulder.

She tensed. "No. They are still here. I see them." My chin quivered, and I gave myself a minute to pull myself together. I leaned to the side and clicked the classical music playlist, hoping the soft melody would soothe her. Her eyes closed, and I sat on the edge of my chair waiting for her breathing to slow. I took one last look at the row of photos that lined the windowsill. The framed picture of her and my grandfather on their fiftieth wedding anniversary sat right next to a photo of the two of us. God, why couldn't I be sixteen again. Life was so much simpler. After a kiss to the top of her head, I tucked the blanket up under her chin. My gaze paused on the quote that sat in a frame on her nightstand.

"All the things that live die. This is why you must find joy in the living, while the time is yours, and not fear the end. To deny this is to deny life. To fear this is… is to fear life."

A smile touched my lips. That quote hit me square in the chest. as if God had just given me a sign confirming I was doing the right thing.

Now it was time to hit that curveball out of the park and go get my guy.

TWENTY-SIX

MARCO

LOGAN'S PHONE BEEPED. "WE GOT HIM. WE GOT THE SON OF A bitch! The judge just issued the warrant. The cell towers picked up a signal from his mother's house in Germantown."

Miguel Perez was the leader of the Los Diablos street gang that took over a good portion of Hunting Park. Perez was no angel. He was wanted for storming into a known drug house and killing three people, including a woman who was five months pregnant. His rivals, a group called the Schuylkill Rangers, were peddling their own poison, which on most days was heroin and sometimes fentanyl. Depending on the demand in the streets. We were also trying to connect him to the warehouse fire from Nicetown last month.

Perez was a firebug, using arson for a tool for extortion, intimidation, and murder. He and Benny Castro did a short stint at the same lock-up before he was sent up to Muncy, an interesting tidbit that we stumbled upon during our investigation. This little game of cat and mouse was getting old, and I was sick of him being one step ahead. I was ready to get him off the streets.

Logan shot me a pointed glance as the images pinged to our screens. It was a photo of two young kids, sitting on a park bench. They didn't look older than fifteen as they both drank a 40 from a brown paper bag. Even with his disheveled appearance, I recognized Benny's tattoo on his left arm. Miguel Perez was the kid next to him, laughing and patting him on the back.

"Looks like we have our connection between these two dirtbags," I said, staring down at the picture. Miguel had been a thorn in my side for the past nine months, and it was time to end this.

"Has the area been evacuated?" I asked Logan.

"All clear."

"Let's roll."

I wanted to get there before anyone else did. This was my homicide case. I've spent months chasing down leads. And the victims' families, no matter how tainted their loved one's life choices were, they deserved justice. If anyone was going to get the satisfaction of taking him down, it was going to be me.

By the time we pulled up to his mother's neighborhood, it was dark outside. The house sat on a street with only one working streetlight. The rest had their bulbs shot out by thugs who preferred to do their work in the dark. I swept the area, searching for anything that might feel off. The only thing that stood out was the white Cadillac parked in front of the garage.

"SWAT is on the way," Logan said, as he typed the license plate into his computer. A prickle of unease traveled down my spine. I ran my hand along the steering wheel, hoping I was just being paranoid, but something didn't feel right. The neighborhood was quiet. Too quiet. I took a minute to assess my surroundings, allowing my eyes to adjust to the darkness.

I cranked the door open and stepped onto a fresh patch of snow. We kept our heads down as we walked along the side of the house, trying to stay out of sight. There wasn't any movement from the inside of the house, but my gut told me we were walking into a trap. I didn't have time to think or hesitate, so I kept on moving. The area was going to be surrounded in a matter of minutes, and I didn't want any possibility of him slipping through our fingers.

I glanced at Logan out of the corner of my eye as we both focused on not making any noise while our boots moved along the gravel driveway. I drew my gun out of my holster, hoping like fuck I didn't have to use it. My job was to protect and serve, and I intended to uphold my oath. Innocent lives were lost because of the poison these low life drug dealers peddled on the streets. They destroyed these once middle-class communities with their selfish greed. Like an insect infestation, these gangs took over stores and businesses one by one, running good people out of the neighborhoods. Those who stayed were extorted for cash payment for "protection" from rival gangs. And if the business owners couldn't pay in cash, they were more than willing to torture their family members and their children to collect in other ways. These were bad people.

I looked over my shoulder, seeing movement on the end of the street. I gave Logan a nod, letting him know that SWAT had arrived. We circled the house and secured all points of entry, eliminating any chance of him escaping. Once the perimeter was established, I gave my men a nod and banged on the door.

The dog next door started barking and a few flood lights from surrounding houses came on. And that's when all hell broke loose. The door swung open and before I could even react, Perez's gun was aimed at my chest and bullets started flying.

"Get down." Logan shoved me sideways right before our men stormed the house. They wrestled Perez and a handful of his crew to the ground as bullets continued to spray out into the neighborhood through the front window. Glass shattered; footsteps pounded as a haze of gun smoke clouded the air.

"Fuck," I shouted out in pain and held on to my left shoulder. While the vest protected my chest, the fucker got a quick shot that struck me where the vest had stopped. My vision started to blur with an intense pain like I'd never felt before in my arm. He fucking hit me. Blood leaked from the wound in my shoulder as I tried to crawl along the floor.

Logan stripped his jacket off and added pressure to the wound.

Captain Jenkins kneeled down on his knees to get a better look. "Hang on. Ambulance is on the way. There is a lot of blood there… just keep applying pressure and don't let him close his fucking eyes."

Logan hissed out a breath through his nose, and I painfully lifted my head to see what had his face going so pale. Shit! His hands were covered in blood. My blood.

"Marco." I felt a slap to my face. "We're going to get you to the hospital, but you need to stay with us." My eyelids were getting heavier and heavier. They weren't going to stay open for much longer. "It's going to be okay," he said right before everything went black.

TWENTY-SEVEN

AMELIA

"Look Aunt Amelia." Madison turned around in her Cinderella gown. "I got a whole chest full of princess dresses for Christmas."

"That's beautiful," I said, wishing she was a real princess because I could really use a fairy godmother right now.

Drew squeezed her shoulder, stopping her mid-spin. "All right, Maddie, it's time for bed."

"Dad, nooo," she whined. He tightened his grip because when Madison had a breakdown, it wasn't pretty.

"It's already past your bedtime. You need to go upstairs and get ready for bed." He released her shoulder and ran his hand along the top of her brown hair. "If you give me any trouble, I'm sending all your gifts back to Santa."

Madison's lip trembled and then she threw her crown on the floor and stormed up the stairs. Drew tossed his head back in frustration and closed his eyes.

He scooped up the crown and turned to Ava. "Stay here and enjoy your wine. I'll make sure she goes to bed."

Ava pushed the pile of decorative pillows to the side. "Thanks, babe."

Drew winked before making his way up the stairs to his very unhappy little girl.

Ava looked at the mess that was now her family room. There were new toys everywhere. "She's been so out of her routine."

"It's okay. I get it." My fingers traced along the rim of the wineglass.

She curled her legs underneath her. "We need to talk about what happened on New Year's Eve."

I took a sip of my wine and set it down while she kept her eyes on me. "I decided not to go through with the arrangement."

"I'm sorry? What did you just say?" The hope in her voice almost made me laugh.

"I'm not marrying Owen, and I need you to help me come up with some big grand gesture to get Marco back. How's that?"

She flung herself at me, causing us both to fall back on the cushions. "Finally." She pulled back and placed her hands on my arms. "I don't think you realize how happy I am to hear that."

I shook my head with a smile. "I think I have a pretty good idea."

Now that I had officially made my decision, nerves were settling in my stomach, and I would feel a hell of a lot better when Marco took me back.

"Why do you look so sad?"

"Oh, I don't know? Maybe because this is a huge risk. I'm walking away from everything I've worked for and there is no guarantee that he will even want anything to do with me?"

The idea of losing my career, letting down my family, my coworkers, and employees made me sad. It felt like I was losing a part of my identity, but it was nothing compared to losing him. I had to remind myself that I was giving up something big, but what I was gaining was so much better.

She patted my leg in understanding. "That man is crazy about you. I don't think you have anything to fear."

"I hope you're right."

She tapped her chin with her finger. "You need to do something big and loud. Something that will show him, not just tell him."

"What do you suggest?" I asked, just as my cell phone started ringing in my bag. I pulled it out and was ready to hit decline when Marco's name flashed across the top of my screen.

My mouth dropped open. "It's him," I announced, feeling all the air rush from my lungs.

Ava nudged my leg. "This is a sign."

With shaky fingers I hit accept. "Hello."

"Amelia, it's Logan." He paused, and something in his voice had every nerve in my body standing on end. "Marco's been shot."

"What?" I gasped. "Is he going to be okay?"

"He's in surgery now. They brought him to HUP. Text me when you're close and I'll meet you in the main lobby of the hospital."

"I'll be right there." My entire body was shaking as I ran around Ava's house gathering my things. "Holy shit! Marco's been shot."

Ava grabbed me by the arms and spun me around. "I'm coming with you."

I shook my head, feeling tears spill from my eyes. "No, please stay here. I'll call you if I need you."

"You are in no condition to drive. At least let me call you an Uber."

"Okay." I held my bag to my stomach. My entire body radiated with fear from the inside out. This can't be how our story ends. It just can't.

———

As soon as the automatic doors slid open, Logan was waiting for me. "How is he?" I asked as he got close. The lobby was flooded with cops.

"He's still in surgery. We're still waiting for an update."

"Where was he shot?"

"His left shoulder." He looked down at the floor and brought his eyes back to mine. "He lost a lot of blood."

"Take me to the waiting room. I need to be there when he gets out of surgery," I said, not giving a damn about anything other than making sure that he was alive.

Logan grabbed my hand and led me to the elevators. The harsh lighting illuminated the hallway as we walked past the cluster of doctors and nurses gathered around computers on wheels, reviewing patient charts. The sounds of the busy hospital blurred into the background. The only thing I could focus on was getting to Marco's side. We rushed down the hall into the small waiting room at the end.

Now that I was here, the reality of everything finally caught up to me. I slumped down into the first available chair and threw my head into my hands. My sobs came in uncontrollable waves as Logan placed a comforting hand on my shoulder. Strangers stared at me with pity, but I couldn't bring myself to care.

I spotted Quinn across the room, talking to a group of officers huddled in the corner. They all looked anxious and it was staggering to see all these badass men so torn up over one of their own.

Time seemed to tick by in slow motion. All I could do was stare at the door and every time a doctor would come out, I would hold my breath and hope they were here to bring us good news. But as time passed, my mind conjured up the worst-case scenarios. I wanted to fall to my knees and pray—

something I haven't done in years. I would promise anything to have him be okay.

Finally, the door opened, and everything seemed to happen in slow motion. A surgeon in blue scrubs entered the room. He stepped forward. "Rubintino family?"

Logan helped me out of my chair and walked me over to the doctor.

"I'm Doctor Awayda." He shook Logan and Quinn's hand while I waited on bated breath for him to deliver us the news. "The surgery went smoothly. He was very lucky. The bullet just missed the brachial plexus which means he won't have any nerve damage. We were able to remove the bullet and stop the bleeding. There was a small piece of shattered bone that we had to reattach, but other than that, there was no damage to the surrounding tissue or organs."

"Thank God." Logan sighed. "What about blood? He lost a lot of blood."

The doctor nodded. "There was no life-threatening bleeding. He did not need a transfusion."

"So, he's going to be okay?" I asked for confirmation. Dr. Awayda was a Middle Eastern man with a heavy accent. Even though his English was good, I just wanted to be sure I heard him correctly.

He gave me a kind smile. "With some intensive physical therapy, I expect him to make a full recovery."

"When can we see him?" I asked, eager to see him with my own eyes.

"He's in recovery now. They are removing the breathing tube and bringing him to ICU. Just sit tight for a bit and we will get you there."

A couple of officers walked in holding coffees and waters. By the amount of people that were taking up space in the waiting room, it made me wonder who was out protecting the streets of Philadelphia.

"I need to call Marietta and Matteo."

"They are on their way," Quinn said, pocketing his phone. "They are going to be awhile though, because they are driving in from Delaware."

His mom had to be going out of her mind with worry. I was thankful that Quinn handled that call personally. I would not want to be the one to deliver that news.

I spent the next thirty minutes pacing the long narrow hallway. I thought about going down to the chapel and lighting a candle, but I wanted to be close by for when they brought him to his room. My patience was running thin, so I walked over to the nurse's station to get an update.

"Is Marco Rubintino still in recovery?" I asked, looking up at the screen. "They gave me a patient number to keep track of his progress, but I didn't see any change in his status."

"Let me check." She started to type away on her computer and looked up. "They just moved him out of recovery. Intensive care is on the sixth floor, he's in room 2B. He's only allowed two visitors at a time. You can take the elevators on the left."

"Thank you," I said and rushed forward. My heart was pounding as I waited for the elevator to arrive. I sent Logan and Quinn a text, letting them know where I was headed. If anyone was getting to him first, it was going to be me. Once Marietta and Matteo got here, I would have to go back to the waiting room so they could go into ICU.

Sweat gathered on my forehead as I slowly pushed the curtain back. Marco was in a thin white gown; there was an IV pole next to his bed with a machine beeping in the background. Glancing at that monitor, I studied his heart rate and took comfort knowing that as long as it was beeping, he was alive.

I dropped down in the chair next to his bed and sobbed. My strong, solid man looked so weak under the blankets. I looked at his arm, noticing all the bruises from the different IVs they inserted during surgery to keep him alive.

Everything that's happened over the past couple of weeks flashed through my mind like a bad nightmare.

Carefully, I pressed my lips against his forehead. "Please, my beautiful man. I don't know if you can hear me, but I need you to wake up so I can tell you how much I love you." Tears clogged my vision, every emotion I'd been holding back spilled out of me. "I need you to wake up. I would give anything to go back and not let you walk away from me. I'm so sorry."

My sobs were loud and ugly, but I was so overcome with despair I couldn't stop. The thought of losing him forever snapped that rubber band in half that had been holding me together. "I'm so sorry." I brushed my fingers through his hair. Being able to touch him gave me a small amount of comfort. "I need you to open your eyes. I need to see your smile. Please, just wake up. I promise you, if you give me another chance, I will do whatever it takes to earn your trust back. I will prove to you that our love comes before anything else."

There were so many things I needed to say to him. So much I needed to apologize for. I rubbed a hand across my cheek and took a calming breath. When I looked down, his eyes blinked open.

"Marco." I started fumbling around in his bed, searching for the call button. I pressed it repeatedly until I heard the nurse call over my shoulder.

He turned his head to the side, looking confused. "What's going on? Where is Logan?"

"Shh… Don't talk." I steadied my hand on the bed rail and looked down. "Logan is fine. He is in the waiting room with Quinn. Your Mom and Matteo are on their way."

"Amelia." His voice was gruff. "What happened?"

"You were shot in your left shoulder, but you are going to be fine."

He reached for my hand. "You're really here?"

"Of course, I'm here." I broke down and rested my head on his chest, my tears soaked his hospital gown. I needed to feel his heartbeat, but I was careful not to touch his injured shoulder.

"Hey." He attempted to sit up but winced in pain, so I pressed a hand to his right shoulder to guide him down.

"Try not to move."

"It's okay," he said, trying to reassure me that he was fine.

"No, it's not okay," I choked out, unable to keep my emotions contained. I was swallowing my own damned tears. "I thought I lost you. The second Logan called, I came straight here, not knowing if I was even wanted here, or if they would even let me see you." The shame of my actions made it hard for me to speak. "I don't even feel like I deserve to be here right now. Not after everything I put you through."

"Amelia." The commotion outside his room stopped him from saying whatever it was he was about to say.

"It's good to see you awake and talking." Doctor Awayda's smile was kind as he approached the foot of the bed. Another doctor who I didn't recognize walked in and checked the monitors and IVs. "How about we look you over and inspect the wound."

"Can I have something to drink first?" he asked the nurse.

She nodded her head. "Of course."

I grabbed the water pitcher off his tray while she handed me a cup and a straw. He attempted to hold it up to his lips, but I was afraid he was going to pull his IV out, I moved closer so I could help him drink it without incident. I was expecting him to complain, but he didn't seem to mind the extra attention.

"Thanks." He swallowed as the doctors and nurses poked and prodded all along his upper body. He looked exhausted by the time they were finished.

"Everything looks great," Dr. Awayda said as he moved over to the sink to wash his hands. "Your vitals are perfect.

Your pain meds will be wearing off in about," he looked at the clock, "another four hours or so. You should expect a little discomfort, so if it gets unbearable, buzz the nurse. She can give you something in between if you need it." He dried his hands off with a paper towel. "Do you have any other questions for me?"

Marco shook his head and looked to me. "No. I think we're good. Thank you."

"Very well." He squeezed my shoulder and walked out.

Alone finally.

"How do you feel?" I asked, sinking into the edge of his mattress. We still had so much to talk about. I had no idea where we stood, but I wanted to take a minute to appreciate the fact that he was alive.

He tried to push himself up, but I gently pushed him back down. "Marco, please." I looked at the bandage on his arm. "You need to take it easy."

"Amelia, it will heal." He reached for my hand and squeezed my fingers. "I just need you. Please stay. Lie down with me. I need to be close to you."

I didn't even hesitate. I climbed in and laid on my side, so I was facing him. He brushed my hair off my shoulder and that's when I lost it. He held me close as I buried my face in his neck and fell apart in his arms.

He cupped my chin and brushed a fallen tear from my jaw. "Sweetheart.

"Stop. Please, just tell me you forgive me."

"Shh… Let's talk later, okay. I just want to be near you. Whatever we have to discuss can wait. We both made mistakes and I want to fix what's broken between us, but I'm so damn tired and all I want to do is hold you." His eyes drifted closed. He was too exhausted to even fight the sleep that he needed.

TWENTY-EIGHT

MARCO

A TWINGE OF PAIN SHOT UP TO MY SHOULDER. I WINCED AND SAT up, looking around for my bottle of pain meds. My other arm was practically useless as I fumbled with removing the child-proof safety cap. I tossed the two pills down my dry throat, swallowed hard, and leaned back, waiting for the relief to kick in.

The sound of pots and pans banging around in my kitchen had me easing off the couch. I stumbled into the other room, and the sight before me sent a grin across my face.

"What are you doing?" I asked Amelia, who was making an absolute mess in my kitchen. There were mixing bowls and baking sheets everywhere. My countertops were coated with every ingredient I had stored in my pantry.

She stood up and made her way over to the sink so she could wash her hands. "I'm making sauce and meatballs. I figured you were probably sick of hospital food and would appreciate a home-cooked meal."

I leaned over, inspecting the meatballs on the baking sheet. "I didn't know you cooked?"

"I can cook a few things. Just because I was raised with

nannies and a chef, doesn't mean I can't cook. I've been living on my own for a while now, and I haven't starved yet."

I whistled loudly at the red sauce that was boiling over on my stove. "It's petty bold of you to cook this particular dish for an Italian boy," I teased and walked over to discretely turn the burner on simmer before the sauce burned the bottom of my pan.

She rolled her eyes. "I'm sure it won't be as good as your mom's, but it won't taste like Ragu either."

"Come here." I opened my good arm, keeping my injured one secured in the sling. Amelia walked into my chest. "You don't have to do this, but I appreciate the gesture. Thank you."

Her eyes searched my face. "If we are going to be together, I'm going to have to learn to cook for my man, now aren't I?"

There was a dusting of flour on her cheekbone, so I rubbed it off with my thumb. "Look at you going all June Cleaver on me. I didn't realize you were so fond of the fifties era?"

She rolled her eyes. "I'm glad to see you are feeling better. And here I was worried about you."

"You were worried about me, huh?"

Amelia has done way more than she needed to. She's cleaned my house, did my laundry, stocked my kitchen with food, and has pretty much been at my beck and call since I got home from the hospital. Any time I made a noise, she sprang into action. Having her here has been a godsend because there was only so much I could do with one working arm.

"I'm just glad you're okay. I just want us to be okay too."

I swept my lips against hers. "I want to talk to you about a few things before these pain meds fully kick in and I crash."

"Let me just get this tray of meatballs in the oven." She turned and put the cookie sheet on the oven rack and pushed the door shut. After loading a few dishes in the dishwasher, she washed her hands and poured a glass of water. I grabbed her fingers and led her into the living room.

I guided her to sit on my lap, and bit back a curse as my shoulder reminded me that a bullet had torn through it a few days earlier. She noticed me wince and raised an eyebrow. "I'm fine I promise."

"Are you sure?" She didn't look convinced, but I was determined to have this conversation before I was drugged out of my mind.

"The pain has been coming and going, it's not that bad."

"So, what do you want to talk about?" she asked, placing her glass of water on the table.

"What do you think your family is going to say about us?"

She slipped her fingers in the back of my hair. Her touch was soft and comforting and exactly what I needed. Fuck the pain pills. There was no better feeling than this right here. I moaned, feeling the tension from the past few weeks fade away.

"I don't know and I don't really care," she said so quietly I almost didn't hear her.

"I know that's not true, and even if it was, I care." I adjusted her on my lap, unsure how to ask my next question. "What about the engagement? Did you break it off?"

I've been avoiding asking about it because things have been so good lately, and I didn't want to rock the boat. But we couldn't keep dancing around the fact that this conversation had to happen. After all, avoiding it is what got us here to begin with.

"I haven't spoken to anyone yet. My main focus is on making sure your recovery goes smoothly. Once I'm comfortable leaving you, that will be my first stop."

I pulled back and frowned at her. She couldn't be serious. "Amelia…"

She stopped me with a finger to my lips. "When you were in the hospital, I sent an email to my grandfather and told him I was taking some personal time off and I would be in touch soon."

I have noticed that she hasn't been on her phone or laptop since I've been home. The only time she has left my side is to shower or go to the bathroom.

"Sweetheart, you can't keep putting this off."

"Is that what you think I'm doing?" I closed my eyes as her fingers traced along my eyebrow. "Marco, while you were lying in that hospital bed, I made a promise to myself that if you could forgive me, that I would never let anything come between us again. The only thing that matters right now is you." I sat quietly, allowing her words to soak in. "You don't need to worry about that contract. I'm not going through with it."

"Amelia." When I made a move to sit up straighter, she pressed her palm to my good shoulder. I tugged her hand away and met her gaze. "Have you really thought this through? Because I don't want you to resent me or regret your decision ten years from now."

A ghost of a smile played on her lips. I placed my finger under her chin and tipped it back. "Why are you smiling?"

She linked her fingers through mine. "Because you're talking about a future with me."

"Let's not get too carried away. I said ten years. I could get sick of you in ten and a half."

She let out a laugh, and I could feel some of the tension fading away. "I missed you so much."

I studied her carefully. "Are you sure this is what you want? You've worked so hard for this opportunity."

"The only thing I want is to be with you. I didn't realize how empty my life was without you in it."

She felt that way now, but would she still feel that way when the dust settled?

I brushed her hair off her shoulder. "I hate that you have to give up your dreams to be with me."

I tried to put myself in her shoes, and I honestly don't know what the hell I would do if I were in her position. Being a cop was my livelihood. It was my life, my identity. I searched for something to say that would bring her comfort, but my mind came up empty.

"Marco, when Logan called to tell me you were shot, I was at Ava's, brainstorming ideas on things I could do to get you back. I had already made my decision. I don't ever want you to think that I gave anything up for you, whatever I do is for us."

I felt my throat tighten. "You promise me you are okay with this decision?"

"If it's you or my career, I will always choose you. I would choose you over anything."

"I hope it doesn't come to that, but if it does, you will find something else. Your smart, and loyal, any company would be lucky to have you."

She toyed with the loose string on the blanket. "I'm going to talk to my grandfather tomorrow."

My fingers flexed on her thigh. "What about Owen?"

She sighed. "He's going to be pissed, but that's not my problem."

My thumb stroked her cheek. How could something so complicated make the most sense?

"I love you," I told her, but my words didn't feel adequate enough to display how I felt. "I swear on my life that I will make you happy."

"I believe you, and I promise to do my best to be the woman you deserve."

My arms wrapped around her. "What about love me? Do you promise to love me, because that's all I need from you."

She rested her cheek over my beating heart and grinned up at me. "Always."

TWENTY-NINE
AMELIA

I STARED OUT THE WINDOWS OVERLOOKING THE CITY. I'VE SPENT weeks preparing for this meeting, making sure all the numbers matched, going over every single detail for the presentation. This was too important for me not to give it my all.

I walked down to the conference room, reviewing the notes on my iPad. Lisa, the head of my marketing team, rose from her cubical. "Everything is all set. I'm just waiting for Griffith in IT to make a few minor adjustments," she said as I led us down the hallway to the set of glass doors. She followed me inside and went straight to the coffee cart set up in the back of the room.

Owen was the first person to see me walk in. He barely acknowledged me as he fiddled with something on his phone. He either hasn't noticed that I haven't been around or he just didn't care.

I extended my hand to the head of our legal counsel, Neil Buchanan. "Good morning, Neil." He gave my hand a brisk handshake and then went back to going over his notes.

My grandfather rose from his chair. "Amelia." He kissed

the top of my forehead. "It's great to have you back. I hope everything is okay?"

I patted his arm. "I'm sorry I haven't returned your calls. I'll explain everything shortly."

He wrinkled his forehead in confusion, but I was grateful when he didn't press further.

Edward Eastan breezed through the door with his signature navy suit and white satin handkerchief peeking out from the breast pocket. "Let's get down to business, shall we?"

Everyone found a seat while I walked around to the front of the room. "Thank you all for being here. After months of preparation and a great deal of planning, I would like to show you the latest cutting-edge design for hotel suites this generation has ever seen."

For the next hour, I went through each slide and answered every question thrown my way. By the time I was finished, I knew without a shadow of a doubt that I nailed it. Not only would we be upgrading all the guest rooms that would cater to the millennials, but our suites were specifically designed to please our most loyal business travelers. Our sales team has already signed an agreement with a major airline carrier, as well as a government contract that would push our sales results through the roof.

Owen gave a big toothy smile to a few people who congratulated him. Of course, he was trying to steal as much credit as he could. Anyone in this room with half a brain knew he didn't do anything to earn it.

"Great Job, Amelia. Truly." My grandfather's eyes sparkled with pride from across the table. This was going to suck, but it had to be done.

"Thank you." My heart sped up with nerves. "While I have everyone here, there is one more matter of business I'd like to attend to." I looked across the table and tried to keep my expression flat, not wanting to give anything away. My head was telling me this was the right decision, even though my heart wasn't all the way there yet. That was okay though, it would get there eventually. "Effective today, I am handing in my resignation."

My eyes met Owen's from across the table. He looked ready to jump out of his seat. "What?" he asked in disbelief.

Heads spun from every direction, their faces were a mixture of shock and confusion. "I have no idea what is going on here," he stood up, trying to act like he was in charge, "but if you will excuse me, I need a word with my fiancée."

I held my hand up, letting him know that I wasn't done. "Oh, that's another thing. The engagement is off."

He leaned into the table. "Amelia. A word now!"

My smile was tight. I tried to appear confident when inside I was more nervous than I cared to admit. "We can talk privately later. I don't want to waste anymore of the company's time."

Edward leaned back in his chair and narrowed his eyes. "I don't know what's going on, but everyone out. Now!"

Every single person in the room jumped up, grabbed their notebooks, pens and laptops, and dashed out of the room. Neil started packing up his stuff when Edward ordered him to stay.

"I apologize that my decision has caught you off guard, but these past few days have been very hard on me personally." I lowered my head, feeling my palms sweat. "When I first agreed to help Owen run the company, I wasn't seeing anyone at the time."

Owen stood up and braced his hands on the table. "Is this about that fucker who showed up at the engagement party?"

I met his glare, not giving him any reaction whatsoever. "He is someone very important to me, so please show some respect."

"I will do no such fucking thing. We had a deal." His eyes went hard. "You are wearing my ring."

"Actually," I held my hand up, "I stopped by your office before this meeting and left the ring on your desk."

His mouth dropped open and he snapped it shut. "You cold-hearted, fucking bitch."

"Hey now," my grandfather bellowed. "You, young man," he pointed to Owen, "will not speak to my granddaughter like that. I don't care how upset you are."

"Listen, I don't want to fight. I'm just here to hand in my resignation. I understand that this complicates things, but I have to follow my heart. As much as I love this company, I love him more. Words cannot express how sorry I am for letting you all down."

My gaze landed on my grandfather. He looked crushed. Somehow my life had taken a drastic turn, and I never filled him in on it. Somewhere along the way, my loyalties shifted. Maybe it was when I finally realized the extremes he went to in order to seal this deal. The sacrifices I made to get to this point, the things I had to give up just weren't worth it anymore.

"Amelia, is there anything we can say to make you reconsider?" His voice was filled with concern, but it was lacking the surprise that I expected to hear.

"I asked myself that very question before this meeting." My eyes pricked with tears. I knew this would be hard but nothing prepared me for the gut-wrenching feeling. "This company means the world to me, but the cost would be too great to pay. If I have to give him up, then there is nothing for me to reconsider."

The irony of it all, is that I've spent most of my life having one dream, and one night in this very hotel I fell for a man who changed everything.

Owen's scowl transformed into a greedy smile. "I guess that just leaves me. I know this isn't what you both had planned, but I give you my word that this company will be in good hands."

"This company might not have a board of directors to answer to, but don't forget you still have a few hundred employees that don't respect you," I pointed out. "I'm not really sure that you are capable of running this company on your own."

As much as I hated the idea of a private equity firm taking over, this company would collapse under his leadership within the first year if he didn't have someone holding his hand. Everyone in this boardroom knew it.

"That's really not your concern anymore, is it," he said a little too smugly before turning his attention back to the three men at the table. "I suggest you all have a little faith in me. I am more than capable, and I'm the only option you have left, unless you want to sell to a stranger."

My grandfather's chair squeaked as he rested his elbows along the armrest. "Owen, it's not just about having a fancy title and power, it's about the people and pleasing guests. You have a reputation of making bad decisions."

Owen was so sure of himself as he buttoned his jacket. There was no doubt he was expecting to get his way as usual. "While I admit Amelia brought a lot of value to this business, she didn't do it all on her own. She's not some freaking fairy who sprinkles gold dust wherever the hell she goes."

He was so wrapped up in telling us how great he was, he didn't notice the door to the conference room open.

My head snapped up and in walked my mother, her heels clicking along the floor with a confidence that couldn't be ignored.

My grandfather glanced over his shoulder and gave her a questing look. "Tamara, what are you doing here?"

She scanned the room and dropped her oversized bag on the conference table. "Well, Jeffery, I'm trying to help you and Edward save this company by making sure it stays in the right hands. I had a feeling that Owen would try to worm his way into the top position. But before this goes any further, I think there are a few things you and your business partner need to hear first."

Owen squinted his eyes at her. "Excuse me? What the hell are you talking about?"

Dread prickled the back of my neck as she made a show of rummaging through the contents of her bag.

"Tamara." Edward leaned back in his chair, adjusting the cufflinks of his custom shirt. "Why don't you dispense with the theatrics. Whatever you came to say, please say it. We have some pressing business to attend to."

She produced a large manila envelope and placed a stack of photographs on the table. On top, there were pictures of a man and a naked woman in a dirty bathroom stall. He was sniffing a white powder off her breasts. I would recognize that figure anywhere. I clamped a hand over my mouth in disgust, looking down at the photos.

Everyone sat around the conference room table, shell-shocked as more images appeared of Owen and more women, so many women. Some looked very, very young where I questioned if they were even legal. I glanced around the room; my grandfather shook his head, and I'd never seen Edward Eastan so pissed off in my entire life.

"This is bullshit," Owen exploded.

While I suspect that he had secrets, it never struck me they would be this dark. "Where the hell did you even get these?"

She crossed her arms. "I hired a private investigator."

His hands shook with rage as he wrestled the tie off his neck. "What the fuck did you do that for?"

"Do you see this photo right here?" She pointed to an image of Owen and a young blonde, having sex in a lounge chair by a pool. "That girl is sixteen years old."

A gasp flew from my mouth. There have been rumors circulating for years on how Owen had a type. I assumed when they said he liked them young, it meant fresh out of college. Never in a million years did I think he would be that sick.

My mother continued, unfazed by our reactions. "My PI was able to get a hold of your bank statements. Did you think those deposits couldn't be traced? He was also able to track down a few of those girls, and they had a lot of interesting things to say about your sexual preferences. Let me tell you something, Owen, you are a very sick man. Let's see," she started to flip through a stack of papers, "Saints & Sinners sex club, the Pleasure Garden, Scores, the list goes on and on." She ticked everything off on her fingers. "Underage girls, sex clubs, drugs… Should I go on?"

It felt like I was going to get sick.

Edward threw his reading glasses across the table. "I've seen and heard enough." He spun around in his chair "How stupid are you?"

Owen sank down into his seat. "Let's not panic." I could sense his mind working on some bullshit explanation that would save his ass.

Neil took his handkerchief out of his pocket and wiped his forehead. "A drug and underage sex scandal will not be good for the sale of the business."

Edwards nostrils flared. There was no mistaken he had reached his limit. "I warned you, son. I tolerated your unprofessional behavior for years. I looked the other way when you slept with anything that walked. I gave you everything you needed to succeed. All you had to do was work for it! I will not let the reputation of this company go down in flames just because my only grandson is a royal fuckup." Owen's gaze dropped for a brief moment. There was no way he wasn't feeling humiliated as his grandfather continued to dress him down in front of everyone. "I was handing over my company. Pairing you up with a good woman. But this… is the end of the line. You know, for a smart guy, you do some incredibly stupid shit."

My grandfather cleared his throat. "Neil, how can we fix this?"

Neil riffled through the stack of paperwork. "First, we would have to have a new agreement drawn up. You two would have to decide on which direction you wanted to go. Clearly, Owen is no longer part of this decision."

Edward tipped his head back; his eyes were fixed on the gray ceiling. The atmosphere in the room was so tense they could probably feel it fourteen stories down in the main lobby. He cut his eyes to my grandfather; a silent understanding passed between them.

Edward took a deep breath and swiped his hand along his brow "Amelia, this business is just as important to you as it is to us. Which is exactly why you should run it. It's one hundred percent yours if you want it."

"Now, wait a minute..." Owen's eyes widened in panic. "You can't be serious."

"I'm serious as a heart attack," Edward fired back.

"Those photos are fakes. I'll hire the best attorney money can buy and clear this up. I will not be pushed aside. This company is my birthright."

Edward pounded his fist on the table, causing the wall of windows to rattle. "Owen, you can have whatever is left of your trust fund after you pay your legal bills. I have officially reached my limit. You have disgusted and disappointed me for the last time."

Owen stood quickly and kicked the chair across the room. "This is fucking bullshit. You can't do this."

Edward shut his eyes and pinched the bridge of his nose. "Tamara, how many people know about this?"

"Only the people in this room."

"Then it's settled. Amelia, as long as this doesn't get in the way of your personal life, are you ready to take over as the CEO of Eastan West? If you are, the job is yours."

I sucked in a breath. Was I prepared for this? I wasn't sure.

This was as complicated as it gets. I worked hard to get to this point in my career. This company didn't just mean a lot to me, I was proud of it. But my relationship came first. I wouldn't settle for less. "Further concessions would need to made before I could accept the offer. I would need time to assemble the right team to assist me."

Owen charged forward, getting right up in his grandfather's face. "I strongly suggest you reconsider."

"Or what?" Edward gritted his teeth. "You have nothing to bargain with. You are finished."

"I will fight this," he hissed.

"Good luck with that." Edward's face turned to stone. "That's going to be a little hard to pull off while sitting in a padded cell, don't you think?"

"You wouldn't?" Sweat beaded down his temple. His fists clenched at his sides. To an outsider you would just assume he was outraged, but I knew well enough to know better. His eyes betrayed him. He was terrified.

Edward's stare was as cold as ice. "Son, see yourself to the door."

"Fuck this." His face was tight as he stormed across the room. He stopped when he reached my mother. "I always thought you were a nasty bitch."

"I can assure you the feeling is mutual," she said as he tipped a chair over and punched a hole in the wall on his way out.

The stack of papers that were on the table he just blew past scattered all over the floor.

Edward's jaw tightened when the door slammed shut. "Sorry about that."

Neil leaned forward and steepled his fingers under his chin. "We need to make sure he doesn't become more of a problem than he already is."

"Agreed." My grandfather shook his head. "Now we just

need to figure out what we are going to do with him and the fallout from his actions."

"You let me worry about that. Amelia, do you have any questions?" Edward asked, his tone was calm, but firm. This entire exchange gave me whiplash. Things were coming at me so fast I couldn't keep up, but if there was ever a time to take control of my life, this was it.

As I glanced around the conference room, I knew this was where I belonged. I took in a breath, hoping it would calm my nerves and blew it out slowly. "Once the contract is drawn up, I'll look it over and make any necessary revisions."

He tapped his knuckles on the table. "Very well. Now if you'll excuse me, I have some family business to attend to."

Neil stood up and placed his files in his briefcase. "I can draw up a new contract and have it ready in a few days."

My mother cleared her throat. "I'm going to swing by the police station. I'll be able to sleep better at night knowing that I did my part." She gathered up all the photos and stuffed them into her bag. She strode over and placed her hands on my shoulders. "I hope you believe me when I say that I did this for you, not for money."

My grandfather raised his eyebrows in surprise. "You told her?"

"She knows everything." She kissed the top of my head and walked out leaving us alone.

He looked crestfallen. "Amelia, I had no idea. I knew Owen needed to work on a few things, but if I had known that he went this far off the rails, I never would have suggested the partnership. I can't believe I even encouraged you to marry that monster."

"Grandfather, it's okay. You didn't know."

He sighed and threw his face in his hands. "Before I start groveling for your forgiveness, tell me about this gentleman you've fallen in love with."

THIRTY

MARCO

"Mom, please stop fussing over me," I said as she wrapped a throw blanket around my legs.

"I brought over a lasagna, a bowl of homemade Italian Wedding soup, and that breakfast casserole you love," she fired off, too busy to even hear my request. I didn't know what it was with Italian women and why they thought that food was the answer to all of life's problems. She looked at the Target bag on the kitchen counter, remembering something. "Oh, I have to get that ice cream in the freezer before it melts."

She scurried into the kitchen and started putting everything away.

I rolled my eyes in surrender and glanced over at my grandmother who was resting comfortably in the recliner. She pulled a bottle of red wine out of a paper bag. "Marietta, get me a glass and a wine opener while you're in the kitchen, please."

My mother placed her hands on her hips. "Hey, I grabbed that wine for Marco and Amelia."

"Well, Marco is still high from all those pain meds." Her gaze slid to mine, daring me to contradict her. I started to object but thought better of it. "Plus, Amelia likes white wine, and I don't want this to go to waste. This Chianti is the good stuff."

There was a reason why I moved out as soon as I earned my first paycheck. While I was lucky to have these women in my life, one could only take them in small doses.

The doorbell rang. My mom strolled over to answer it, wiping her hands along her apron.

"Expecting someone?"

"It's probably one of the guys," I said, remembering that Quinn and Logan were planning on visiting later in the day.

"Uh…" My Mom paused, peering through the sidelight window. "Definitely not one of the guys."

She opened the door, and I blinked my eyes in disbelief, wondering if the pain pills were making me hallucinate.

"Sienna?" I said as she aimed a big smile at me. There was a time where I would have melted seeing that smile, but now it didn't even faze me. "What are you doing here?"

She waved to my grandmother, but my nonna would rather have her teeth pulled without Novocain than return my ex-girlfriend's smile. "I heard what happened and came right away."

"Where's Antonio?" my mom asked, stepping out onto my front porch and looking out into my front yard expecting to see him walking up the sidewalk.

Sienna's eyes darted across the room; she gave me a nervous smile. "Oh, he's back in California."

I tilted my head to the side. "I'm sorry. I don't understand?"

"Antonio and I are getting a divorce."

The news only added to my confusion.

"I'm sorry to hear that, but what does that have to do with me?" I asked as gently as possible, even though I had a sneaking suspicion that she was quite possibly here for me.

She breezed through my house and perched herself on my

coffee table. "We haven't been doing well for some time. I asked him for a separation right after Christmas." She pursed her lips and I couldn't help but notice the amount of lipstick she had on them. "It's been over between us for a while." She clutched my hand and I just stared at it in disbelief. I didn't dare look into her eyes because she didn't deserve my attention. "I heard about you being shot. I was so upset. I came back for you."

My eyes drifted to my grandmother. She never liked Sienna, and when she finished that big glass of wine, there was a good chance that things were going to get a lot more uncomfortable in this house.

My mother had her arms crossed over her chest in a protective stance; she was watching Sienna closely.

I closed my eyes and tried to figure out how to let her down easy. Sienna wasn't a bad person, just severely misguided. I would like to think that once she thought this through that she would realize that this was messed up. We didn't talk. We didn't keep in touch. Other than this past Christmas, I hadn't seen her in years. This was crazy.

My hesitation must have been a second too long because she reached in with her other hand and cupped my face. "I was so young and stupid." Her eyes filled with longing. "I feel like I gave up on us too soon. I never should have married Antonio, not when my heart still belonged to you. I want another chance. A chance to make things right with you and me."

I turned my head when I heard the front door swing open. Amelia stepped into the room, pulling a piece of rolling luggage. The timing couldn't have been more perfect. She halted in place, and the black duffel bag along her shoulder fell when she caught sight of my ex.

I held my breath, waiting to see how things played out. The last time these two women were in the same room together, things did not go well.

Sienna threw her a phony smile. She always did have a jealous streak.

Amelia set her luggage to the side, appearing cool as a cucumber. She unbuttoned her coat and dusted the snow off her hair. She acted like seeing Sienna was an everyday occurrence. I knew this act wouldn't last long. When I looked closer, I couldn't help but notice how much weight she's lost over the past couple weeks due to all the stress. She was usually strong and vibrant, but the woman standing in front of me looked exhausted. I was eager to ask her how her meeting went today, but my curiosity would have to wait.

"I didn't realize we were expecting company?" Her eyes shifted to me. She didn't appear all that happy with our uninvited guest.

I quickly removed my hand from Sienna's. "Don't look at me like that. I had no idea she was stopping by. I'm just as surprised as you are."

Sienna smirked. "Is there trouble in paradise already?"

I pinched the bridge of my nose. "Sienna, cut the shit."

Her shoulders slumped forward. "Please, Marco, I really would like to speak to you alone."

"Sienna, we have nothing to talk about. Go back to your husband and your children. Be happy. Antonio is a good guy. Your life is there with them."

Her face paled. "I don't want to go back to him. That's what I came here to talk to you about."

Aside from her physical appearance, this woman bears no resemblance to the woman I knew. The woman I spent years trying to get over.

I studied her with a guarded expression. "If I would have known that you were going to pull a stunt like this, I would have told Antonio the second I got your first letter. How do you think he would feel if he knew that you were begging me to take you back when you were pregnant with his child?"

I should have warned my cousin a long time ago, but I felt

like he was getting exactly what he deserved. Now that there was a family with kids hanging in the balance, my perspective has changed.

Her shoulders straightened. "You told me I was the love of your life."

"Yeah, when I was eighteen and New Kids on the Block had just topped the charts."

Was she insane?

She shook her head. "No, I know you haven't had a serious relationship since me. You forget that I'm a part of this family and people talk. You never got over me. I made a mistake. You can't hold it against me forever. We belong together."

She didn't get it, and I wasn't even sure wanted to. "Sienna, this is crazy talk. You don't know what you're saying."

"I know that I want you."

"No. You want what you can't have."

"Enough." Amelia stalked across the room and lifted Sienna up by her arm. "You've overstayed your welcome. It's time for you to go."

Sienna tried to pull her arm away, but because she was in a ridiculous pair of heels, she ended up swaying on her feet. Once she found her balance, she glared at Amelia. "Marco and I have history. You've only known him for weeks when I have known him for years. Just because you've been sleeping in his bed, that doesn't give you the right to speak for him. You are nothing. You are nobody."

"You're right about one thing, what you had is history. It's in the past." Amelia sneered. "So, I suggest you buy a new god damned watch and learn how to tell time, because right now, yours is up."

If it weren't for my throbbing shoulder, I would jump from the couch and remove her myself. Regardless of my physical limitations, I needed to handle this once and for all.

"Sienna," I sharpened my tone. "It's time for you to leave."

Defeat swam in the depths of her teary brown eyes. "You can't mean that?"

"I am dead serious. Go back to your life in California, or not. I really don't give a damn, but there is nothing left for you here."

"I can't believe this." She sniffed.

"Oh, believe it," my Nonna said from the recliner where she was holding up a cell phone. "I have it all recorded. Now, I just need to figure out how to send this to Antonio. Amelia, what buttons do I push to do that?"

Sienna's eyes flew around the room in a panic. "You don't need to do that, Sophia."

My mother walked over to the door and held it open. "Goodbye, Sienna."

She looked at me one last time. "I will always regret what I did. If I could go back and do it all over again, I would never have cheated on you. You are the best man I have ever known." She shifted her attention to Amelia. "I hope you realize how lucky you are."

She took one last glance over her shoulder as my mother ushered her outside.

She stood vigilant by the window and waited for Sienna's car to drive away. Once she was satisfied that Sienna was indeed gone, she trudged over and plucked the wine bottle out of my Nonna's hand. "Let's go. It's getting past your bedtime."

After the two gathered their things and said goodbye, I breathed out a sigh of relief.

Amelia eased down and crawled into my arms. I stared at her face, looking for any sign that she was upset. "I'm sorry about that," I said, brushing my thumb across her hair.

"I love you." She breathed into my neck. "But your ex is a

horrible human and if she ever shows her face in this house again, it won't be pretty."

"Duly noted," I said, pulling her in for a kiss. "In fact, I think you should just move in and stake your territory."

Her hands paused on my chest. "Excuse me?"

"Move in with me? Help me make this house a home. If this isn't where you want to live, we'll look for something else."

She tapped her lips with her finger like she was thinking it over. "Can we get a dog?"

A deep chuckle rumbled through me. "If that's what it takes for you to say yes, then sure."

She wrapped her arms around me and smiled. "I'm going to hold you to that, you know."

Just the feel of her in my arms made everything else feel lighter. "Sweetheart, whatever you want. Whatever you need, it's yours."

EPILOGUE

"Is this your office?" Marco asked as we passed the receptionist's desk and made our way to the end of the hall.

I opened the door and smiled. "This is it."

He walked over to the windows and looked out at the Philadelphia skyline. "I would love to see the view at nighttime when everything is all lit up."

"That can be arranged," I said, admiring the handsome man in my office. It's been a little over a month since the shooting, and even though his arm was still in a sling, he's made great progress.

"So," I pushed a few folders aside and leaned on the edge of my desk, "what do you think will happen to Owen?"

After the man who shot Marco was arrested, they looked further into his crimes and discovered the list of people connected to his underage sex ring. Owen's name was at the top of the list. Talk about a strange coincidence.

"From what I've been told, it's pretty messy. Everything was handed over to the Feds. My guess is that he's going to be gone for a very long time. I know Logan was appreciative for you handing over his company laptop."

My skin crawled just thinking about it. "I'm just glad nothing was linked back to our corporate account."

He crossed the room and stopped in front of me. "Well, I'm just grateful that none of his filth touched you." He moved in between my legs. "Because I would personally destroy him," he said, tucking a piece of hair behind my ear and staring into my eyes. "You know that there isn't anything I wouldn't do for you, right?"

"I know and that's why I love you."

He pulled me into his chest. "I have a surprise for you."

I twisted in his arms and looked up. "Really? What is it?"

"Come with me." He grabbed my hand and led me down the hall to the elevators. He grinned over his shoulder when he realized I was going with him without asking a single question. Didn't he know by now that I would follow him anywhere?

We got off on the tenth floor and I smiled into the mirror as we passed it by. We stopped at room 1005 and he reached into his back pocket and pulled out a key card.

"I take it by the look on your face that you remember this room?"

I nodded my head like an idiot until he pushed the door opened. It took a moment for my brain to register what I was seeing. While I remembered this room vividly, it looked very different than the last time we were here together. There were rose petals and tea light candles scattered everywhere. But that wasn't what got my attention. My eyes flooded with tears at the gold letter balloons that spelled out Will You Marry Me? placed over the wall of the bed.

Marco got down on one knee and pulled out a black velvet box. I sucked in a breath and tried to speak, but the lump in my throat choked off my words.

"I never believed in fate until our eyes locked across the bar during the middle of a snowstorm. I was so nervous when you gave me your hand and let me lead you here to this very room. Our first kiss was like nothing I ever experienced before. I only wish I could remember the exact moment when I fell in love with you. I don't know how or when it happened, but I know I'll never love this way again." He blew out a shaky breath. "Now, I can't imagine going to bed at night without kissing you, or holding these hands for the rest of my life. I can't imagine my heart beating for anyone else but you. I can't guarantee that there won't be tough times. We will probably have to work at this every day, but I can promise you that if you say yes, you won't regret it. So, Amelia, will you marry me?"

I framed his face in my hands. "Marco, before I met you, love was just a word. And now, as I look into your eyes, I know why I never felt it with anyone else before. Every time I'm with you, I find more reasons to love you. I can't imagine going through this life with anyone else but you. Yes, my answer to you will always be yes."

He slid the ring onto my finger. The feeling of contentment settled into my bones. It wasn't until this moment that I realized my entire life was spent chasing the wrong dream. This man was everything I could ever want and need in this lifetime.

Marco stared at the emerald-cut diamond with smaller stones encrusting the band. His fingers skimmed across my hand before he pressed a kiss to my finger and stood up. I folded my arms along his neck as he wiped the tears off my cheeks.

"You know you're stuck with me now, right?" he said, before sealing his lips to mine. He kissed me like he never wanted to stop. There was no doubt in my mind that I was going to love this man forever.

I pulled away and admired my ring. "This is perfect."

"You're perfect. I don't ever want you to forget this moment because I'm going to be honest with you." His tone turned serious. "I will mess up from time to time. I will say stupid things. I will annoy you and get on your last nerve, but you will never doubt my love for you or regret saying yes to me. I promise to always put us first above anything else."

"I'm not worried about any of that. I know that no matter what life throws at us, we will be okay. If it's all we have to survive on is love, then I am confident that ours is strong enough to see us through."

He smashed his lips down on mine and poured everything he was feeling into the moment. When he pulled back, his smile made my heart skip a beat.

"God, why did I wait so long to ask you?"

I laughed against his chest. "You don't think we are rushing things a bit?"

We've technically only known each other for a little over three months. This would seem absurd to some people, but I guess when you know, you know. Besides, I was done caring about what other people think. If his shooting taught me anything, it's that life can change in an instant. There were no guarantees that the people we love today will be here tomorrow.

"We can have a long engagement if you want."

"Marco, I don't need time or convincing. I know in my heart that this is right."

His fingers went to my waist. "You know what I think?" He slanted his mouth over mine and kissed me soft and slow. "I think it would be a shame to let this room go to waste."

"It sure would, especially with all the work I put into renovating these rooms."

His eyes lit up and those damn dimples popped out. "I'd be willing to leave you a five-star review on Trip Advisor if that will help."

I was pretty sure my entire face was split into a smile. "What do I have to do in order to get such a glowing review?" I asked as he started to strip down.

"Take everything off except the ring." He smirked.

I was so far gone for this man it wasn't even funny.

He leaned his leg on the bed and cupped my face. The tenderness in his gaze made my eyes burn. "Thank you for saying yes."

My fingers played with the ends of his hair. "Like I could ever say no to you."

He raised an eyebrow. "So, anal?"

A laugh tumbled out of me. "Except that."

He shrugged. "It was worth a shot."

"I love you."

He pressed a sweet kiss to my lips. "And I'm going to spend the rest of my life making sure you always do."

———

Are you ready for Logan and Ava's book? Whatever You Want is a second chance at love, single parent romance with a few twists and turns you won't see coming. You can start their story here: https:// geni.us/TmsCI

Before you go, I wrote a really cute Bonus scene for Marco and Amelia. You get a sneak peek at their life and adorable kids. Just subscribe to my newsletter, and this welcome gift will be sent right to your inbox.

Sign-up HERE
Already Subscribed? CLICK HERE

Or Scan:

ALSO BY S. JONES

THE PROTECTIVE SERIES

Whatever It Takes

Whatever You Need

Whatever You Want

THE ATLANTA ARROWS SERIES

Fumbled Love

Fumbled Beginning

Fumbled Arrangement

THE HARD SERIES

Hard to Love

Hard to Stay

Hard to Leave

ABOUT THE AUTHOR

S. Jones is a contemporary romance author from Central New York. She has a strong passion for writing and reading stories that will rip your heart out before it's put back together again.

If she's not buried in her writing cave, she's usually reading or planning out her next vacation.

She loves to travel to new places and spends all her free with her husband, two adult children and her dog, Winnie.

When the weather permits, you can find her outside walking her golden retriever, or enjoying a nice cocktail by the pool. She loves cooking and entertaining for her family and friends.

When she's not holding a glass of wine in one hand and her kindle in the other, she loves to hear from her readers at:

authorsjoneswrites@gmail.com